The ——
SURVIVALIST
—— (Judgment Day)

Books by Dr. Arthur T. Bradley

ॐ ॐ

Handbook to Practical Disaster Preparedness for the Family

The Prepper's Instruction Manual

Disaster Preparedness for EMP Attacks and Solar Storms

Process of Elimination: A Thriller

The Survivalist (Frontier Justice)

The Survivalist (Anarchy Rising)

The Survivalist (Judgment Day)

The Survivalist (Madness Rules)

The Survivalist (Battle Lines)

The Survivalist (Finest Hour)

ॐ ॐ

Available in print, ebook, and audiobook at all major resellers or at:
http://disasterpreparer.com

The SURVIVALIST
(Judgment Day)

Arthur T. Bradley, Ph.D.

The Survivalist
(Judgment Day)

Author:	Arthur T. Bradley, Ph.D.
Email:	arthur@disasterpreparer.com
Website:	http://disasterpreparer.com

Illustrations used throughout the book are privately owned and copyright protected. Special thanks are extended to Siobhan Gallagher for editing, Marites Bautista for print layout, and Nikola Nevenov for the illustrations and cover design.

ISBN 10: 1495265471
ISBN 13: 978-1495265471

Printed in the United States of America

This is a work of fiction. Names, characters, businesses, places, events, and incidents are either the products of the author's imagination or used in a fictitious manner. Any resemblance to actual persons, living or dead, or actual events is purely coincidental.

FOREWORD

Religions teach that every man and woman will eventually be judged. Most faiths believe that mankind's final judgment will follow an apocalypse, a cleansing of its sinful footprint from the Earth. Christians believe in the Second Coming, Hindus in Pralaya, Jews in Rosh Hashanah, and Muslims in the Day of Resurrection. While specifics differ, many religions share this common thread of judgment and reckoning, followed by rebirth and eternal life.

Even before this final judgment, however, most would agree that there must be accountability and justice in everyday life. Whether such judgment is found with the pounding of a gavel, at the wrong end of a gun, or from the firm hand of our Creator, everyone must eventually answer for their transgressions.

Some would follow the Code of Hammurabi, forcing an eye for an eye. Others would advocate a softer, more learned approach to dealing out justice. But when blood is spilled and loved ones are lost, it falls upon a few to ensure that those who committed the offense learn that nothing is without consequence.

Retribution is not always swift; nor does it resurrect those who have been lost. It does, however, allow hands to stop wringing and tears to be wiped from bloodshot eyes. Fear of judgment is rarely enough to keep evil at bay, but it remains a righteous beacon to those who have suffered. If this light of equity were ever to fade, darkness would surely threaten to overtake us all.

ঌ ঌ

"Conflict follows wrongdoing as surely as flies follow the herd."

John Henry "Doc" Holiday

1851–1887

ঌ ঌ

Nakai was a short man, lean and strong, with leathery skin, thick black hair, and eyes lined with deep creases, as if he had been squinting at the sun his entire life. He wore a set of wrinkled black fatigues and rested his hand on the butt of a Sig Sauer P226 pistol as he watched over the operation. Directly beside him was an eighteen-wheeled tractor-trailer with the bright red words "Wonder Bread" painted on its side. Four other trucks, each with different markings, formed a procession of rigs behind the first.

A huge black man, carrying an AK-47 equipped with a tactical stock and holographic red dot sight, hurried up to him.

"We're almost ready," he said. "Five minutes, tops."

Nakai nodded. "Put two vehicles to the front and two to the rear, with a fifty at each position."

"Roger that," the big man said, his eyes narrowing slightly as he scanned their surroundings.

The buildings in the Federal Law Enforcement Training Center were quiet except for the rumble of the trucks' giant diesel engines. The bodies of three US Marshals lay on the blacktop only a few steps away. A small pool of dried vomit lay beside the closest man's mouth.

"What is it, Jeb?" Nakai asked, following his lieutenant's eyes. "What do you see?"

Jeb shook his head. "Nothing. I just don't like this, that's all."

"We've killed men before."

"Not like this, we haven't."

"Killing is killing."

Jeb rubbed his hand across his chest.

"I can feel the gas crawling on my skin like a bucket of spiders."

Nakai patted the man's thick shoulder.

"It's in your head. The sarin dissipated within an hour or two. You know that."

Jeb nodded, but the scowl never left his face.

"How many rifles did we get?" Nakai asked, hoping to get Jeb's mind off the gas.

"Two thousand, maybe. All M16s. They look like old infantry training rifles. Serviceable, but they wouldn't be my first pick."

"Only two thousand?"

Jeb shrugged. "It's what we found. I didn't figure you wanted us hanging around looking for more. Not after what we did here."

"No," he said, shaking his head. "If they haven't already noticed that the post's gone quiet, they will soon. We need to be gone before they come looking for answers. As for them," Nakai motioned toward the dead marshals, "we did what we were hired to do. Our customer wanted to make a statement."

"I get that. But why?"

"You know I don't ask that kind of question," growled Nakai. "All I care is that we're paid for what we do."

"That's all good," Jeb said, motioning to a nearby soldier to hurry it up. "But in case you haven't noticed, the world's gone to shit. What are we going to do with more money?"

"Who said anything about money?"

Jeb stared at him. "What then?"

"We're getting the only thing that really matters anymore."

"And what's that?"

Nakai pressed his lips together in a tight smile.

"A place at the table."

☙ ❧

Deputy Marshal Mason Raines would have traded anything in his truck for a good pair of binoculars. He stood in the back of his black Ford F150, leaning over the top of the cab, straining to see the convoy of tractor-trailers and HMMWVs as they spilled out of the Federal Law Enforcement Training Center in Glynco, Georgia. His giant Irish wolfhound, Bowie, pressed up against him, looking back and forth between Mason and the trucks down on the highway.

It had been less than twelve hours since Mason had raced out of the center, terrified by the thought of being poisoned by whatever gas had been used to kill his fellow marshals. Night had come and gone, as had his panic. When he returned to survey the scene early the next morning, he discovered that the center had found new occupants.

For the past hour, he had watched as a sizable group of soldiers loaded scores, perhaps hundreds, of crates into tractor-trailers. Even at a distance, he could see that the men wore matching black fatigues—not official military garb, but uniforms nonetheless. At first he had thought that these men were some kind of makeshift force, like York's Free Militia, which had been formed in response to the nation's lawlessness. After watching them for a while, though, he changed his mind. Unlike Alexus's ragtag army, the men loading the trucks were efficient and coordinated in their movements. There were also sentries set up all around their operation. It seemed much more likely that they were a professional paramilitary organization.

The most pressing question was whether they were responsible for the death of the marshals. Given their timely arrival and obvious intent to pilfer something from the center, it seemed likely. That brought him to his second question. What exactly were they taking? Mason couldn't imagine anything stored there being important enough to stage a chemical attack, killing hundreds of lawmen in the process. As far as he knew, FLETC didn't house anything other than basic law enforcement training equipment. But these men had indeed found something, and whatever it was, it required numerous tractor-trailers to haul it out.

As the trucks began to file out Gate 2, Mason dropped to the ground and climbed back into his pickup. He was about two hundred yards away and parked in the yard of an abandoned house that offered a clear line of sight. The tractor-trailers all had different markings, suggesting that they had been picked up en route to the operation. Finding an armada of serviceable trucks would have been easy enough. The Superpox-99 virus had left more than five million such vehicles littering the roadways, some abandoned by their drivers, others acting as their final resting places.

Two armored military HMMWVs, painted in simple desert tan, led the convoy. Two others protected the rear. Men stood ready behind Browning M2HB .50 caliber machine guns perched atop two of the four vehicles. Mason took a quick tally of the number of men. Two sat in each tractor-trailer, and four were in each HMMWV, for a total of twenty-six well-armed soldiers. Unlike the militia Mason had fought in York, or even the convicts in Boone, he suspected that these men would not be easily overcome. If he were to have any chance of fighting the small army before him, it would require expert tactics and more than a little luck.

Before any such confrontation, however, he needed to get some answers. Were they to blame for the horrific murders? If so, why had they done it? How he was going to get those answers was unclear at the moment. The one thing he did know was that he couldn't afford to squander the good fortune he'd had in catching them red-handed.

As he watched the convoy turn west toward the Golden Isles Parkway, Mason started his truck and eased out into the road behind them. Bowie moved around in the bed of the truck before finally sticking his large head through the sliding rear window and whining loudly.

"Don't worry," Mason said, reaching back with one hand to rub Bowie's head. "We're not going to let them get away. But we'll need to be careful. These men are more dangerous than any we've fought so far."

S tanding on the front porch of his cabin in the Blue Ridge Mountains, Tanner stretched both arms over his head like a grizzly bear reaching for a beehive. He yawned and exhaled with a loud *yee-aww-uhh*. Squirrels darted up nearby trees, and insects quieted for a moment as life all around him tried to make sense of the terrifying sound.

Samantha stepped from the cabin with a red plaid blanket wrapped around her shoulders, and lowered herself into one of the worn rocking chairs.

"Morning," she said, pulling her legs up into the seat.

He nodded to her.

"Best morning I can remember."

"Because you're home?"

"Because I'm free." He smiled and looked around. "And yes, because I'm home. I didn't know if I'd ever see this old place again. Did I tell you I built it with my own two hands?"

"Four times, now."

His face took on a faraway look as he ran his fingers over a large wooden totem that stood beside the porch.

"Mind if I ask you something?" she said.

"Probably not."

"What did you go to jail for? Killing someone?"

"Two someones actually." His smile faded, and he looked off toward the sun that was beginning to peek over the trees.

"What did they do?"

He took a deep breath and let it out slowly.

"They hurt a friend of mine. And that's something I don't ever let slide."

"Why'd they do that?"

"Like most people, they took her for less than she was—a stripper, maybe a little more when money was tight."

"And the two guys? Who were they?"

"A couple of Army grunts out for a little weekend fun. The kind of men I normally cut a little slack, on account of what they do for our country."

"But not this time."

"No. Not this time."

Samantha's eyes were fixed on Tanner.

"What, uh..., what did they do to her?"

He swallowed hard. "They thought it would be fun to tie her to the bumper of their car and have her run along behind it for a while."

She cringed. "Why would anyone do something like that?"

"They were lit—maybe jacked up on a little something. Who knows?"

"Did she die?"

"No."

"But she got hurt."

He sighed. "Yeah, she got hurt. Let's just say she wasn't going to be dancer anymore."

"So, you killed them for it? Right then and there?"

Tanner shook his head. "I caught up with them behind a bar a couple of nights later."

"And then what?"

"They laughed and joked, and acted like the whole thing was some big party game."

"I'm guessing that was a mistake."

He nodded. "You might not have noticed, but sometimes I lose my temper. That was one of those times."

"You've killed a lot of people since we've been together. But none of them were good people." She shrugged. "Maybe it's okay if you lose your temper with really bad people."

He grunted. "The authorities didn't agree."

After a moment, she asked, "Do you think they'll try to put you back in jail someday?"

"Nah."

"Why not?"

"For one thing, there aren't any jails left. And even if there were, they have worse problems than me running around. Who knows? Someday, people might even say I was one of the good guys."

She looked at him with doubt in her eyes.

"I'm pretty sure they won't."

Tanner laughed. "No, I guess not."

He came over and sat in the chair beside her. They sat for several minutes, rocking quietly, listening to the sounds of the forest all around them.

Samantha eventually broke the silence.

"How long are we going to stay here?"

He looked over at her. Samantha was clean and well rested—a far cry better than when they had arrived at the cabin two days earlier.

"You ready to leave already?"

She shrugged.

"You must be missing your mom something awful."

She shrugged again. "I guess. But I've always been kind of a loner."

"What is it then? You worried about her?"

"Not much. My mom has lots of people protecting her. What about you? Aren't you worried about your son?"

He shook his head. "Now that I know Mason made it through the pandemic, I'm sure he'll be fine."

"How can you be sure? We've seen so many awful things."

Tanner rubbed the stubble on his chin and smiled.

"I haven't told you much about Mason."

"No," she said, searching his face. "Just that he was a marshal. And a good man. Better than you, you said."

"That part's true. What I didn't tell you is that he's incredibly good at two things."

"What're those?"

"The first is that he can pull and shoot a pistol better than any man I've ever seen. Maybe better than any man left alive, things being as they are."

"I once saw a cowboy shoot a silver dollar flipping through the air. Think he could do that?"

"I don't know. Maybe. But I doubt he'd see much point in it. Mason has a different set of skills. He's the kind of man who can keep his nerve when staring into another man's eyes, knowing that one of them is about to die."

"That must come in handy, him being a marshal and all. What's the second thing?"

"He's what the military called a brilliant tactician. He got some big fancy medals for it too."

"My teacher was a tactician."

"Really?" Tanner said, surprised.

"Yep. He could do algebra without ever taking out his calculator."

Tanner smiled. "I see. Well, my son was a different kind of tactician."

He thought for a moment. "Let me give you an example. Let's say you and I came across three men who wanted to eat us for dinner."

"That's nasty," she said with a disgusted look.

"What do you think I'd do?"

She furrowed her brow.

"Is this some kind of trick question? You'd smash their heads in, and probably take their wallets too."

"Oh, you know me so well," he said, grinning. "Mason would handle it differently. He'd probably lure one man away to an ambush, instigate a fight between the other two, and then shoot the lone survivor. When it was all said and done, they'd all be just as dead, but he would have been able to fight each one on his own terms."

"Ah, I see," she said, nodding. "So, he's smarter than you too."

He growled softly.

She giggled, and Tanner couldn't help but chuckle too.

"You sure you're ready to go back out there?" he asked. "You've seen how ugly it is."

"I think we need to."

"Why? Don't tell me you're getting tired of my charming company."

She gave him a little smile.

"It's not that."

"What then?"

"I want to ask you for a favor."

"What kind of favor?" he said, squinting with suspicion.

She reached under the blanket and brought out a small slip of folded paper. It looked like it had been folded and unfolded dozens of times. Tanner recognized it immediately as the note that Booker Hill had left behind. In it, Booker had asked that whoever found the note pass along one final message of love to his young daughter living in Salamanca, New York.

"Salamanca is hundreds of miles away," he pointed out.

"Six hundred, but they're not all out of our way."

"And how exactly would you know that?"

"I looked at one of your maps in the cabin before going to bed last night."

"Ah," he said, turning back to look out at the trees. "You've given this some thought."

"My mom will have more important things to worry about than this note. If we don't deliver it ourselves, his daughter's never going to see it. Not ever."

"It would mean not getting back to your mom for a while longer."

"I know," she said, staring at him. "But what's a few more days either way?"

Tanner studied her for a minute. Young Samantha was becoming a very different person than the awkward eleven-year-old he had met just a few weeks earlier. Things like courage, strength, and purpose were becoming more than just spelling words.

"All right then," he said. "We'll go to Salamanca."

"Just like that?"

"You'd rather I throw a big fuss? Maybe stomp my feet and shout like an ogre?"

"You do look a bit like an ogre," she said, laughing.

"You trying to butter me up?"

"It's just that I thought you'd say no. You didn't want to go before."

"True."

"So, what changed your mind?"

"I don't know. I'm rested. My belly is full of food. And my wounds are healing." He touched the two-inch gash on his forehead that had been stitched with fishing line. "Being back at nearly a hundred percent has improved my already sunny demeanor."

"Now that you mention it, you do seem like a happy ogre," she said, grinning.

"Besides," he added, "if it's important to you to deliver Booker's message, who am I to say otherwise? You're half of this team, right?"

She nodded. "I am."

"But I do have one condition," he said, holding up an enormous finger between them.

"What's that?"

"After we hand over the note, we head straight to Virginia to see your mom."

She raised her hand as if making a solemn pledge.

"Deal."

 споро

By noon, they were almost ready to leave. The Escalade they had taken from a house in northern Atlanta was loaded with freeze-dried food from the pantry, as well as six gallon-sized jugs of water. Given their previous challenge of finding drinking water, Tanner would have taken even more, had he been able to find suitable containers. He also transferred fuel from the red Hummer parked in front of the cabin over to the Escalade. According the digital fuel gauge on the dash, they could travel nearly five hundred miles on what was now a full tank of gas. Unfortunately, that wouldn't be quite enough to make it to Salamanca, which meant they would have to either refuel along the way or, more likely, swap to another abandoned vehicle.

Tanner set the Smith and Wesson Model 29, .44 Magnum on the dashboard. He had yet to fire the weapon since taking it from a backwoods kidnapper hiding in an old military bunker. It was fully loaded, but after those six rounds were spent, he suspected the weapon would become about as useful as a brick. Finding ammunition for such a rare caliber would be difficult, if not impossible. Fortunately, his trusty Remington 870 Police Magnum shotgun, loaded with triple-aught buckshot, sat on the floorboard beneath his legs, and more than forty unfired shells were stuffed in his backpack.

Samantha leaned her Savage .22 Varmint rifle against the inside of the SUV door. She only had a couple of dozen rounds for the rifle, but Tanner assured her that, by the time those ran out, they would have found another box or two. With billions of .22LR rounds having been sold every year for decades, the existing supply would probably outlast mankind.

Tanner unfolded a large map and studied it one final time. The drive from his cabin to Salamanca, New York, was almost exactly six hundred miles. His planned route would take them north along Highway 221 as far as Wytheville, Virginia. From there they would veer onto I-77 and eventually onto I-79, the latter of which would take them all the way over to Morgantown, West Virginia. At that point, they would detour around Pittsburgh, which was likely to be as hellish as Atlanta had been. The final couple of hundred miles would be traveled along two-lane highways as they snaked their way across the entire state of Pennsylvania and up into New York State.

Unfortunately, much of the trip had to be made by interstate, thoroughfares that were not only blocked by millions of vehicles but also frequented by every imaginable danger. While he didn't like the risk that the journey posed, Tanner accepted that the decision to go had already been made. Whether they were traveling to Virginia to take Samantha to her mother, or to New York to deliver a note to a girl who anxiously awaited her father's return, they would have to face the world in which they lived.

Danger was a part of life, now more than ever before.

He started the Escalade and listened to the engine.

"You hear that?"

Samantha rolled down her window and listened.

"I don't hear anything."

"That, darlin', is the sound of another adventure about to begin."

President Glass stared at the phone as if she was waiting for news on whether a loved one had survived a lifesaving surgery. The Secretary of Defense, General Kent Carr, had assured her that he would find Samantha. But for the past forty-eight hours, his special task force had turned up nothing. What was supposed to have taken only a few hours had now stretched into days. Somehow, Samantha had disappeared. And while President Glass drew a modicum of comfort that her daughter had been spotted alive, she couldn't shake the dreadful worry.

Finally, she could wait no longer. She snatched up the phone and dialed General Carr's closed-circuit number.

He answered on the second ring.

"No news yet, Madam President."

"You said it would only take a few hours."

"We're doing all we can. She's apparently left the Atlanta area."

"But how? Why? Why would she run like this?"

"My guess is she's afraid."

"Of what? Our soldiers?"

"Perhaps."

"What do you mean perhaps?"

General Carr hesitated. When he spoke, his voice was barely above a whisper.

"Ma'am, I think we should meet in person."

"Why? What's going on?"

"Not over the phone. Let's talk in private."

"In private?"

"Somewhere out of the way. Not in the main conference areas."

"There's not another pandemic, I hope," she said, forcing a nervous laugh.

"No, ma'am. It's something else."

"Is it serious?"

He paused. "Yes, ma'am, I'm afraid it is."

అ ఇ

A single overhead fluorescent light lit the small, nondescript conference room. There were only six chairs, and one of them tilted to the side because of a missing set of casters. The room was located in the far northwest corner of the Mount Weather Emergency Operations Center, an area that President Glass rarely visited. She wouldn't even have known about the room, had it not been for her Chief of Staff, Yumi Tanaka, who had assured her that it was the most secluded meeting spot in the entire center.

As Yumi and President Glass stepped into the room, they found General Carr already waiting inside, pacing nervously in front of a long, narrow window.

He immediately nodded to the president, his lips pressed tightly together.

"Madam President."

"General Carr," she replied, searching his face for clues as to the purpose of the clandestine meeting.

He said nothing as her security detail came in and quickly searched the room. When they were satisfied, they looked to President Glass for instructions.

"I'll be fine," she said. "Please wait outside."

The three agents went out into the hall and took up positions.

General Carr turned to Yumi.

"Miss Tanaka, if you wouldn't mind, I'd like a word with the president alone."

Yumi seemed a little put off but said nothing as she turned to leave. President Glass reached over and placed a hand on her arm.

"General, Yumi can be trusted with anything we have to say."

"I'm sure that's true," he said, offering Yumi an understanding smile. "However, I still think it's best that we discuss this matter in private. For now, anyway."

President Glass considered protesting, but the look on General Carr's face told her to let it go.

"Very well." She turned to Yumi. "Dear, please wait outside with the agents."

Yumi nodded, not quite hiding the worried look on her face.

After Yumi closed the door behind her, President Glass turned back to face General Carr.

"Okay, General, what's this all about?"

"It might be best if we sit," he said, sliding a chair out for her and then taking a seat himself.

She reluctantly sat on the gray metal chair, finding it cold and hard.

"This must be serious," she said. A thought suddenly hit her like a punch from J. Gordon Whitehead. "Oh, my God, it's Samantha, isn't it?"

He quickly shook his head.

"No, no. Nothing like that."

"Thank God." She took a deep calming breath. "What is it then?"

General Carr placed his hands on the table as if needing the laminated wood to help steady him.

"We've received word that chemical weapons have been used on our soil."

"What? Where?" she demanded. This was not at all what she was expecting to hear.

"It occurred at the Federal Law Enforcement Training Center in Glynco, Georgia."

She furrowed her brow, confused.

"That doesn't make any sense. Who would do such a thing? Who *could* do such a thing?"

"That's just it. No one outside the military has ever possessed chemical weapons. Not in the US, anyway."

"Then where did they come from?"

"We recovered a serial number from one of the Mk-116 bombs. It traces back to a large batch of chemical weapons decommissioned more than forty years ago."

"If they were decommissioned, shouldn't they have been destroyed?"

"Indeed, they should have been. However, records indicate that some of the bombs were never properly accounted for."

"So, what are you suggesting? That someone within our government or the military is involved in this attack?"

"I don't see how else they could have gotten the weapons."

"But who would do such a thing?"

He shrugged. "With the limited resources we have left, we may never know."

"How many weapons are we talking about?"

"There were a total of twelve bombs declared missing. Of those, we have confirmed that three were used on the law enforcement center."

"My God, are you saying that someone has nine more of these chemical weapons?"

"I have no way of knowing for certain, but I think it's prudent to assume so."

President Glass sat back in her chair and began unconsciously twisting a curl in her hair as she considered the significance of the attack as well as the missing weapons.

"How many people were killed?"

"A little over three hundred."

"And injured?"

He shook his head slowly.

Her face took on a pained expression.

"All police officers?"

"Marshals. This attack essentially destroyed what little remained of the Service."

"All of them?"

He shrugged. "There might still be a few scattered about the country, tending to loved ones. But the Marshal Service as a whole is no longer viable."

Tears formed in the corner of her eyes.

"Those were good men and women."

"Yes, ma'am."

"Why would anyone do this?"

He pulled out three black and white photographs from under his jacket and spread them out on the table. They were glossy satellite images, zoomed out far enough that the entire FLETC compound was visible.

"This is the law enforcement center?" she asked.

"Yes, and if you'll look here," he said, pointing to several rectangular blocks near the west side of the compound, "you'll see five large trucks."

"Military trucks?"

"No, commercial tractor-trailers."

"What are they doing?"

"We think they're stealing weapons stored at the center."

"What kind of weapons?" she asked, leaning down to study the photographs.

"Assault rifles."

"Any heavy weapons? Tanks, artillery, stuff like that?"

"No, ma'am."

President Glass shook her head.

"That doesn't make any sense. Why use chemical weapons to steal a few assault rifles?"

"Not a few, Madam President—a few thousand."

She grimaced. "That's... bad, but still, why the chemical weapons? Surely, they knew this would draw our full attention."

"Exactly."

Her eyes grew wide. "You think that's what they wanted?"

"I do."

"For what reason? To frighten us?"

"Maybe. Or perhaps it was meant as a warning."

"What do you mean?" She didn't like the sound of that at all.

"Madam President, I believe they may be planning to stage an attack."

"On what?"

"That I don't know." He started to say more but then fell silent.

"Don't hold back on me now, General. What is it?"

"It's my job to worry, Madam President."

"Given the state of our nation, I'd say that worry is in all of our job descriptions. Tell me what's on your mind."

"What if they are planning to attack Mount Weather?"

"Here?" she exclaimed. "Why would you think that?"

He took a deep breath.

"As I said the other day, our government is currently held in the lowest regard by what remains of our population." When she started to argue the point, he held up his hands. "Whether that's fair or not is beside the point. What matters is that there are people out there who wish to do us harm— to do *you* harm, Madam President."

She thought about his warning before replying.

"I trust your judgment, General Carr. If you say we're in danger, then I believe you. But surely we can fend off any attack they could muster."

"If they attempt a direct assault, yes. We have four thousand soldiers in the area as well as numerous gunships and armored vehicles. Plus, we could quickly call in what remains of the country's air support, if needed."

"Then we're fine," she said with a tentative smile.

"I'll agree that we're safe enough from a conventional attack."

"But?"

"What if their goal is not to take over the compound, but only to kill those inside? Preventing them from setting off a few chemical weapons might prove nearly impossible."

"If they do that, we'll just retreat to the huge underground bunker beneath the facility. Isn't that the whole point of having it? They can't get to us in there."

"That's true if we have time to seek shelter. But the attack might occur suddenly, making a tactical retreat impossible. Remember that sarin is nearly undetectable until infection has occurred. By the time the alarm was sounded, it would already be too late for many."

"Then what should we do? Have everyone carry around gas masks?"

"While that might be prudent, I don't think it would ultimately prove effective. Using a gas mask requires training. Also, they have to be carefully fitted to each individual."

"Well, what other options are there?"

"The only way to guarantee your safety is to move you to an undisclosed location."

"Evacuate?"

"Yes, ma'am."

She stared off at the small window, her thoughts momentarily returning to Samantha.

"Where would I go?"

"There are at least half a dozen highly secure locations. The most obvious would be the NORAD Cheyenne Mountain Complex, near Colorado Springs. Unfortunately, they are having difficulty generating enough electrical power to continue operations."

"NORAD isn't operational?"

"No, ma'am."

"This just keeps getting better and better. Where else?"

"There's Site R in the Raven Rock Mountain near Fort Detrick, Mount Pony in Culpeper, The Greenbrier in West Virginia, and—"

President Glass raised her hands.

"Okay, enough. I get it. There are other rocks under which I could hide. But that's why we came here in the first place. Mount Weather has a huge underground complex. I can't see the point in leaving this hole in the ground only to hide in a different one."

He fell silent, seeing that she had already made up her mind.

President Glass reached across the table and briefly placed her hand on his.

"I appreciate your concern, General. I do. But I'm not running and hiding. Not from some unknown enemy whose intentions aren't even clear at this point."

"I suspected as much. Still, I had to try."

"Here's what we'll do. You work to figure out who's behind the attack, and I'll ensure that we take a few extra precautions around here."

He gave a reluctant nod.

"Yes, ma'am."

"Are we good?"

"One more thing. I think it might be best if we keep this between the two of us." He glanced at the door to make his point.

President Glass followed his gaze and nodded.

"Okay," she said in a cautious tone. "This stays between us for now."

Nakai lowered the M22 binoculars and leaned his head back in the HMMWVs passenger side window.

"Someone's following us," he said, trying to talk over the rumble of the diesel engine.

Jeb didn't bother asking whether he was sure. If Nakai said someone was following them, then someone was following them. He possessed an almost unnatural sense about such things, and that, Jeb suspected, was one reason he was so damned hard to kill.

"How many?"

"One person in a black, or maybe dark-blue, pickup truck."

"Could it be someone traveling in the same direction?"

Nakai shook his head. "I spotted the truck when we left the center. Whoever he is, he knows where we've been and what we've done."

"One man shouldn't be too hard to clean up."

Nakai studied his wristwatch.

"We have eighteen hours to deliver these rifles to Lexington. General Hood won't be happy if we're late."

Jeb glanced at his own watch.

"There's still plenty of time. The drive from here is maybe nine hours."

"That's true if this is the only problem we encounter." Nakai thought for a moment. "Stop the convoy briefly, and leave two men behind to find out who he is and why he's following us."

"And then?"

"Leave his body for the dogs."

&ro &o

Standing at the edge of the overpass, Mason studied the convoy nearly a half-mile ahead of him on I-95. The soldiers had stopped briefly but were once again starting to get underway. Mason had maintained what he believed to be a safe distance for the past twenty miles and doubted that they could have spotted him. Still, they had stopped for no obvious reason, and experience had taught that it was better to be safe about such things. He would take additional precautions for the next mile, as well as drop back a little further in his pursuit.

Navigating a convoy of eighteen-wheelers down a congested interstate was a slow process, and Mason was confident that it wouldn't be too hard to catch back up. He had no idea where they were headed, but their current course took them straight toward Savannah, Georgia. Unless Savannah was their final destination, they would be forced to detour around the logjam of cars surrounding the city. Unlike Mason, the soldiers had opted to boldly travel the interstate, obviously confident that they were the most dangerous thing on the road.

Mason eased his truck off the overpass and down onto the interstate. He left his foot off the gas pedal, letting the truck coast while keeping a steady stream of abandoned vehicles between him and any would-be ambush that might lie ahead. When he was about a quarter of a mile from where the convoy had paused, he swung his truck in behind a burned-out camper and stopped.

Bowie immediately sat up on the seat beside him, the dog's head nearly touching the roof the cab. As soon as Mason opened the door and stepped out, Bowie hopped down and began sniffing the cars around them.

Mason took a moment to quickly inspect his rifle. During his time as an Army Ranger, he had found that Colt's M4 assault rifle was a remarkably reliable weapon. Like all firearms, however, it required that the operator keep it properly maintained and ready for action. Other than a few scratches from when he had thrown it to the ground during a firefight in Boone, the weapon looked to be in virtually new condition.

He ejected the magazine and set the weapon on the seat, one round still in the chamber. He pulled another fully-loaded thirty-round magazine from the bed of the truck as well as a roll of duct tape. Flipping the second magazine upside down, he taped the two together. He seated the dual magazine into the M4 and flipped it around a couple of times to make sure there wasn't any interference on either end. It worked perfectly. He now had sixty rounds at his disposal, enough for most one-man firefights.

"Come on," he said to Bowie. "Let's go do a little recon."

They moved slowly, but steadily, keeping their eyes on the road ahead of them. When Mason got to within fifty yards of where the convoy had stopped, he squatted down behind a silver Lexus. Inside was a woman's corpse, topped with a mop of long red hair. She had been decomposing for more than three weeks, and her body had burst on the seat into a puddle of dark blood, guts, and human waste. Her flesh was as dry as parchment, and it was splitting open along jagged seams. Bones stained with dried blood peeked out through her elbow joints as the skin began to sag and fall away. The car's windows were partially open, and a steady stream of black blowflies buzzed in and out.

The rotting corpse was hardly unique. Most of the cars around him had decaying bodies inside, people who had fled the cities when the outbreak reached its crescendo. Flies worked relentlessly to clean up the mess, leaving behind their maggot children to do much of the dirty work. In a few more months, only bones, hair, and cadaver stains would remain of the billions who had perished. Until then, the grotesque horror show would continue.

Bowie propped himself up to peek in through the window. When he was satisfied that there was nothing tasty to eat inside, he dropped back to the ground and walked in a small circle before lying down beside his master. Leaning around the front of the Lexus, Mason took a long moment to study the interstate. Nothing moved, and there were no sounds of life. He shook his head slowly, a little disappointed that his instincts had driven him to take an unnecessary and time-consuming detour.

Bowie tipped his head up and took several deep sniffs, his moist black nose sponging up odors from every direction. Then he looked over at Mason as if to ask, *Don't you smell that?*

Mason smelled the air, searching for anything that didn't belong. There were many odors, human decay and gasoline being the strongest. But there was something else too—a faint hint of cigarette smoke. He caught it only for an instant, but the smell of burning tobacco was unmistakable. He scanned the cars ahead of him, hoping to see a wisp of smoke rising into the air like an ethereal arrow pointing to his enemy. No such luck.

He studied the road for places where someone might hide. There were plenty of cars, most smashed into one another or pushed to the side of the road. While someone could certainly hide inside, the loss of mobility would put them at a significant disadvantage. Professionals wouldn't do that, he thought. Then he saw it. Three giant concrete pipes sat beside the road in a deep culvert, a small Toyota pinned beneath one of them. Mason could only assume that they had rolled off a tractor-trailer as it plowed its way through the stalled traffic.

The pipes were roughly lined up end-to-end, creating a makeshift tunnel with small gaps between the sections. The heavy concrete pipes were easily eight feet in diameter, making them traversable even when standing upright. It was an incredibly solid defensive position, providing cover, shooting ports between the pipes, and only two ways in or out.

Something dark crossed the gap between two of the pipes.

Mason's heart quickened. The question of whether or not someone was inside had been answered. Now what? Getting any closer without being seen would be difficult.

There were plenty of places around him to use as cover or concealment, should he choose to engage in a firefight, but none were as good as the pipes. The M4's 5.56 mm rounds had no chance of penetrating the ten-inch-thick concrete. His best bet was to draw them out. Unfortunately, luring trained soldiers out of a defensive position was nearly impossible. Every infantry soldier knew the merits of putting something bulletproof between himself and the enemy.

A second option, albeit a more dangerous one, was to stealthily approach from one end of the structure. There was enough roadway clutter that Mason thought he could probably low crawl his way to the culvert without being seen. Once there, he could snake his way to the end of the far pipe and pop in like an unwanted in-law. At that point, the pipes would act to trap the men. The biggest unknown was how many men were inside. If there were too many, even the element of surprise might not be enough to win the day.

Fresh out of ideas, Mason decided to give it a go.

"Stay put," he whispered, giving Bowie a quick pat on his side.

Then he turned away and leaned his M4 against one of the tires. Low-crawling twenty yards on asphalt covered in broken glass without being detected was going to be hard enough. Trying to do it while pushing a rifle ahead of him seemed all but impossible. Next, he lay flat on the ground, head first, with his legs splayed out behind him.

Bowie whined softly but didn't move.

Keeping his head pressed against the pavement, Mason began to shimmy his way forward. The low crawl offered the smallest silhouette to anyone who might be keeping an eye on the road, but it in no way guaranteed that he would remain undetected. To keep from drawing attention to his motion, he kept his progress slow, advancing only a few inches at a time. He carefully snaked around cars, pausing any time he made a noise. After nearly five full minutes, he arrived at the grassy embankment on the far side of the road. The smell of cigarette smoke was stronger now.

Believing that he was out of their direct sight, he rolled slowly down the embankment to the bottom of the small gulley and into a puddle of cool, muddy water. The first pipe straddled the ditch, with the end lying almost directly above him. He lay there for nearly a minute, listening. The only sound was that of boots scrubbing across concrete. He waited a little longer and was rewarded for his patience with the sound of voices.

"You see anything?" a man asked.

There was no answer.

"Hey, jackass, I asked you a question."

"If I saw something, don't you think I'd tell you?" a second man said with a strong New England accent. "Finish your damn cigarette, and look for yourself."

"Yeah, yeah, a couple more drags."

Two voices meant at least two men. There could easily be more, however.

Mason quietly slid his Supergrade from its holster. It wasn't the right weapon for the task, but it was what he had. The full length of the pipes was probably only about fifty feet, well within his range, but if anyone made it out of the end pipe, Mason would be at a serious disadvantage against their long guns.

He glanced over and saw Bowie peeking at him from around the Lexus. The dog would help whether he wanted him to or not. If someone made a run for it, Bowie would give chase. It was in his nature to do so, and nothing Mason said or did was going to stop that.

Mason had no way of knowing whether anyone was looking down at his end of the pipe, and he couldn't chance raising his head up to get a better look. He would hold the advantage of surprise, and that would have to be enough. Worrying that Bowie might decide to come check things out for himself, Mason decided to move sooner, rather than later. He pushed up and rolled to a kneeling position, swinging the Supergrade into position.

Two men, dressed in black fatigues, stood in the chain of pipes. One man was very close, perhaps eight feet away, holding a cigarette up to this mouth with one hand, and resting the other on an AK-47. His left ear was completely missing, sliced off as cleanly as Van Gogh's. The second man was all the way at the far end of the pipes. He had an M4 rifle up and ready as he peered out to watch the road.

Mason immediately sighted in on the far man and fired two shots in rapid succession. The first bullet caught him under the ribcage, and the second in the neck as he tumbled backward. At the sound of the gunshots, Bowie bolted from behind the car, barking as he raced toward Mason. Van Gogh spun around, shock and confusion on his face.

"Drop it!" Mason commanded, quickly adjusting his point of aim. At eight feet, he could empty the magazine into the one-eared man before he could get his rifle in hand.

Van Gogh glanced at his partner and then back at Mason. After only a short deliberation, he released his rifle, letting it clatter against the concrete pipe. At that same instant, Bowie raced around Mason and scrambled up into the pipe.

Mason shouted for him to stop, but Bowie tore ahead. At the sight of the snarling dog, Van Gogh turned and ran. Mason jumped to his feet and raced around the outside of the pipes, hoping to cut him off. The soldier was remarkably agile, making it out the far end of the pipe, with Bowie hot on his heels.

They raced out onto the freeway, the man finally turning and screaming while holding his open hands out toward the dog. Bowie hunched his back and began to slowly advance, snarling, without a hint of mercy.

"Bowie!" shouted Mason.

Bowie tipped his head to the side to acknowledge his master's call, but refused to take his eyes off the soldier.

Mason approached and placed one hand on the dog, trying to calm him.

"Easy, boy," he said, careful to keep the Supergrade pointed at Van Gogh.

Bowie relaxed, letting his fur settle along his back.

"Keep that monster away from me," Van Gogh pleaded, his voice trembling.

Hearing the fear in the man's voice, Mason thought he saw his way in.

"That depends on how cooperative you are. My dog hasn't eaten in a couple of days, and right now, you look a lot like a ribeye steak."

Van Gogh bent slightly, and his gaze flicked toward his boot knife.

Mason shook his head.

"That's not going to end well for you."

Van Gogh gently pulled the knife out with two fingers and tossed it a few feet away.

"Smart," said Mason. "Now, drop to your knees, and lace your fingers together on top of your head."

Shaking slightly, the man did as he was told, his eyes never leaving Bowie.

Mason glanced back at the soldier he had shot. The man's body was half out of the pipe, blood dripping from his neck down into the gulley. He was definitely out for the count.

"I assume you two were waiting for me?" he said, turning back to his prisoner.

Van Gogh didn't answer.

Mason shrugged. "Okay, dinner it is." He loosened his grip on Bowie, and the dog immediately lunged for the soldier.

"All right, all right!" the man screamed, leaning away. "Yeah, we were waiting on you."

"Why?"

"Just to find out who you were. That's all."

"Uh-huh, and then put a bullet in my head, right?"

Van Gogh started to deny it but stopped himself.

"Hey, man, I was just following orders. This wasn't personal."

"I assume you're a private contractor?"

He nodded. "I used to be regular army, but the pay was shit, you know?"

"Who are you working for now?"

"Look, the best thing you can do is turn around and walk away from this. I'll tell my boss that you got away. Simple as that. He's not going to come looking for you. Why would he?"

"He won't need to," Mason said calmly. "I'm going after him."

"That's suicide. Nakai is—" Van Gogh caught himself. "Shit!"

"Who's Nakai? Another mercenary?"

"It doesn't matter what you know. If you go after him, he'll kill you for sure. I'm telling you, you should let this one go."

"I'm touched that you're so concerned for my wellbeing. Really, I am. Did you feel that way about the marshals you murdered back in Glynco?"

The man's face turned pale.

"Listen, I had no part in that. I swear to God. That was Nakai all the way. Most of us showed up after it was already done. We were only there to pick up the guns."

Mason smiled. Van Gogh was a veritable gold mine of information.

"That's what this is about? Guns? It must have been a hell of a haul to need five tractor-trailers."

Van Gogh shrugged. "Not so many. A couple thousand rifles, maybe."

"Why did you need the guns?"

He shrugged again. "They're not for us. We we're hired to deliver them to a guy named Lenny Bruce. He's building a little army up near Lexington. It was just a job. That's it."

"All right, you're doing great. You may actually live through this."

"There's no need to kill me. I'm nothing more than a grunt left behind for a little clean up. You know how it is."

Mason nodded. "Believe me, I do. Now tell me about your boss, Nakai."

"There's not much to tell. He was Force Recon. A badass, through and through."

"What else?"

Van Gogh pointed to Mason's handgun.

"He can pull one of those faster than Jesse James."

"What about with a rifle?"

"He carries an Aug. Very skilled with that too. Like I said, it'd be better to walk away from this one."

"What else?"

"He's careful. I don't think he trusts anyone—no one other than Jeb."

"Who's Jeb?"

"Jeb's like his foreman, big and mean. I once saw him kill a man in the mess tent with a fork. Shoved it right through his eye."

Mason thought about what Van Gogh had revealed. While it could all have been carefully crafted bunk, he didn't think so. The man seemed incapable of telling a lie, let alone keeping a secret.

"Okay, final question."

Van Gogh looked up, wondering what would happen after that.

"Who hired Nakai?"

"I don't know."

The words came out too quickly to be a lie, but Mason thought he would push a little to see what else Van Gogh might know. He loosened his grip on Bowie, and once again, the dog began growling and inching forward.

"I swear to God I don't know!"

"What *do* you know?"

"Look, all I heard was that a general buddy of Nakai's might be the one who called us in. That's it, I swear. I don't have a name or nothing."

Mason's hand closed onto Bowie's collar, and Van Gogh sighed with relief.

"A general?"

He shrugged. "It was just what I heard. Could be shit—I don't know."

Mason stared at the man, trying to decide what to do with him. He had been as helpful as anyone could ask, but he was also involved in what had happened at Glynco. Mason thought about it long and hard, and in the end, mercy won out over revenge.

"Pick up your knife."

Van Gogh's worry quickly turned to panic.

"Listen, man, I told you—"

"Pick it up and start walking." Mason pointed in the direction that the convoy had traveled.

"Why? Even if I catch up to Nakai, he'll kill me for sure when he finds out that I talked to you. And he'll know, believe me."

"I don't care where you go. Just get out of my sight before I let my dog use your gonads for jawbreakers."

Bowie stared at Van Gogh, licking his lips.

"Fine, fine," he muttered, getting to his feet. He walked over and carefully picked up his knife and slid it back into his boot. "No need to be like that. I'm gone already." He turned and began hiking north along the interstate.

When he was about thirty feet away, Mason called out to him.

Van Gogh stopped and looked back over his shoulder.

"You should consider a new profession."

The man looked confused.

"Why's that?"

Mason slid his Supergrade back into its holster.

"Because you scare too easy."

"It's too bad we couldn't stop in Boone," Samantha said, looking out her window at long rows of trees that were beginning to get their full spring foliage.

"We have what we need. Best if we just roll on for now."

She nodded noncommittally.

They drove past a pack of wild dogs standing on the side of the highway. The animals watched the Escalade pass, their heads tipped up and their eyes sharp with interest. Perhaps it had been quite some time since they had seen anything moving on the road. More likely, they were staring at its occupants, imagining the taste of fresh meat. They chased the car for a short time, running up alongside the SUV, barking and growling. They only stopped after Tanner swerved and ran over the lead animal, breaking its neck with the seven-thousand-pound vehicle.

"Damn dogs," he said.

Samantha winced but didn't say anything. They had seen countless packs of dogs, many of which had undoubtedly once been loving pets. The lack of human companionship, not to mention their eating of cadavers, had turned them from loyal companions into ruthless pack animals with a taste for human flesh. And while Samantha was the first to defend animals of nearly every size and shape, she held no love for the dogs. Since her very first encounter with them on a dark highway, she felt only fear and loathing for the beasts.

"What do you think Isa will say to us?" she asked.

"Who?"

"The little girl we're going to see."

He shrugged. "She looks pretty young in the photo. I doubt she'll have much of anything to say."

Samantha imagined their meeting with dreamy eyes. Something suddenly occurred to her.

"I was thinking—um, maybe you should let me do the talking."

He glanced over at her.

"What are you saying? That I'm scary?"

"You're the scariest person I've ever met."

"Thank you," he said with a wicked smile. "That's the nicest thing anyone has said to me in a long time."

"No, really. You're scarier than Frankenstein."

He chuckled.

"You're so scary that a great white shark would put on tennis shoes and run up the beach to get away from you."

His chuckle turned into a laugh.

"I mean it," she said, getting into the spirit of it. "If the boogey man was in your closet, he'd stay there until you left for work."

"Okay, okay," he said, holding up one hand while trying to stop laughing. "I got it. When we find the girl, you can do the talking."

She nodded thoughtfully. "Yeah, that's probably a good idea."

Tanner saw the sign for I-77 ahead. A long string of cars jammed the on-ramp, but the off-ramp was relatively clear. He drove over the median and started up toward the interstate. As they came to the top of the ramp, he brought the Escalade to a full stop. All four lanes were filled with cars. A narrow path had been pushed through the automotive bedlam, but it was by no means straight or easy to follow.

"Do you think we can get through this?" she asked.

"If others can, we can," he said, easing the car forward.

"We'll have to go slow, or we'll end up walking... again."

"Hey, that was one time. And I was new to this whole apocalypse thing."

"You almost got me eaten."

Tanner rubbed a small scab on his face.

"We've all had our close calls with hungry critters."

She turned to him with a serious look on her face.

"Promise you won't ever let anything eat me."

He glanced at her.

"And what exactly would you have me do?"

"You know," she said, biting her lip.

"You'd rather I put a bullet in you than let zombies munch your brains," he said, trying to lighten the mood. "Is that it?"

She nodded. "Promise me."

He gave her a long look.

"Okay, I promise."

"Do you want me to do the same for you?"

"Unh-unh."

"Why not?"

"If something's going to eat me, I want it to have to work for its food."

"You probably wouldn't taste as good as me anyway," she said in a very matter of fact way.

"What makes you say that?"

"In all the horror movies, monsters always want to eat the children. I figure they must know that we taste better. It's only logical."

Tanner shook his head. He had become accustomed to conversations with Samantha going in odd directions, but her quirky comments never failed to amuse him.

She rolled down her window and took a deep breath.

"Ugh! It smells like dead people."

"I can't imagine why."

Tanner noticed something in the road up ahead and gestured for her to take a look. Pieces of roadkill were spread along the yellow center line, hunks of meat and bone run over so many times that they were no longer recognizable. An RV sat parked on the side of the interstate with long black skid marks extending behind its rear tires. A human leg, with a bright blue tennis shoe still attached, lay beside the RV. A little further up was an arm. Beyond that rested what was left of the torso. Splashes of blood were everywhere, as if the famous expressionist painter Jackson Pollock had gotten busy with a bucket of red paint.

"Gross," she said, making a face. "What do you suppose happened here?"

Tanner slowed the Escalade.

"Nothing good."

They eased by the carnage, searching for clues.

"I bet the dogs did this," she said.

Tanner looked to his left and saw the naked body of a woman staked to the ground in the grassy median. A heavy piece of rebar protruded from her stomach like the flagstick at a golf course.

"No," he answered, his voice cold and hard. "This wasn't dogs."

Without further explanation, he punched the gas and sped past the bloody massacre.

∾ ∽

Parked on the shoulder of I-77, Tanner and Samantha sat inside the Escalade, finishing a lunch of freeze-dried spaghetti and a powdered juice drink.

"Good?" he asked, tipping the pouch up to pour the last drops of spaghetti sauce into his mouth.

Samantha looked down at her pouch. It was still half full.

"I'm not Italian," she said, "but I'm pretty sure that spaghetti isn't supposed to be thin enough to slurp through a straw."

Tanner tossed the wrapper out the window and pulled a couple of chocolate bars from his pack.

"You want one?"

She nodded, sliding it into her shirt pocket.

"Even chocolate might not save this meal," she mumbled as she opened her door. "I'll be back. I'm going to pee."

"Take your rifle."

"To pee?"

"If I had to count the number of times I needed a rifle when peeing—"

She held up her hands, surrendering.

"Fine. I'll take it."

As Samantha walked away from the Escalade, Tanner rolled his window down. If she got into trouble, it would be easy enough to hear her call for help. One benefit of civilization dying was that the world had become incredibly quiet.

He stared out the window at endless miles of cars and trucks, wondering if society would ever get back where it was before the pandemic. It could go either way, he thought. Enough damage had been done that the world could just devolve into chaos. And while he might not want to openly admit it, he was okay with that.

ॐ ॐ

Samantha walked slowly up the grassy embankment toward a small thicket of trees and bushes, the spaghetti sloshing around in her stomach like a bathtub filled with warm water. If she missed anything most of all from her previous life, it was the food. What she wouldn't give for a plate of her mom's buttermilk fried chicken. Maybe with a cob of corn and a slice of Texas Toast on the side. She licked her lips but tasted only the remnants of the rehydrated spaghetti sauce.

She reminded herself that there were people all over the world eating far worse things to stay alive, but it only consoled her until the next spaghetti burp. Someday, she thought, I'm going to have that fried chicken again.

She stepped around a three-foot-high boulder, looking for a place to relieve herself. Before she could zero in on the right spot, a deep rumbling sounded from the interstate below. She instinctively sought cover, ducking behind the large rock. When she peeked over the top, she saw a long line of motorcycles weaving in and out of the stalled traffic, heading south in the northbound lane—directly toward Tanner.

She started to stand and run for the Escalade but realized that she would never make it in time. With her heart pounding, she squatted back down and slid the rifle off her shoulder.

ॐ ॐ

The sound of motorcycle engines vibrated the air like lions warning off would-be predators. Tanner knew what was coming even before spotting the long procession of bikers winding their way through the endless gridlock of cars.

He leaned out the window and searched for Samantha. She was nowhere in sight. Had she already seen them? Hopefully, she had at least heard them and would exercise a little common sense by staying put until they passed. Unfortunately, Samantha Glass and common sense were words rarely used in the same sentence.

Tanner opened his door and stepped out of the Escalade. He left the shotgun on the seat, but slid the .44 Magnum into the back of his waistband. Neither weapon would be enough to overcome a gang like the one that approached, but if it came down to it, the pistol might provide a slight deterrence. Sometimes being a hard target was enough. He stepped around to the front of the Escalade and leaned back against the grille, making it impossible for anyone to see the huge pistol pressing against the small of his back.

The motorcyclists split left and right, approaching him from both sides. There were at least twenty of them, and each one appeared to be armed. They spread out, stopped, and began revving their engines to create a mindless cacophony of angry noise.

Despite the overtly threatening action, Tanner was grateful for the deafening sound. There was no doubt that Samantha now knew of their presence. For his part, he stood casually leaning against the car while scanning for their leader. The man was easy enough to find, wearing a distinctive black helmet designed to look like the alien hunter from *Predator*, complete with built-in nylon dreadlocks.

Tanner had been around men like these for much of his life, and he knew that his best chance of surviving the encounter was to play it cool. He fully expected that they would test him, and if he showed weakness, they would kill him for sport.

After a few seconds, Predator raised one hand into the air, and the entire gang killed their engines in unison. Several of the riders, including the leader, pulled off their helmets and dismounted. Predator was a tall man with a thick black mustache that wrapped around to merge with long bushy sideburns.

"Whatcha doin', big man?" he asked, showing off a silver front tooth.

"Just finished having my lunch," Tanner said with a yawn.

"Out here?" the man asked, waving his arms. "On my highway?"

Tanner shrugged. "What can I say? This is where I was at lunchtime."

Predator leaned around to peer into the Escalade.

"Anyone else in there?"

"Nope. I'm what you'd call a loner."

He motioned for a couple of his men to take a look. They circled around and looked in through the side windows. When they were satisfied, they both shook their heads.

"I can see from the tat on your arm that you did some time," said Predator. "What were you in for? Purse snatching?"

Several bikers laughed and pushed against one another like high school jocks.

"How'd you guess?" Tanner said with a smile.

Predator squinted his eyes, studying him.

"You know... I was going to ask if you wanted to join my merry band. But I'm beginning to think that you'd just be a pain in my ass. Am I right?"

Tanner nodded. "Afraid so."

"Then we got ourselves a bit of a dilemma."

Tanner didn't like the sound of that. Any time a thug felt the need to use the word *dilemma*, dollars to donuts he was planning on killing you.

"No dilemma," said Tanner. "We both go on our way, no worse for the wear."

Predator made an almost imperceptible nod, and one of the bikers suddenly lunged forward, stabbing a small stiletto at Tanner's gut.

Tanner sidestepped, caught the man's wrist, and twisted it hard. The ulna snapped with an audible *snick*, and the man dropped the knife. Tanner leaned forward and hit him with a half-fist to his Adam's apple, sending him stumbling back with blood bubbling from his mouth.

Two other men moved in on him. One carried a pipe wrench, and the other a long red cattle prod. Tanner stepped forward and kicked the first man in the groin, lifting him off the ground and sending his eyes rolling up in his head. He immediately doubled over and toppled sideways on the pavement, groaning.

The second man stabbed forward with the cattle prod. Tanner knocked it away and punched him hard on the jaw. Teeth separated from gums, flying across the hood of the Escalade. He too fell to the ground, moaning and cupping his bloody mouth.

Tanner whipped the .44 Magnum out from behind his back and leveled it at Predator. A dozen or more bikers scrambled to raise their own firearms.

"They'll kill you if you pull that trigger," Predator said. His face was beginning to lose its color.

"I'm sure. But that won't help them reattach your head."

Predator glanced left and right at his men. It was the type of impasse that was difficult to see how to get past. Before anyone could offer a way forward, the man with the cattle prod rolled over and stuck it to Tanner's calf. One hundred thousand volts of electricity shocked his system, causing every muscle in his body to spasm. The pistol fell from Tanner's grip, clattering to the ground, as his legs buckled under him.

∾ ∿

Nearly a hundred yards away, Samantha watched the situation unfold. Tanner was impossibly outnumbered. Even he couldn't possibly hope to fight all of the bikers. When he finally fell to the ground, shaking and twitching, she knew that it was over. She was alone, now and forever. Until she got eaten by the dogs, anyway.

To her surprise, the men didn't immediately shoot him. Instead, they danced around, laughing, and repeatedly poking him with some kind of red stick. Each time they jabbed him, his body jerked and flopped on the asphalt. When they finally tired of their sadistic fun, they tied thick white cords around his wrists and ankles, and attached the other ends to the back of four motorcycles. Samantha watched, horrified, as they climbed on the bikes and slowly stretched him out straight, like a prisoner being put to the rack. When he was finally spread-eagled, the crowd of bikers cheered, raising their weapons into the air.

"No, no, no," Samantha muttered, lifting her rifle and resting it on top of the boulder. It was up to her now. She knew that.

She looked down the gun sight, lining up the rear peep hole with the front reticle before sweeping the crosshairs over the crowd. The men on the motorcycles began to pull harder, slowly lifting Tanner's body off the ground as the cords drew taut. He struggled to pull free, but the lack of slack in the restraints made it impossible for him to get any sort of leverage.

Samantha took a deep breath and let the sights settle on one of the bikers who was stretching out Tanner. The man was revving his motorcycle, looking back over his shoulder, laughing. She heard Tanner's voice in her head.

Any day now, darlin'.

She let out half of the breath and squeezed the trigger. The gun emitted a sharp *pop*, but neither the report nor the slight slap against her shoulder even registered. The man brought his hands to his chest and toppled sideways off his bike.

She cycled the bolt, swung left, and sighted on the second biker. Squeeze. A second *pop*. A second man down, this time clutching his stomach as he dropped to his knees.

Bikers began diving behind cars. Others started their engines and raced away. Most stood dumbfounded, unable to hear the rifle pops over the roar of the motorcycles. The two remaining bikers who had been pulling Tanner began to drag him across the asphalt, like horses pulling a runaway stagecoach.

Samantha cycled the bolt and shifted her aim to the third man. He was moving, but she used the rock as a pivot point, never letting the reticle drift behind her target. Squeeze. Another *pop*. The man jerked, then lost his balance and fell back off the bike, slapping his head against the pavement. More bikers dove for cover, finally understanding that they were taking fire.

Nearly free, Tanner sat up and began tugging on the final remaining tether, pitting his might against that of the motorcycle.

Samantha cycled the bolt and squeezed again. The final bullet caught the last biker in the middle of his back about the same time that the cord snapped. Instead of falling off the motorcycle, the rider leaned forward and gunned the engine, racing down the interstate.

Shouts rang out, panicked bikers pointing off in seemingly random directions. Tanner scrambled to his feet, hopped the side railing, and ran for the edge of the forest that paralleled the interstate. Still unsure of how many people were shooting at them, no one dared to try and stop him.

As Samantha ducked back behind the boulder, two things occurred to her. The first was that she had just shot four people. And the second was that she no longer had to pee.

Mason's mind was racing as he swerved around cars and the occasional dead body lying on Highway 17. He now had both a name and a destination. Nakai was apparently to blame for the murders, and Lexington was where they planned to drop their cargo. If Mason had anything to say about it, they were never going to make that delivery.

The plan was simple enough. He would get ahead of them and set a trap of some sort. Once he had them stopped, he would figure out a way to overcome what were some pretty serious odds against him. How he would accomplish such a feat wasn't important at the moment. Right now, all that mattered was disrupting their plans. With chaos, he thought, comes opportunity.

Highway 17 paralleled I-95 all the way up to Savannah. The roads crossed at two points, either of which Mason could use to get back on the interstate and set his trap. The first crossing was only about ten miles ahead, not far enough to ensure that he wouldn't encounter Nakai and his men before he was ready.

The second was twenty miles beyond that, at the town of Richmond Hill, a place made famous in the 1930s and '40s when Henry Ford built a huge plantation there. The community, which only measured a few miles on a side, was skirted by the Ogeechee River on one side and I-95 on the other. And while it wasn't in their Chamber of Commerce brochure, Richmond Hill struck Mason as an ideal spot to ambush a gang of murderous mercenaries.

When he was about halfway to Richmond Hill, Mason came across a long row of RVs and tents set up along the opposite side of the highway. His first thought was that the inhabitants were probably a group of survivors like those he had met back in Sugar Grove. Carl Tipton and his family had been moving westward in search of a viable community in which to settle down. Perhaps these people had decided to stop looking, choosing instead to set up one of their own.

Mason slowed his truck as he approached the first RV. A gaunt man stood in the shadow of an outstretched awning, a rifle hanging from his shoulder. He watched Mason warily but didn't ready the weapon. Not wanting to risk driving by the entire convoy without knowing their intentions, Mason pulled to the shoulder on the opposite side of the interstate.

Careful not to seem too threatening, he climbed out of his truck slow and easy. Bowie hopped down next to him, and immediately sniffed the air. Even Mason could smell the odor of something cooking. Given his recent run in with a family of cannibals, however, he was reluctant to draw any conclusions about what might be on the grill.

The rifleman across the street called out over his shoulder, and within a few seconds, others began peeking out from their tents. Surprisingly, no one moved out into the sunlight. Mason raised a hand and waved—a simple gesture used for centuries to indicate that one's hand was free of weapons.

Three men finally stepped from the lead RV, immediately opening black umbrellas over their heads. They huddled together and started across the road toward him. Fortunately, none of them appeared to be carrying a weapon.

Bowie growled at the strange sight of three men carrying umbrellas on a sunny spring day. Mason leaned down and patted him.

"Be good. We don't need any more enemies. Besides, if you're nice, they might feed you something."

Bowie looked up and blinked, his growl changing to a soft whine.

Mason patiently waited for the three men to approach. He didn't want to be out in the open, nor did he want to move too far from the rifle sitting ready in the cab of his truck. As they got closer, he could see that the men's faces were dotted with the remnants of dried scabs. They must be survivors of the Superpox-99 virus. He stood a little straighter, letting his hand hang ready by his Supergrade.

The group consisted of an old man and his two grown sons, both of whom strongly resembled their father. All of them squinted, trying to protect their eyes from the daylight. As they got closer, Mason saw that the men's eyes were almost completely black, their pupils expanded to their natural limits. The edges of their eyelids were also stained, as if they had been caught in the rain after putting on a heavy coat of mascara.

Mason nodded to them, watching their hands for any sudden movement.

Detecting his concern, the old man smiled.

"We're not looking for any trouble, mister." He spoke with a slow southern drawl, a dialect that had been perfected across generations to put people at ease.

Mason thought about it for a moment and then extended his hand.

The old man seemed surprised by the gesture.

"Aren't you afraid of catching the pox?"

"I've been told by people I trust that, by the time the pox scabs, it's no longer contagious."

The man quickly shifted the umbrella to his left hand and shook Mason's hand with the other.

"I believe that to be true as well. Still, it's been a long time since we've been treated with that kind of respect." His voice broke, and he wiped at what looked like a drop of ink pooling in the corner of his eye.

Mason looked away for a moment, allowing the man to collect himself.

"I'm Robert Sterling, retired district judge for the city of Charleston, South Carolina. God rest her soul. These are my boys, Dean and Colton."

"Deputy Marshal Mason Raines. Good to meet you folks."

Judge Sterling's mouth turned up in a smile.

"Deputy Marshal? How about that. It's been a while since we've seen any lawmen."

Colton, the younger of the two, said, "The last lawman we saw was a city cop from Savannah. He wasn't as... as enlightened as you are."

"How's that?" asked Mason.

"He tried to put me down because of my condition."

Mason nodded. He had seen his fair share of hatred for those infected, some of it deserved, and some of it not.

"Are you out on business, Marshal?" asked the judge.

Mason took a moment to consider the question.

"I suppose I am."

"Pursuing bad men?"

"The worst."

He nodded. "From the look in your eye, I can see they've crossed the wrong man."

Mason pressed his lips together but said nothing. Bowie gave a little whine as if reminding his master to introduce him.

Judge Sterling squatted down and petted the dog.

"What's your name, big fella?"

"That's Bowie."

Both Dean and Colton stepped over and gave Bowie some petting as well. For his part, Bowie returned the affection with sloppy licks to each man's face.

"Are you hungry, Marshal?" the judge asked, standing back up. "We're grilling a deer that one of the men shot last night. You're welcome to your fill."

Bowie looked up at the judge with a sense of urgency.

"Plenty for your dog, too," he said, smiling.

While the food certainly smelled delicious, Mason couldn't afford the delay.

"I appreciate the offer. Unfortunately, I need to get out ahead of those I'm after. It looks like my best bet is to cut them off at Richmond Hill."

Judge Sterling's face filled with concern.

"Don't do that, Marshal."

Dean and Colton both shook their heads as well.

"No, sir," said Colton. "You want to stay clear of Richmond Hill. We know. We were there."

"What's wrong with Richmond Hill?"

"That place has been completely overrun by survivors of the pox. Hundreds, maybe thousands, of them by now."

"They came down from Savannah," added Dean.

Mason was confused. "I hate to state the obvious, but aren't you three—"

"They're not like us, Marshal," the judge said. "These people are something else. Not fully human anymore, I think."

"How's that even possible?"

"I don't really know. Some of us who caught the pox stayed pretty much the same, save for these damned eyes and stiff joints. But others..."

"Others, what?"

"Well, they changed. They grew bigger, stronger. And their minds changed too. They can't think straight any more. Worst of all, they developed an intense hatred for anyone who wasn't infected."

"The pox drove them crazy?"

"Not just crazy. They've lost some intelligence along the way. They can't drive cars or operate any kind of technology. Oh, they can do simple things, but not like before."

"They're like Neanderthals," added Colton. "Big, stupid beasts that only want to tear you apart."

"Did they try to kill you too?" asked Mason.

"No," the judge said, shaking his head. "Even though we didn't change like they did, they never held that against us."

"Not yet, anyway," added Dean.

"Then why did you come out here and set up this camp?"

The judge looked over his shoulder at the long row of tents and RVs.

"That's a fair question. The truth is we couldn't stand to watch their brutality any longer. It was horrifying to witness. We weren't strong enough to stop them, so we did the only thing we could—we left."

Mason nodded. What they told him seemed to reconcile with his experience with Erik, the infected man who had come to his aid in Boone, and the stories that others had told him about the berserker violence they had witnessed.

Judge Sterling's face grew long and serious.

"Please, Marshal, listen to us about this. Steer clear of Richmond Hill."

Mason met the man's eyes but said nothing.

The judge frowned. "You're going there anyway, aren't you?"

Mason nodded. "Richmond Hill is my best chance. If I don't stop them there, I'm not sure which direction they'll turn. So, yes, that's where I'll make my stand."

Judge Sterling sighed. "Okay, but for God's sake, get out before dark."

"I'll try." Mason nodded to each man. "I'd best be on my way."

"Before you hurry off," said Dean, "let me get your dog a treat." He wheeled around and hurried back to one of the tents. When he returned, he was carrying a large bone. There was still plenty of bloody meat attached to it, as well as a little fur.

Bowie's eyes grew wide, and he gave a little bark. Dean held out the bone, but before taking it, Bowie looked up at Mason. He nodded, and the big dog leaped forward, snatching the bone from Dean's hand.

"You got yourself a fine animal there," said Judge Sterling.

Mason patted Bowie on the side as the dog began tearing off snippets of flesh from the bone.

"You don't know the half of it."

⌘ ⌘

Mason found the outskirts of Richmond Hill to be as deserted as nearly every other small town in America. There was an outdoor shopping center to his left that had its windows smashed, and a mom-and-pop store on his right that advertised the best boiled peanuts in all of Georgia. Up ahead was a sign for a Motel 6 and, beyond that, a Burger King. Contrary to Judge Sterling's warning, he saw no signs of murderous crazies roaming the streets.

He pulled over and stopped at the on-ramp to I-95. Almost directly above him were two three-lane overpasses, one traveling south, the other north. He smiled. The overpasses presented an opportunity to disrupt Nakai's plans.

He climbed out and dug through the supplies in the bed of his truck, finally finding a box of ten-penny nails. The three-inch nails were the perfect size for what he had in mind, long enough to get the job done and still easy enough to be worked with pliers. He knelt down and dumped a small pile of the nails on the concrete beside his truck. Bowie sniffed them and then looked up at him.

"Just watch."

Using a pair of heavy pliers, he bent two nails, each into ninety-degree angles. Overlapping them, he twisted the nails around one other until the four tips pointed off at orthogonal angles. Then he clipped the head of each nail. He picked up the four-pronged spike and touched the tips with his finger. Not perfect, but sharp enough.

Working as fast as he could, he repeated the process a couple dozen more times. When he had finished, he tossed the pliers into the back of the truck and scooped up a large handful of the improvised caltrops.

"Come on," he said, turning and running up the on-ramp.

Bowie tore after him, barking as he ran.

When he got to the top of the ramp, Mason saw that a Greyhound bus had jackknifed and tipped over, and was now leaning on the edge of the overpass. The bus was wedged against the concrete barrier, and Mason doubted that it could be moved by anything smaller than a bulldozer. A dozen cars from the other two lanes had been pushed out of the way to form a narrow passageway across the overpass. Nakai's convoy would have to squeeze between the bus and cars, making it an ideal choke point. Rather than simply tossing the caltrops on the open pavement, Mason moved from one side of the road to the other, carefully placing them like candles on a birthday cake.

He stepped back and studied the trap. The caltrops were all but invisible when standing more than a few feet away. Getting past them would require careful clearing of the road—a time consuming process that would probably have to be conducted on hands and knees. Moving the cars or bus would be even more difficult, and the heavily congested ramps on and off the interstate would prevent the convoy from taking a detour.

Mason grinned with satisfaction. The trap wasn't perfect, but it was pretty darned good.

෴ ෴

Mason lay flat on his belly, peeking out from the tree line on the opposite side of the interstate. Pine cones poked into his side, and the occasional bug crawled along his legs as nature reminded him that he was not entirely welcome. Bowie leaned up against him, snoring softly. The convoy had taken nearly an hour to arrive, and that was about fifty-nine minutes longer than the dog's attention span.

Bowie finally stirred when he heard the tractor-trailers' engines groaning as the trucks powered up the steep incline leading to the Richmond Hill overpass. Two things had changed since Mason had last seen the procession. The entire convoy was now traveling more tightly together, keeping their heavy weapons closer to the payload. And the HMMWVs had shifted so that there were now three at the rear of the convoy and just one at the front. Mason suspected the shift in position was due to Nakai worrying about him coming up from behind. As luck would have it, both changes worked in Mason's favor.

The lead HMMWV rolled across the overpass, followed closely by the first tractor-trailer. To Mason's surprise, the HMMWV rolled right over the area where the caltrops had been placed without even slowing. The tractor-trailer, however, was not as fortunate. The front right tire blew first, followed by the left a couple seconds later, pitching the nose of the truck down toward the road. The driver locked up his brakes and skidded sideways into the bus that leaned against the edge of the overpass. The rest of the convoy ground to a stop, and two dozen armed men scrambled from their vehicles.

Mason smiled. The ferocious lion had been stopped with nothing more than a tiny thorn.

෴ ෴

Even before the tractor-trailer's tires blew, Nakai knew that something was wrong. The two men left behind had yet to return. Their orders had been simple enough. Catch, question, and kill their pursuer, and then use an abandoned vehicle to return to the convoy. That had not happened. Normally, he would have left them with a radio, but instinct told him not to risk anyone gaining access to their communications. He had to assume that the man following them had somehow managed to kill the two soldiers. He also had to assume that whatever those men knew, his pursuer also now knew.

Nakai and Jeb both stepped from the lead HMMWV and walked cautiously back toward the crippled truck. Two soldiers were climbing down from the cab with AK-47s.

Nakai motioned for Jeb to go on ahead.

"Check the road."

Jeb nodded and continued across the overpass.

Nakai squatted down and studied the truck's left tire. He worked out a twisted piece of metal from the tread and studied it. Two nails carefully bent together, their heads removed. This was no accident. It was a trap.

He didn't need to tell his men to prepare for an assault. They were already doing so. Soldiers manned the two .50 caliber machine guns, rotating them to get maximum coverage of the area. The rest of his men were taking up defensive positions behind the interstate's concrete barriers and the armored doors of the HMMWVs.

Within seconds, Jeb hurried back across the overpass, carrying another of the improvised caltrops.

"We got trouble," he said, tossing the twisted nail to Nakai.

"Yes," he answered, standing back up. "The question is what kind?"

"If this is the same man who's following us, he's a soldier, someone trained in improvised weapons."

"So it seems."

"The nails won't hurt the HMMWVs' honeycomb tires, but the trucks can't cross until we clear this bridge."

Nakai took a moment to consider their predicament. The lead tractor-trailer would be a pain to move now that it had collided with the side of the Greyhound. Crumpled metal had a way of grabbing hold of everything it came into contact with.

"Transfer the cargo to the other trucks. Then get this one pulled out of the way," he said. "Once that's done, sweep the overpass. And let's be quick about it."

"It'll be dark by the time we finish."

Nakai nodded. He didn't like being caught in the open at night, but he didn't see a way out of it. Whoever had set the trap had done so with careful deliberation. His goal had been to slow them down, and that was exactly what he had accomplished.

"Have the men set up a perimeter on this side of the overpass. It looks like we're going to be here for the night."

"Roger that," Jeb said, turning to leave.

"One more thing."

Jeb looked back over his shoulder.

"Sweep the tree line on each side of the road. A quarter-mile each way."

"You think he's close?"

Nakai squinted, scanning the trees.

"I do."

Tanner darted through the trees, his body stinging from a dozen small burns from where the cattle prod had touched him. When he was about a hundred feet in, he cut left and sprinted up a steep slope, heading in Samantha's direction. About halfway up, he nearly barreled into her as she came stumbling down the hill, rifle in hand.

"Come on!" he said, turning to his right and running deeper into the forest.

They ran for nearly ten straight minutes, weaving through the thick maze of trees and brush. When they finally stopped, both were panting heavily.

"Rest," he said, gasping for breath. He turned to face the way they had come, bracing himself against the trunk of an oak tree.

Samantha dropped to her knees and then toppled back onto the seat of her pants, landing in a thick pile of leaves.

"Anyone... following... us?" she gasped, struggling to catch her breath.

Tanner could no longer hear the motorcycles, nor could he see anyone coming through the trees.

"I think we're clear."

"Good." She stretched out her legs and laid the rifle across them.

Tanner waited several more minutes before allowing himself to relax. When he was finally certain that they had made a clean getaway, he moved over and flopped down next to her.

"Thanks," he said.

"For what?"

"For what you did back there. You saved my life."

She looked down at the rifle.

"Do you think I killed them?"

"I sure as hell hope so."

"I don't think my mom would want me shooting people."

He shrugged. "Most mothers want their kids to do whatever it takes to stay alive. Is yours different?"

She shook her head.

"I want to tell you something," he said.

She let her eyes slowly drift his direction.

"What?"

"I'm not one to blow sunshine up your skirt. You know that, right?"

She squinted at him. "I have no idea what you just said."

He smiled. "I'm saying I don't give out meaningless praise."

"So?"

"So, you should believe me when I say that you're something special."

"What do you mean?"

"Scared as you were, you fired four shots at moving targets probably a hundred yards away. And from what I saw, you didn't miss a single one. That's grade-A sniper material in the making."

She managed a little smile, but tears pooled at the corners of her eyes.

"I don't want to shoot anyone else."

He put his arm around her.

"I don't want for you to either. But what we want to do, and what we have to do, are often two different things. Understand?"

She nodded.

"The next time I'm being pulled asunder, I expect to hear your rifle."

"Asunder?" She grinned, wiping at the tears. "New word?"

He smiled and pulled her close.

"I try."

They held one another for a long time. When Samantha finally sat up, she seemed better.

"What now?" she asked.

"Now we assess and survive. Just like every other day."

"Okay," she said, looking around at the forest. "Where do we start?"

"We start with what we have."

"All I've got is this." She held up her rifle. "And it only has one bullet left."

"I don't suppose you have any spare rounds in your pocket?"

"Nope," she said, patting her pants. "Too bad you lost your shotgun."

"I've got something better," he said, pulling out a folding knife, equipped with a three-inch blade and titanium frame.

She looked at it with skepticism.

"That's better than a shotgun?"

"When you're stuck in the wilderness, it is."

"I don't see how."

"Tell me something. What can you do with a gun?"

"Kill things, of course."

"Anything else?"

She thought for a moment.

"No, I don't guess so."

"Exactly." He flipped open the blade, and it made a metallic *click*. "A knife, on the other hand, can save your life in all kinds of ways."

"Like how?"

"You'll see. I bet I'll use it half a dozen times before the sun comes up."

She took a moment to study the knife, trying to decide whether it was indeed the miracle tool he professed it to be.

"Even so, we don't have any food or water. Or even blankets to stay warm."

"Nope," he said with a big smile. "It's all gone."

"And you're happy about that?"

"Of course not. But half an hour ago, vicious road warriors were trying to make me look like Stretch Armstrong. Sitting in the woods with a knife in my hand is a step in the right direction, wouldn't you say?"

"Well, yeah," she said. "You know, you're right. It's not so bad." She glanced back the way they had come. "I don't suppose we can just go back and get our stuff?"

He shook his head. "Too risky. Besides, they probably took everything we had of value."

She turned her attention back to the forest. It seemed to go on forever.

"Which way should we go?"

"The interstate is back to our west," he said, pointing. "If we travel north and parallel it, I'm sure we'll find a small town before long. Once we do, we can get a car and some supplies. Then we're back in business and on our way to Salamanca."

"And how will we know we're walking north?"

He pointed up at the sun, which was already past its midpoint.

"Leave it to the sun and the stars to get you moving in the right general direction."

"Do you think we'll find a town or at least a house before dark?"

"Sure," he said with a confident voice. "How far can it be?"

๛ ๛

Tanner and Samantha wandered north for nearly three hours, trudging up and down hills covered with trees, briars, and kudzu. To their dismay, they found no signs of civilization. As the sun slowly started its descent behind the tree line, they finally came across a small campsite. It consisted of a fire pit, ringed in heavy stones, and a flat grassy area where tents had once been pitched. The campsite didn't appear to have been used in many months, and the only traces of man's footprint were a handful of empty beer cans and a ring of large stumps positioned around the fire pit.

"Looks like we're camping here for the night," he said, picking up the beer cans and examining them.

She turned slowly in a full circle.

"Here?"

"Why not? The ground is flat, and it even has a fire pit."

She looked at him with furrowed brows.

"What good is a fire pit without a fire?"

"Ah," he said, giving her a knowing look. "Do you still have that chocolate bar?"

The question surprised her. She pulled the candy from her pocket. It felt warm and soft.

"It's melted," she said, being careful not to squeeze it.

He took it and carefully set it on one of the stumps.

"Gather us some wood. I'm going to see if I can build us a fire."

Her eyes widened. "Are you one of those survival experts who can start a fire with two sticks?"

"Believe me, that's harder than most people think."

"Then why should I bother with the firewood?"

"Because I'm going to show you a magic trick."

She looked doubtful.

"Get going," he said, waving her off. "We need wood. Lots of it."

She reluctantly turned and began gathering sticks and twigs from the campsite's perimeter. Tanner continued talking while she worked.

"Shelter, heat, food, and water. If we can get those, we're golden."

"I'm sure I don't have to tell you," she said over her shoulder, "but we don't have any of those."

Tanner stacked several small twigs, dry grass, and pine needles into a small teepee structure. Then he spit on the bottom of one of the beer cans and wiped it clean with his t-shirt. When he was satisfied, he unwrapped the candy bar, pinched off a piece of melted chocolate, and smeared it on the bottom of the can.

Samantha watched him as she continued picking up firewood.

"What in the world are you doing?" she asked.

"I told you. Magic," he said, as he began to rub the chocolate around with the tips of his fingers, like he was polishing a pair of jump boots.

She snorted and wandered off to pick up more sticks. When she returned with an armful of wood, Tanner was examining the bottom of the can.

"Come see," he said.

She hurried up next to him.

"What is it?"

He tipped the can so she could see the convex bottom. It was as reflective as any mirror she had ever seen.

"Wow, it's really shiny."

He nodded. "Now watch."

He held the can near his teepee structure and tilted the bottom up to reflect the sunlight. A bright spot appeared on the pile of dried tinder.

"I get it," she said. "It's like a magnifying glass."

"Exactly. The shape of the can reflects and focuses the light. Make the surface shiny enough, and the spot gets real hot, real fast."

They both watched the bright spot illuminating the tinder. In less than a minute, a thin trail of white smoke started streaming up from the grass. Seconds later, a flame flashed to life.

"Whoa!" she exclaimed, clapping her hands.

Tanner quickly knelt down and blew softly, nursing the fire to life.

"Don't blow it out," she warned.

"My breath gives it a little more oxygen to burn."

Samantha looked down at the flame and smiled.

"That's the coolest thing I've ever seen."

"It is, isn't it?" He glanced over at the small pile of firewood that she had gathered. "Get some more wood. Bigger branches, if you can find any on the ground."

"Right," she said, hurrying away.

When she returned the second time, it was nearly dark, and she found a good-sized fire burning in the pit. Tanner was breaking off leafy branches from nearby trees and tossing them back toward the campsite. She dumped the wood beside the fire pit, exhausted.

"Is that enough?" she asked in a tired voice.

"No," he said, without even looking. "Get some more."

Unable to take her eyes off the fire, she slowly turned and went in search of more branches.

By the time she returned, he had constructed a simple shelter by tying one of his shoestrings between two trees and leaning the green foliage against it. He was busy weaving in smaller branches, leaves, and dried grass to create a thatched roof.

"Not bad," she said, dumping the branches onto what was now a respectable pile. She noticed a mound of dandelions and kudzu sitting on one of the stumps. "What are those for?"

"That's dinner."

"Weeds?"

"Those plants are quite nutritious."

She picked up a dandelion and smelled the bright yellow flower.

"We can eat this?"

"Sure." He tossed a large pile of pine needles under the lean-to and crawled in to spread them out. "Come over and try this out."

Samantha walked over and sat beside him on the pile of dried needles.

"It's kind of cramped under here."

"Good. That way we won't get cold."

"I don't suppose you have some magic way of getting us water."

He held up a couple of the empty beer cans.

"That's what these are for. But you'll have to wait until morning to see that trick. Right now—" He froze. "Hand me your rifle. Slowly."

"Why?" She looked around, stiffening with fear.

"Shh," he whispered. "Pass it here."

She carefully handed him the Savage .22 rifle.

He brought it to his shoulder, slowly swung left, and then fired into the darkness. The shot was followed by a quick rustle of the brush. Tanner hopped to his feet and raced out into the forest. He was only gone for a minute, and when he returned, he was carrying a large rabbit by its hind legs.

Samantha stared at it with a mixture of fascination and horror.

"Is it dead?"

He set it down on a rock beside the fire.

"It is."

"Are you going to eat it?"

"No, *we* are going to eat it," he said, opening the knife.

"Unh-unh. Not me."

"No?"

"I told you. I don't eat animals. You know, other than chicken and hamburgers."

"Rabbits are like nature's wild chickens."

She eyed the dead rabbit.

"Nature's wild chickens?"

"It's true. I'm surprised you didn't know that with all your schooling."

"But how can you eat it? It's so furry."

"We have to undress it first. Come on, give me a hand." Tanner lifted the rabbit by its hind legs and held them out to Samantha.

She shook her head.

"Just hold it all ready," he said. "I'm hungry."

She reluctantly reached out and gripped the rabbit's hind legs. They were warm and soft.

"It's heavy," she said, her hands shaking.

"Do you want to close your eyes?"

She looked at the rabbit and then back at him.

"No."

He nodded. "That's my girl."

Tanner used the pocket knife to cut a small notch in the top of the rabbit's hide. Samantha flinched as he slipped a couple of fingers into the hole and peeled the skin down its body until it pulled free, leaving only two small fur-covered feet. He then did the same thing in the other direction, pulling the rest of the skin up over its head.

"There's no blood," she said, surprised.

"There's a little on the inside, but rabbits are mostly meat and bones."

He reached down and snapped the rabbit's four ankle joints and used the knife to cut them off. After that, he placed it on a stump and severed the head.

"This is where it gets a little messy. You still good?"

She nodded, unable to look away.

With the rabbit still lying on the stump, he lifted up the pink flesh on the belly and carefully sliced it open from neck to groin. A thin layer of blood covered his fingers as the organs bulged out.

"You want to be careful not to cut the internals. Especially the bladder or sex organs." He reached down into the pelvic area and lifted the bladder up and out. Then he split the pelvis open with a quick slice. "Hold him while I pull out the innards," he said, lifting the rabbit back up and handing it to her.

When she grabbed it by the front legs, she noticed that her hands were no longer shaking.

"If you do it right," he said, "everything comes out with a little tug." He pulled the organs down and out through the pelvic split and set them aside. "There. Now we cut it up." He cut off the two back legs and then the two shoulders. Finally, he split the body into two pieces, setting all six pieces in a neat row. "Voilà!"

"That's it?"

"Other than looking the rabbit over to make sure that it doesn't have tularemia." He quickly examined the rabbit's organs, picking up the liver and checking it carefully. "If it does, you'll usually see white spots on the liver. This one's good." He held it out for her to take a look.

"I expected it to be bloodier," she said. "It looks kind of like..."

"Like a raw chicken?" he teased.

She shrugged. "Sort of, yeah."

"I told you—nature's wild chickens." Tanner scooped up the rabbit's organs and skin and tossed them into the fire. "Never leave anything that might draw scavengers."

She nodded. "Right."

He dug though the pile of sticks until he found a couple that were green enough not to easily ignite. Then he poked the end of the stick through one of the back legs and added a shoulder and half of the body. Next, he stacked a few smaller rocks on each side of the fire pit to act as supports. When he was satisfied that the setup wouldn't accidently drop his kill into the fire, he set the skewered rabbit in place.

"Should I do the other half?" she asked, looking at the rest of the meat.

"Only if you want to eat."

Without answering, she mimicked what he had done. When she had it ready, she laid her stick on the rocks beside his.

"How long will it take to cook?"

He lowered himself to the ground and leaned up against a stump that was already warm from the fire.

"Not long. Maybe thirty minutes. It's better to cook it slowly."

She looked over at the pile of dandelions and kudzu.

"Are you still going to eat those?"

He patted his thick belly.

"In case you didn't notice, I don't waste food."

She nodded her approval and moved over to sit beside him. The fire felt good.

After a few minutes, he rotated his half of the meat so that it would cook evenly. She did the same. The odor of sizzling meat permeated the entire campsite.

"Wow," she said, licking her lips, "it smells delicious."

He smiled but said nothing.

For the next half-hour, they watched the meat cook, turning from a creamy pink color to a crispy brown. When it was finally ready, Tanner lifted the skewers from the fire and pulled off all six pieces of meat. After letting them cool for a minute, he held out one of the legs to her.

Samantha looked at it for a moment, obviously trying to decide whether or not to accept his offering. Surrendering to hunger, she reached up and took the meat. She stared at it for several seconds without moving.

"Something wrong with it?" he asked.

"I was just thinking that... well, you know, that we should offer some kind of thanks. I mean you took this creature's life."

"Fair enough," he said.

"Really?"

"Sure. Why not?"

"But you're a Buddhist."

"Doesn't mean I'm not thankful."

"Okay then," she said, bowing her head. "Dear God, Tanner and I want to say thanks for the food. Even though this rabbit never did anything to us, we had to kill it to stay alive. Well, just to be clear, I didn't kill it. He did." She glanced over at Tanner. "Anyway, please don't hold it against him." She shrugged. "Amen."

"Amen," he said, immediately pulling off a piece of the crispy flesh and stuffing it into his mouth.

She closed her eyes and took a small bite of the meat.

"Well?" he said, licking his fingers.

She nodded.

He smiled and passed her some of the dandelions and kudzu.

"Think of this as your salad."

She bit off the top of the dandelion. It was a little bitter but certainly no worse than the spinach leaves her mom made her eat. She took another bite of meat, and before long, she was shoveling it in almost as fast as her giant wilderness companion.

B y the time Nakai's soldiers reached the part of the tree line where Mason had been hiding, he had already repositioned himself further down the interstate. He and Bowie now lay beneath a large pine tree, partially buried under a mound of straw. In his years of serving as an Army Ranger, Mason had been on countless reconnaissance missions, and he was no stranger to hiding, or waiting. Both required a calm sense of purpose that not every man possessed. As for Bowie, he seemed to find the entire experience terribly boring and used the time to nap the final hours of the day away, only occasionally stirring to rustle the pine straw.

Despite being nearly three hundred yards away, the convoy remained easy enough to see with its bright headlights and the fast-moving shadows of soldiers working to clear the overpass. They had managed to pull the damaged tractor-trailer back off the bridge and were in the final stages of sweeping the roadway of homemade caltrops. With the fading light, however, their search had become tediously slow. Soldiers were forced to crawl on the ground, scrubbing their hands across the asphalt like metal detectors in search of a lost Rolex.

As darkness took hold, the soldiers retreated to the protection of the convoy. The mercenaries had set up a defensive position with the tractor-trailers arranged end to end along the inner and outer lanes of the interstate. Bright lights beamed out, reflecting off a light fog that was beginning to form. Two of the HMMWVs had been positioned in the gap at the front of the convoy, and the other two at the rear. Each pair of HMMWVs consisted of a light reconnaissance vehicle as well as a more heavily armored model. The heavy vehicles were particularly dangerous because they were each equipped with a pedestal-mounted Browning M2 .50 caliber heavy barrel machine gun—true cannons of death.

Mason had yet to fully flesh out his plan, but what he did know was that the key to stopping the mercenaries was disabling the tractor-trailers. If he could take out a few more trucks, Nakai would not only fail to deliver the goods, his team would be hamstrung with thousands of pounds of equipment that couldn't easily be moved. That, in turn, might force the soldiers to separate, some staying behind to make repairs, while others drove ahead to complete a partial delivery. Dividing the mercenaries into more manageable groups struck him as a reasonable next step in his one-man war. Mason was absolutely confident that, in the end, he would be facing off against Nakai. For now, though, he forced his thoughts to remain focused on inflicting damage on every front.

He studied their position for an easy way to disable another truck. A few bullets to the tires would do it, but the rifle's muzzle flash would announce his position as clearly as hanging a road flare around his neck. No, he thought, his handiwork would have to be done up close and personal. A large rag soaked in gasoline should do the trick. If he could get up to one of the trucks and stuff the rag into the gas tank, it would only take a flick of his lighter to ensure complete chaos. If he were lucky, the fire might even take out two or three trucks.

Bowie stirred, finally sitting up and turning his head from side to side as he surveyed the sounds of the night.

"Are you about ready to move?" whispered Mason.

Bowie pressed a cold wet nose against his cheek.

"All right. Let's get back to the truck and gather a few things. We've got a busy night ahead of us." He stood and brushed the pine straw off his shoulders and back.

Bowie scrambled to his feet too, shaking his entire body to send needles flying in every direction. He looked up at Mason with excitement in his eyes.

Mason nodded to him.

"Stay close."

❧ ❦

Nakai stared out at the night. The enemy was out there, watching him. What he would have given for one of his patrols to have caught the man. Nakai's questions were as obvious as they were irrelevant. What were the man's motivations? What did he hope to accomplish? Was he acting alone or as part of a larger force? While Nakai would have liked to know the answers, he needed none of them. He had learned a long time ago that surviving combat starts and ends with killing the enemy. Everything else was noise.

His first thought had been that General Hood had betrayed him, setting up him and his men to take the fall for the chemical attack. However, after consideration, he realized that it simply didn't add up. For one thing, Hood would have sent a more formidable attack force. Also, he wouldn't have resorted to primitive techniques to stop the convoy.

This enemy, while limited in his capabilities, seemed driven by a personal vendetta. The most reasonable conclusion was that he was a marshal who had somehow managed to escape the gas attack. Perhaps he had been outside the center gathering supplies or conducting some other course of business. Unfortunately, men with revenge in their hearts were often even more dangerous than professional killers.

A car's headlights suddenly lit up the dark from the bottom of the off-ramp. Nakai and the other soldiers instantly turned their weapons in its direction. The car was easily five hundred yards away and didn't appear to be moving. It was just sitting there, facing up the ramp from the small town of Richmond Hill.

Jeb appeared from around one of the tractor-trailers. He was carrying his AK-47 and had donned a black bulletproof vest.

"The bridge is as clear as its going to get," he said. "We'll sweep it one more time in the morning to make sure that nothing new has been introduced."

Nakai nodded, not taking his eyes off the distant headlights.

"What do you make of that?" he asked.

"It's probably the bastard who's been causing us all this trouble."

"Perhaps," Nakai mused, "But why announce himself?"

Jeb thought for a moment.

"Maybe he wants to meet. A parlay of sorts to talk things out."

"What about you? Would you like to get a good look at this man?"

"What I'd really like to do is put my knife in his eye," Jeb said, sliding his hand down to the pommel of his twelve-inch Kukri machete.

Nakai considered his next move carefully. They were probably not in any direct danger while in a defensive position, but only a fool ignored a determined enemy. The longer he delayed dealing with him, the more damage they would be forced to endure.

"Let's you and I go hunting."

❧ ❧

When the headlights first flashed on, Mason was bent over, scuttling across the interstate with Bowie at his side. He immediately pulled the dog behind a nearby car, squatted down, and waited. When nothing happened, he peeked out and saw that a single set of high-beams were shining up the off-ramp. It wasn't the mercenaries. They were as surprised as he was, turning all their guns in the car's direction. Who then? The townspeople of Richmond Hill? Some other threat? Whoever it was, they were drawing the attention of a dangerous group of men, and for that, he was thankful. It should make it easier for him to get his supplies and sabotage one or more of the tractor-trailers.

He shuffled forward, carefully climbed over the median, and dashed across to the cover of trees on the opposite side of the interstate. Bowie stayed close by his side, moving as quietly as his size allowed. When Mason got to the tree line, he turned and hurried to the on-ramp located a couple of hundred yards past the overpass. Unlike the off-ramp, the single lane exit was quiet and dark, with only the occasional squeak emerging from the mash-up of abandoned cars, as they slowly settled against one another.

Mason started to step out from the trees when Bowie crossed in front of him and let out a low warning growl. He squatted down and laid his hand on the dog's side. There was a persistent rumble deep in its chest.

"What is it, boy?" he whispered.

Bowie stood very still, staring off into the night.

Mason followed the dog's stare down the long stretch of asphalt leading toward Richmond Hill. After a moment, he saw them—a series of shadows moving among the jagged column of abandoned cars. At first, there were only a few indistinguishable shapes, but as he watched, their numbers quickly grew. Five—ten—twenty—fifty.

Mason pulled Bowie back into the tree line a few feet and took a knee. As the crowd drew closer, he saw that the procession of shadows were actually people infected by the virus. They clustered together, shuffling stiff and bent over, hiding behind cars as they advanced up the on-ramp. There were so many that he soon lost count. As he watched them snake up the ramp, Mason was struck by how much they looked like an army of undead, seemingly mindless and set only on bloody violence.

But he understood that this was not truly the case. They were not zombies; just poor souls infected by a mutating virus. Neither were they mindless. The group moved quietly and with purpose. They were also coordinated, staying in small clusters, rather than in a single mob. But what set them apart most from mindless, flesh-eating zombies were their tactics. They had drawn the attention of the soldiers to the off-ramp using the headlights and were now attempting to mount a sneak attack on the convoy.

One thing that was not in question, however, was their violent intent. There was an electric charge to the air, a feeling that he had experienced many times when war was at hand. The strange sensation was not unique to Mason, as he had known many soldiers who claimed to feel it as well. Whether it was a natural sense of foreboding or something more extra-sensory, he couldn't say. What he did know was that a terrible battle was about to begin.

಄ ఴ

Nakai carried a Steyr Aug A3, and Jeb an AK-47, as they worked their way down the steep slope covered in knee-high grass. They maintained a distance of about fifteen feet apart, both of them taking care to stay well outside the persistent shine of the bright headlights. As they got to the bottom of the slope, they split left and right. Jeb immediately sought cover behind a black Ford Crown Victoria that looked like it had once belonged to an FBI agent, while Nakai advanced to stand with his back against the brick wall of a convenience store.

The sky was clear, and stars shone down like millions of shards of broken glass. Both men took several minutes to let their eyes adjust to the darkness. The air was cool and filled with enough humidity to make breathing noticeably more difficult.

The vehicle with the bright headlights was still far enough away that Nakai couldn't quite make it out. It was big. That much he could tell—a truck, maybe. His enemy would not be inside, but he would likely be close.

He moved ahead carefully, watching out of the corner of his eye to keep pace with Jeb. They separated further and further as they advanced. By the time they got to within a few paces of the vehicle, they were coming at it from nearly ninety degrees apart, Jeb from the driver's side and Nakai from the rear.

The vehicle was a tow truck, heavy, with lots of torque. It could haul a car out of a ditch as easily as a parent might lift a toddler from the tub. The whole truck was canted to the left, the result of something heavy smashing into the driver's side quarter panel. The bottom half of the door was crumpled so badly that Nakai doubted that it would even open. He advanced a little further to see the passenger-side door. It too was dented, and the window had been smashed in. Someone had obviously leaned in and flipped on the lights.

Jeb shuffled up to the mangled driver's side door and quickly popped up, muzzle first, to peek in through the window. It was empty. He stepped around to the rear of the vehicle, squatted down, and motioned to Nakai that no one was inside.

Seeing Jeb's all clear, Nakai turned to survey his surroundings. The street was filled with abandoned and broken-down vehicles, most of them crashed or skewed at odd angles, no doubt the result of people trying to push their way through the congestion. His prey could be hiding in any one of them, planning his next move, or perhaps just waiting for morning.

Nakai could make out the dark but familiar sign for a Motel 6 not far down the street. Half a dozen smaller buildings lined the sides of the thoroughfare, most of them unrecognizable in the night. Other than the tow truck, there wasn't a single light to be found anywhere—no candles, no flashlights, not so much as a flicker of someone lighting a late-night smoke. It was as if the town had died in its entirety. That struck him as strange. Even the hardest hit communities had their share of survivors. Why was Richmond Hill different?

As if in answer to his question, the wind shifted, and he caught the sound of faint whispers. Someone was out there. Someone who didn't want to be discovered.

ॐ ॐ

Peeking out from behind a huge pine tree, Mason took a moment to consider his next course of action. If he did nothing, the hundreds of infected men and women who were secretly snaking their way up the on-ramp would soon swarm the mercenaries. While Mason held no love for the soldiers of fortune, he needed to capture Nakai alive. Not for any honorable intention, such as seeing him convicted in a court of law, but rather, to use whatever means were necessary to discover the man's employer. If Nakai died, so would Mason's only link to whomever had masterminded the attack on the marshals.

It would take but a single shot to draw the attention of the mercenaries and spoil the ambush. Once alerted, the soldiers would chew them up with the .50 caliber machine guns. But in doing so, it would put Mason back on uneven ground against an army of trained soldiers. Despite his recent success in slowing their convoy, he saw no clear way to actually defeat them.

No, he thought, I will wait and let the enemy of my enemy do my bidding. If Nakai and his men triumph, they will be weaker and fewer in number. Even if they lose, Nakai might find a way of escaping. He was, according to Van Gogh, a very dangerous man. And dangerous men often found ways to survive.

❧ ☙

Nakai motioned for Jeb to approach. The big man rushed across a small parking lot and moved up beside him. Nakai was peeking around the corner of a small grocery store.

"Do you see him?" whispered Jeb.

Without answering, Nakai stepped back and motioned for him to take a look.

When Jeb leaned around the corner, he saw dozens of men and women moving along the dark street. Their bodies were stiff, and they shuffled along like their knees didn't bend quite right. They made very little sound other than heavy breathing and the scrubbing of their shoes across the asphalt. They all moved in the direction of the off-ramp to the interstate. Most of them carried primitive weapons—pipes, sticks, knives, and shovels.

Jeb ducked back around the corner.

"Night of the frickin' dead!"

Nakai nodded.

The two men stood in the shadow of the building and watched as the mob slowly passed. When the infected arrived at the tow truck, they stopped and began banging on the hood, shouting at the soldiers on the interstate above them.

"What the hell?" Jeb looked astonished. "Do they really think they can draw us out? Even if they did, those sticks and shovels wouldn't hold up against rifles."

Nakai said nothing as he gazed up the long off-ramp. He played out possible scenarios. Even using the cover of cars, anyone who tried to charge up the ramp would be shot to pieces. Were they really that stupid?

But they didn't advance. Instead, the infected began shouting unintelligible obscenities as they continued taking great pleasure in beating the hell out of the tow truck.

A thought suddenly occurred to Nakai. His eyes scanned the night, looking for confirmation. Then he saw it—the back door.

"Shit," he spat, pushing off the wall, and bringing the Aug up to his shoulder.

"What is it?" asked Jeb, raising his own weapon.

"They're a decoy. We've got to warn the men."

⁊ ⁋

Looking out over the roof of the HMMWV, Lieutenant Tripp gripped the handles of Browning M2 .50 caliber machine gun. Corporal Finn stood down at ground level, ready to help spot for him. They both listened to the sound of crazies beating the paint off the car at the end of the off-ramp.

Finn seemed especially agitated.

"First, they turn on the lights. Now, they go ape shit. What the hell, Lieutenant?"

"It must be pus pockets," said Tripp.

"I say we give 'em a taste of Ma Deuce," Finn said, using the familiar moniker for the heavy gun.

"You heard our orders. We don't fire unless a threat is confirmed. You want to be the one to explain to Jeb why we broke silence?"

Finn shifted his weight back and forth from foot to foot.

"Not me, man. You're the gunner."

"And I say we wait." Tripp looked around at the rest of the men. Most had weapons up and ready, facing down the ramp.

A distinctive burp of gunfire suddenly sounded from the town below. Finn looked up at Tripp.

"That's an Aug. Nakai's giving us the go ahead."

Tripp wasn't so sure.

The burping of the Aug was quickly joined by the *thump thump thump* of an AK-47 as gunfire flashed at the bottom of the off-ramp. Men looked around at one another. Most stared over at Tripp, who was the ranking officer in Jeb and Nakai's absence.

Feeling the pressure, Tripp raised his arm and dropped it sharply. Before his hand had even reached his side, the mercenaries let loose with long strings of small-arms fire. As had been the case for generations, when things got confusing, soldiers were most comfortable resolving matters with a little snap, crackle, and pop.

Finn looked up at him and nodded.

"It's time, Lieutenant."

Tripp swung the weapon over and lined up the bore sight with the headlights shining at the bottom of the ramp. Most of the small arms didn't have the range to accurately target the car, which was sitting at around five hundred yards. The Browning M2, however, was a beast all its own.

Tripp used his thumbs to depress the butterfly trigger, sending a single slow-fire burst of .50 BMG rounds hurtling toward the headlights. The thunderous sound of the heavy machine gun sent percussion waves that rattled windows and jarred teeth. Almost instantly, the right headlight went out, and sparks flew as the heavy slugs, moving with more than ten thousand foot-pounds of energy, chewed through the front end of the tow truck.

The second .50 caliber gunner joined it, firing a short burst at the remaining light. It hit a little short, but he quickly walked it up on target. With his second firing, metal found metal, and the ramp went dark.

⮜ ⮞

Mason heard the unmistakable sound of an Aug firing down at street level. Was it Nakai? Van Gogh had said that Nakai preferred the Aug. But what was he doing down there? A thought suddenly occurred to him. The lights must have lured Nakai out. Maybe he even thought it was Mason. It had been too good an opportunity for the mercenary to pass up.

More gunfire sounded. This time from an AK-47, the rhythmic pumping of rounds also easily recognizable. Nakai was not alone.

Mason turned back to the on-ramp. The infected had worked their way quietly up the ramp and were gathering at the top. There were easily two hundred of them now, all pressed together as if waiting for someone to give the order to attack.

My Lord, he thought, they're going to be hard to stop. But if he was right, and Nakai was indeed away from his men, Mason no longer needed to worry about the outcome of the battle. He only needed to find Nakai. The rest of the mercenaries could rot in hell for all he cared. What goes around comes around.

More gunfire sounded, this time from soldiers on the interstate. Assault rifles first, followed by the big .50 caliber machine guns. The barrage of gunfire was apparently the cue that the silent horde had been waiting for because they began rushing across the overpass. With all eyes turned to the firefight, not a single soldier had yet to see them. If that didn't change soon, what could have been a one-sided shooting match would turn into a medieval bloodbath.

❧ ❦

Corporal Finn saw the enemy about three seconds before they broke through the perimeter. For a moment, his mind refused to accept what he was seeing. Hundreds of creatures raced toward him, climbing over cars and leaping onto his fellow soldiers like bloodthirsty savages.

Finn bumped Lieutenant Tripp's leg.

"Lieutenant!" he yelled. "Incoming!"

Lieutenant Tripp looked first to Finn, and seeing the horror on his face, whirled around to find the madness that was already upon them. He swung the heavy machine gun around and held down the butterfly trigger, letting loose a thunderous volley of lead. Dozens of the infected were torn apart, arms, legs, and heads exploding, drenching everything in huge sheets of blood. He continued to track them even though his own men were caught in the crossfire and being cut in half by the horrific .50 caliber bullets.

Other soldiers joined in, turning their fire in the direction of the infected. But the creatures were relentless, fighting to the death while hacking and clubbing with pipes, sticks, and axes. For every soldier, there were a dozen of the infected, and in less than a minute, only a few of the mercenaries remained.

Corporal Finn was trying to swap rifle magazines when they finally overran his position, clawing and beating him until he was little more than a mound of bloody meat. Tripp held out a few seconds longer, the barrel of his Browning steaming in the night as round after round pelted the relentless army of monsters. But he too was soon pulled down and savagely torn to pieces. As the last mercenary fell, the only sounds that remained were that of the mashing and hammering of bodies.

❧ ❦

As soon as Nakai and Jeb opened fire, the infected at the base of the off-ramp turned toward them and charged. The Aug and AK-47 both functioned flawlessly, as did their operators, dropping creature after creature. But the monsters were no longer easily brought down, taking several rounds to stop each one. Within seconds, both men knew that it was a fight they could not win.

"Fire and smoke!" yelled Nakai.

Without hesitation, Jeb ripped an M67 fragmentation grenade from his web gear, pulled the pin, and hurled it toward the creatures. At the same time, Nakai rolled a smoke canister that immediately began spraying a thick gray cloud.

Both men turned and dove in the opposite direction.

The grenade's explosion rocked the street, lifting the back end of the tow truck off the ground and ripping arms and legs from several of the infected. But it wasn't nearly enough. In the thick cover of the billowing gray smoke, both men scrambled to their feet and ran.

Nakai's first inclination was to head back toward his men, but he could already hear their screams. Long strings of gunfire erupted, but what was most telling was the bellowing sound of the .50 caliber as it pounded their own position. Things had already gone to shit. Two extra rifles would not determine the outcome of the battle.

Not knowing which way to go, Nakai and Jeb ran east along Ocean Highway. The four-lane road was lined on both sides by restaurants, hotels, and gas stations. Jeb looked over and saw dozens of the infected survivors pouring out of a Scottish Inn.

"Christ!" he said, pointing. "They're sleeping in the motel rooms."

Without pausing to look, Nakai turned right and cut across a long parking lot. Jeb stayed close at his heels, watching their six. They ducked behind a Domino's Pizza and paused for a moment to get their bearings. Screams and gunfire continued from the overpass a few blocks behind them.

Nakai scanned the street.

"We've got to get off this main road. The whole town is nothing but pus pockets."

"I'm with you," said Jeb. "But we don't know which way is which."

Nakai pointed back the way they had come.

"Well, we know that way is death." He swung his arm around to point in the opposite direction. "Let's put a little distance between us and them. Maybe we can find a place to hole up until morning."

≈ ≪

Mason and Bowie stayed well inside the tree line, slowly working their way up the steep slope so they could get a better view of the interstate and the town below. The fighting on the overpass was dying down, and it was clear by the lack of gunfire that good old-fashioned sticks and stones had won the day.

Richmond Hill was dark and clear. The infected that had been beating on the tow truck had evidently pursued Nakai and his partner. Most of the rest had gathered at the top of ramp to enjoy the barbaric festivities.

The question at hand was where had Nakai gone? Richmond Hill was not an overly large town, perhaps three miles in each direction, but that would be impossible for Mason to cover on foot. Not to mention the fact that aimlessly wandering the town at night would be pure suicide. His only hope was that Nakai would be forced to open fire and give away his position.

Mason sat on the ground and leaned back against a tree. Bowie circled the tree a couple of times, sniffing squirrel droppings, fermented nuts, and nature's other interesting odors. When he was satisfied there wasn't anything to eat nearby, he flopped down and rested his head on Mason's lap.

"I know this hasn't quite worked out as planned," Mason said, rubbing the dog behind its ears. "But at least we're not down there."

Bowie scooted closer until half his body was lying across Mason's lap.

"Let's watch for a while. If they give up their position, we'll go in after them. If not, we'll stay in the trees and search them out in the morning. Sound good?"

Bowie closed his eyes and slid his tongue in and out of his mouth a few times, content to wait as long as necessary.

�� ��

"There!" Nakai said, pointing to a fenced-in business directly ahead of them.

The *Jack Rabbit Storage* facility consisted of a small manager's office and two long sheet-metal buildings divided into rental units. The side of the office building had a cartoon painted on it of a rabbit wearing tennis shoes. The entire property was surrounded by an eight-foot-high chain-link fence.

They sprinted to the main entrance and inspected the large motorized gate. It was not only closed up tight; it was also chained shut. Nakai scanned the setup for an easy way in. The gate and fence were both topped with barbed wire, but where they attached, two different height poles had been used. He smiled. The staggering of barbed wire was a mistake frequently made by commercial fencing companies.

He quickly scaled the fence, pulled himself up along the taller pole, and stepped over the barbed wire on the lower fence. Then he carefully climbed down inside the facility. Jeb covered him until he was safely back on the ground, and then he repeated the same method of entry. They quickly walked along the fence line to determine how defensible the compound might be. They stopped when they came to a huge hole cut in the fencing.

"I knew it was too good to be true," muttered Jeb. "Something's been coming and going around here."

Both of them turned to face the small brick office building. The front door was partially ajar, but it was dark and still inside. Nakai held his finger up to his lips, and Jeb nodded. Both men leaned their rifles against the brick wall and drew their blades. Nakai readied a black Ka-bar knife, and Jeb his Kukri machete.

Nakai held his fingers in the air, counting down: *three... two... one!* They rushed the door and split left and right.

A dark shape immediately jumped at Jeb, screaming with bloodthirsty fury. He sliced upward with his machete, cutting the man from groin to gut and sending warm blood and entrails spilling out over his hand. Jeb kicked him away to maintain distance, and swung the blade in a huge figure eight. Twice his Kukri met meat and bone, and both times it came out the other side.

Nakai felt strong hands grab him from behind, trying to pull him down. He spun and stabbed the man's torso with quick motions. After the fifth stab, the man fell forward against him, blood gurgling from his mouth. Nakai shoved him off and turned, pressing his back against the wall.

A third infected man pushed his way past them and stumbled out into the night. He was bleeding from the hip and shoulder. Nakai darted out after him, and Jeb immediately stepped back and covered his retreat, windmilling his blade to prevent anyone from following.

The infected man only made it about ten feet before Nakai came up from behind, pulled his head back, and cut him from ear to ear. As he lowered the body to the ground, he scanned the night. The air remained quiet and still. When he was satisfied that they hadn't been detected, he turned and hurried back into the building.

Jeb was about five feet inside the room, fighting with a fourth man. They were struggling for control of the machete. Before Nakai could intervene, Jeb flipped the infected man over his hip and drove the machete deep into his chest. He ripped it free and spun back to face the room. Nothing moved.

They stood for nearly a minute, listening to the sounds of their own heavy breathing.

"I think we're clear," whispered Jeb.

"For now."

They went back outside and dragged the body back into the building.

"What do you think?" Jeb asked, looking around. "Want to hole up here for the night?"

Nakai thought about it a moment, and then shook his head.

"Let's go find an open storage unit. They're less likely to stumble upon us if we're out of the way."

They went back outside, closed the door, and recovered their rifles. Then they walked slowly down the long row of rental units. About halfway down, they found several that didn't have locks on them. Nakai went to the middle one, set his rifle down, and prepared to slide the door up.

Three... two... one!

President Glass studied the three men sitting across from her, trying not to let her gaze rest on General Carr longer than on anyone else. Despite her position, she had never considered herself very good at keeping secrets. She liked to lay her cards on the table early and often in order to make the best possible decision. But she had agreed to keep their discussions about the chemical attack private until they knew more, and that was exactly what she intended to do.

She had called the meeting under the guise of having a general discussion on national security, but in truth, she hoped to learn more about who might have the means and inclination to conduct such a heinous crime against the US Marshals.

"Gentlemen," she started, "I've asked you here to have a frank discussion about the security and recovery of our nation. We've experienced serious deterioration of every national infrastructure, and I believe it's more important than ever to remain vigilant against both foreign and domestic threats. General, let's start with you. Have you had time to assess how secure we are from those outside our borders?"

General Carr had a large stack of folders, all marked with various Secret and Top Secret cover pages, but he refrained from opening any of them.

"Madam President, our enemies largely remain the same—only their capabilities are diminished. Russia was devastated and is in a situation as tenuous as our own. St. Petersburg is the only city that remains even under partial government control. It is not expected that the current communist authority will remain in power for much longer. As for China, every major city is now uninhabited, except for the infected survivors of the virus. The rural areas fared a little better, mainly because the residents had less exposure. Our best guess is that, in time, the farmers will once again rise up and take control of their country."

"And their nuclear arsenals? Are they secure?"

"To be honest, we don't know. We have very little insight into either country at this point. What I can say is that we haven't seen any military action that could be considered threatening. Unfortunately, that doesn't mean that a launch, accidental or otherwise, could not occur. With that said, experts have assessed the threat as being unlikely."

"Unlikely that we'll all die in a nuclear fireball?" she said. "That's not very reassuring."

"No, it isn't, but you indicated that you wanted an open and honest discussion. It's what we know at this point."

She nodded. "Yes, I'm sorry. Please go on, General."

"Not much remains of the so-called Axis of Evil. Iran's population and infrastructures were decimated, including its military. A few ruling clerics remain, but their previous anti-American rhetoric has been toned down as they look for allies to help them recover."

"They're looking to the US to provide relief?" she said with a tone of incredulity.

"Everyone is looking for help, ma'am. Iran is just one of many."

"And North Korea?"

"North Korea collapsed from within. Its leaders were summarily executed, and the country is now in the hands of what remains of their military. Again, the rural nature of the country spared many of the farmers, but most will likely starve before the year is out. Experts are suggesting that South Korea will be invited in to help stabilize and unify the peninsula."

"That sounds positive. And China won't oppose this?"

"With an estimated one billion people dead in China alone, they simply don't have the means to take an offensive position against anyone."

"A billion people? Could that be right?"

He shrugged. "It's an educated guess but probably not far off the mark."

"My God," she whispered.

"Military threats are not our only concern," said Tom Pinker, the Secretary of Homeland Security. Pinker was a serious man who seemed more suited to running a spy agency than serving in a cabinet position. He was small in stature, barely five feet tall, but he had a commanding voice and a knack for sifting fact from bullshit.

"Go on," she said.

"Our border with Mexico is now essentially unguarded, and there are thousands of illegals crossing over every day."

"Why? Surely, the promise of a better life has lost some of its luster, given the condition of our country."

"As bad as it is here, it's far worse in Mexico. Drug cartels now run the country, and survivors are being brutalized in every possible way. The biggest problem for us is not the influx of illegals but the actions of the cartels. They have already taken control of several US border towns, and before long, they will look to extend their reach."

"And can we stop them?"

He shrugged. "That depends."

"On what?"

"On whether we continue to take a defensive posture or adopt one that is more aggressive."

She was unsure of exactly what he was implying.

"Spell it out for me, Tom."

Pinker cleared his throat.

"Vice President Pike and I were discussing the matter yesterday. He believes, and I agree, that we should consider striking the major cartels as a deterrent to future aggressions."

"In other words, you want to hit them first?"

"Yes, ma'am. Even with our diminished military, we could conduct operations that would greatly hamper their ability to disrupt the United States. It would all be very low risk to our remaining forces. Tomahawk missiles and air strikes could do what was needed."

"Attacking citizens of another country could be construed as an act of war."

"I think we're past that, Madam President. Mexico is essentially without a government at the moment."

She turned to General Carr.

"General, what do you think of a preemptive attack on Mexico's cartels?"

"This is the first I've heard of it," he said, obviously irritated by not being included in the discussion with Vice President Pike. "However, I wouldn't dismiss it out of hand. Our country has enough to worry about without drug cartels moving in."

She nodded. "Okay, we'll take that up with the generals. What else, Tom?"

"The situation on the northern border is very different. Canada wasn't hit as hard as the US, and we've already received formal complaints that many of our residents are crossing over in search of food and emergency supplies."

"Does that strike anyone else as ironic?" she asked. "Immigrants are rushing in from the south while our citizens are fleeing to the north?" She didn't wait for an answer, waving away the question. "It doesn't matter. The

Canadians will have to deal with it for now. We're not going to put what few resources remain toward keeping people from leaving the country."

"Yes, ma'am," he said, jotting something down on a pad.

"How are we doing inside the borders?" she asked. "Are we still being plagued by infighting?"

"We are, but Jack might be better able to answer that." Pinker turned to Jack Fry, the Director of the Federal Emergency Management Agency.

President Glass had known Jack for longer than any of the other men, and she considered him a close friend. Shortly after she took office, he had been involved in an auto accident that left him paralyzed from the waist down and confined to a wheelchair. Despite his injuries, he had not lost his almost grandfatherly way of dealing with those around him.

"Jack?" she said.

He smiled warmly at her.

"Ma'am, I'm afraid that it's gone from bad to just plain awful. Violence and lawlessness are spreading to every corner of the country. Of course, we're still trying to get supplies out, but given that they now require full military escort, we've had to greatly reduce the number of relief convoys."

"What about air drops? Can't we drop food and supplies using cargo planes?"

"General Carr and I have been working on that," he said, gesturing to the general. "The problem is one of putting supplies in the hands of law-abiding citizens and not violent militias. Also, there are obvious issues with the availability of planes, fuel, and crew. But challenges aside, we will begin a campaign of air-dropping supplies in the coming weeks."

"But that's not going to be enough, is it?" she said. It was more of a statement than a question.

"No, ma'am, it won't be nearly enough."

"Which means that people will continue to resort to taking what they need."

He nodded. "I'm afraid so."

She turned back to General Carr.

"How are we with clearing a few major cities? Places where we can provide security and supplies for those who remain."

He opened one of his folders and removed a map. On it were symbols denoting different military units. There were surprisingly few of them.

"We've begun moving forces to establish supply routes," he said, moving his finger across the map. "Our plan is to start with three cities: Denver, Norfolk, and Olympia."

"Why those cities?"

"Norfolk and Olympia provide port access, and Denver is centrally located. All three are small enough to be cleared in a reasonable time frame. A city like Los Angeles or New York would be years in the making."

"All right," she said. "And how long do you think it will take to clear these three cities?"

"That's tough to say for certain. We have two issues to deal with. The first is handling the infected survivors, some of whom are more cooperative than others."

She raised an eyebrow at him.

"Tell me you're not planning to just go in and kill them all."

"No, ma'am. Those who have devolved will be put down. The rest will be registered and allowed to stay on."

"Registered?"

"Yes, ma'am. It's the only way to monitor their health."

"You want to make sure they don't go crazy."

He nodded. "That's right."

"What else must be done besides dealing with the infected? I imagine getting the bodies out will be a nightmare."

"Indeed. Massive cleanup teams will come in behind the combat force to get rid of the bodies."

"How exactly?"

"We're planning to use mobile incinerators."

"We can't bury them?"

He shook his head.

"Okay, she said. "So, I'll ask again—how long will it take to clear the three cities?"

"Our best guess is four months."

"That long?"

"Yes, ma'am. It's important that we get them cleared before winter arrives. But understand that four months refers only to the time to clear the city and ensure that they are habitable."

"What does that mean?"

"It means that they will no longer function as modern cities."

"Go on."

"We'll have to ration food, water, and fuel. Beyond that, these new colonies, for lack of a better term, will function like huge bazaars in which people must trade goods and services."

"You're telling me that, in many ways, these people will still be on their own."

He nodded. "That's right. Life won't be easy, but it should be better than it is now."

"Will they have electricity?"

"No, ma'am. That's still some time off."

She shook her head, clearly disappointed.

"And this is the best we can do?"

He gave her an understanding smile.

"We'll try to do better."

"If I'm hearing you correctly, even if this operation is successful, the entire United States will be reduced to a few colonies. What about the rest of the country?"

"It will remain much like it is today."

"Lawless, in other words."

"While some of the country is indeed lawless," interjected Jack, "other parts are being taken over by militias, warlords, cartels, and religious cults."

"That doesn't make me feel better, Jack."

"No, ma'am."

She sat quietly for a moment, thinking.

"It's going to take some time. That's what you're all really telling me, isn't it?"

All three men nodded.

General Carr added, "In a way, we're like the early Roman Empire, hoping to spread our influence across a violent continent. And you know what they say..."

She smirked. "Yeah, yeah, I get it. Rome wasn't built in a day."

❧ ❧

Vice President Pike could almost feel Yumi Tanaka's naked breasts pressing against his back, her sharp fingernails digging into his shoulders. She had left more than two hours earlier, sneaking away when there was little chance of her being discovered, but the perfumed smell of her body had not yet left his bed.

Their relationship continued to deepen, which was both comforting and troubling to him. On the surface, it was driven by a nearly insatiable desire, but hidden beneath were undeniable feelings. He found it odd that they never spoke of such things, but he thought he knew why. For one thing, he was much older than Yumi, and both surely recognized the fleeting nature of their relationship. Also, the truth was that he didn't want to love Yumi, nor, he suspected, did she want to love him. They were both users in every sense of the word. But somewhere along the way, and purely by accident, their souls had brushed a little too closely, and a bond had been formed. So fight it or not, every time she stepped into the room, he felt his stomach tighten and his heart skip a beat. He accepted that it was childish and stupid, but also completely out of his control.

Even the memory of Yumi's touch, however, was not enough to relieve Pike's worry. He tossed and turned, struggling to clear his mind. Insomnia was the first of many physiological symptoms that he experienced when plans went awry. And things had definitely gone awry. Problems had plagued him from the very beginning. The kidnapping of the President's daughter, Samantha, had gone terribly wrong when her bodyguard threatened to expose their plan. The subsequent air attack was botched, and the girl not only walked away, but managed to find a traveling companion who rivaled Spartacus.

Agent Sparks, one of General Hood's most trusted men, was still looking for the girl. Once he managed to pick back up her embedded transponder signal, he should be able to make short work of the problem. But he had already missed her twice. Who was to say that she wouldn't elude him a third time—or a fourth? Samantha was wily if nothing else.

Then there was the attack on Glynco. According to General Hood, that was the only operation that had gone off without a hitch. The marshals had been easily dispatched and the weapons seized. Within hours, the rifles should be arriving in Lexington and delivered to Lenny Bruce, a zealot who was building his own version of a utopian society, known as Fresh Start.

Lenny was smart and charismatic, someone who could win most arguments with words. When that failed, however, he was not above sending someone over with a pair of pliers to ensure that his point of view was better appreciated. Lenny had held many stations in life, including city councilman, tent evangelist, and white supremacist.

He had managed to recruit nearly a thousand men, mostly convicts, but the community was quickly attracting families with nowhere else to turn. By all accounts, he was a true believer, a man who saw a brighter future now that the country's government had all but disintegrated. For his vision to come to fruition, however, what remained of the corrupt establishment had to be put down. That was how he fit into Pike's plans.

Lenny was not so different from the mercenaries that General Hood had contracted. He would fight against the establishment, embarrassing President Glass and making it clearer with each passing day that she was losing control of what little remained of the nation. When she was finally out of office, either by having stepped down or by being forced out, Pike would lead the country back to its former greatness.

The thing that bothered him about the Glynco attack was that he had not yet been briefed. The murders had surely been discovered by now, which could only mean that President Glass was intentionally keeping it from him. But why? The reality of it was that she was keeping him at arm's length on a number of things. It occurred to him that isolation was her weapon of choice. She might be unwilling to confront him directly, but like every woman he had ever met, she was perfectly capable of giving him the cold shoulder.

Equally disturbing was that General Hood, the Head of Special Operations Warfare, had also been kept in the dark. Given his position and the use of chemical weapons in the attack, Hood should have been brought in from the very beginning. His exclusion meant that President Glass, or perhaps her Secretary of Defense, General Carr, was growing more suspicious, more careful.

But Pike was certain that suspicion was all it was. There was no connection between the attack and either himself or General Hood. The weapons had been hidden away for decades, a trail so cold that no one could uncover it. And any investigation of the attack would point to a shadowy group of mercenaries—yet another violent act of forces battling for control. In the unlikely event that the mercenaries were ever found, General Hood would make sure that they were obliterated and unable to implicate him.

All Pike needed to do was continue working behind the scenes to set the stage for his ascension to power. Just as Napoleon had been welcomed by turmoil-ridden France, so too would he be called upon to bring order to a post-apocalyptic America.

CHAPTER
10

Samantha was dreaming about being a rabbit chased by a hungry fox when a hand squeezed her shoulder. Startled, she abruptly sat up.

"Huh? What?"

"You thirsty?" asked Tanner.

She looked around. The sun hadn't quite come up yet, but it would be light soon.

"Very," she said, swallowing.

"Come on, then. I'll show you how to get some water." He handed her a couple of the empty beer cans with the tops cut off. "You'll need to take off one of your socks."

"My socks? Why?"

"Just do it," he said, pulling off his own boot.

She did as he instructed, taking off one of her socks and then slipping her boot back onto her bare foot.

"Now, follow me," he said.

When they got to the edge of the campsite, he squatted down and rubbed his sock across a large patch of green clover.

"Feel," he said, holding out the sock.

She touched it. "It's wet."

"It's dew." He set one of the beer cans on the ground and squeezed the sock over it. A few drops of water dripped into the can.

"That'll take forever," she said.

"We'll see."

Without another word, they got busy mopping their socks across plants of every sort, collecting the moisture that had condensed as the temperatures cooled through the night. To Samantha's surprise, by the time the sun started peeking over the trees, they had managed to fill all four cans.

She held up one and examined the water. It was mostly clear, but several small twigs and plants floated on the surface.

"Is it safe to drink?" she asked, sniffing it.

"Maybe. But let's boil it to be safe."

She looked pointedly at his sock.

"Good idea."

They set the cans of water in the campfire's hot embers, and their socks on a rock nearby to dry. Before long, the water began to bubble. Tanner used his sock like an oven mitt to pull the cans out of the fire pit and set them on the rock to cool.

"By the time the water cools, it'll be safe to drink."

"Where'd you learn all this stuff?" she asked, sitting down to put her sock back on.

"The question is what have you been learning?"

"What do you mean?"

"Somewhere along the way, people became too dependent on the comforts of the system. Hardly anyone knows how to find water, work the land, or catch their own food. Humans have forgotten what it takes to survive on good old Mother Earth."

"And that's important?"

"You tell me."

She pondered on it for a moment, watching the steam rise off the water.

"I guess it is now."

Tanner gave her the thumbs up.

A thought tickled her, and she giggled.

"What?" he asked.

"I always thought of you as my protector. But in a weird way, you're sort of my teacher too."

He smiled. She was finally getting it.

ঌ ◌

Tanner kicked dirt over the last of the smoldering embers.

"You ready?" he asked.

Samantha took one last look at their campsite and nodded.

"Yeah. Let's go find breakfast."

"Cheerios?"

She grinned. "Froot Loops."

He looked up at the sky to get his bearings, and then spun slightly to the left and pointed at the forest.

"North would be that way."

They walked steadily and with a sense of purpose for a good hour, up and down sloping hills covered in dense growth. Without anything larger than a pocketknife at their disposal, they were forced to push their way through thick brambles covered with thorns as sharp as fishing barbs. By the time they finally broke out into a wide clearing, they were bleeding from a dozen scratches on their hands, arms, and faces.

Ahead of them lay an open stretch of farmland nested in a shallow valley. The valley easily spanned a mile from north to south and many more than that from east to west. The interstate was visible a few hundred yards off to their left, and they could see the outline of a small town about a mile ahead.

Tanner pointed in the direction of the town.

"See?" he said. "I told you we find something."

"Yeah, but you forgot to mention the part where we'd be spending the night in the forest."

"It wasn't so bad, was it?"

"No," she said, shaking her head, "I guess not. Besides, when I get back to school, I'm going show my class some of the cool tricks you taught me. Like you said, everyone should know that kind of stuff."

"All right then," he said, marching ahead. "Onward."

They pressed across the open farmland that lay fallow and neglected. Rye grass and weeds were slowly taking over patches of fertile soil. After about twenty minutes, they came across a small two-lane highway that meandered its way into town. The road was surprisingly clear of abandoned cars. Even though it wasn't a straight shot into town, they opted to walk the highway because they were tired of pouring dirt out of their boots.

A few hundred yards ahead, they came across two signs. The first welcomed them to Bland County, Virginia, and the second identified the road as Highway 656. The middle digit had been painted over with red paint, so that the sign now read "666."

Samantha stopped and studied the highway marker.

"In church, they said 666 is a bad number. Have you ever heard that?"

Tanner dodged the question, saying, "It was probably just kids having fun with a can of spray paint."

She paused to study the small buildings several hundred yards in the distance.

"Maybe we should skip this town."

"You itching for another night in the woods?"

She shrugged.

He looked over at the interstate to their west.

"If we run into those motorcyclists again, I'm going to need a way to thank them for their hospitality. Unless you have a better idea, I think we're going to have to chance it."

She hesitated and then nodded reluctantly.

They walked for another ten minutes before arriving at the edge of the small county seat of Bland. There was a large elementary school to their left, with a matching gymnasium adjacent to it. Both buildings had been badly burned by a fire that looked to have originated from inside the school's cafeteria. Like the highway, the parking lot was empty except for a couple of school vans, both of which had been destroyed by the fire.

The road ahead of them forked. Highway 656 veered right to intersect with the main thoroughfare, and Jackson Street went off to the left.

"Which way?" she asked.

"Let's go right up to the main street. Better chance we'll find something we can borrow."

"Borrow? Is that convict code for steal?"

"The way I see it, anything not nailed down is up for grabs."

She didn't argue the point. Samantha had long since abandoned any notion that taking from those who had passed was morally wrong. The world had become a giant abandoned flea market, and rummaging through what had been left behind was the only way to survive.

They turned right and hiked for another long block. They passed a small house, easily a hundred years old, with a mobile home parked out back. The house looked like it had already been ransacked, its front windows and door both broken in. A beige pickup truck, with its hood propped up, sat in the front yard. Tanner took a quick look inside the vehicle. The floorboards had been eaten away by rust and chicken manure, and sharp springs poked up through the faded vinyl seats. He shook his head, and they continued on.

When they reached the main intersection, they turned left and headed deeper into Bland. Another half-block up, they found a pontoon boat sitting on a small trailer in the center of the road. Whoever had been pulling it was long gone.

"I don't suppose that will get us very far," she joked.

He chuckled. "Not unless God decides to bring down another flood."

Samantha looked up at the cloudless blue skies and shook her head.

Tanner walked around the boat, giving it a quick once-over. It was in fine shape, not that that made any difference one way or the other. The only weapon he could find was a fiberglass-handled fishing gaff, about four feet in length. The hook felt sharp enough, and he figured that it could do some damage with enough force behind it. He lifted it out of the boat.

Samantha eyed the gaff warily.

"What's that for?"

"You hook fish with it," he explained.

"I know that. I meant what are you going to do with it?"

He flipped it hook side up and began using it as a walking stick.

"Anything to help an old man on his way."

She made a face that said she wasn't buying it but said nothing else.

Another fifty yards up, they came upon another old white house on the right. This one didn't appear to have been broken into.

"Let's check it," he said.

As they walked up the front steps, Samantha pointed to a white "S" that had been painted on the glass storm door.

"What do you think that means?"

"Don't know," he said, trying the knob. It was locked. "Maybe the 'S' was used to mark homes that were safe from the virus." He peered through the small window in the door but couldn't make out much inside. "Let's go on a bit further. I'd hate for them to return home and find us munching on their goodies."

"Like what happened before," she said, thinking back to Professor Callaway and his daughter, in the town of Hendersonville, North Carolina.

"Hey, that worked out okay."

"Yeah, after you blew up the entire town."

He shrugged. "It wasn't the whole town."

They continued on, checking other houses spread out along the street. A few of the homes were marked with the same "S" painted on their doors. Those that weren't marked had been broken into and cleaned out of anything useful. The only logical explanation was that the townspeople had marked the homes still inhabited, and scavenged from people who had either passed or simply left their property behind.

A little further up, they came to small church. The same white "S" was painted in the middle of its bright red door. The sounds of people speaking in unison were coming from within.

"Should we go in?" she asked.

Tanner hesitated a moment, looking around. He shook his head. They had yet to see a single living person on the street or in any of the homes, and something felt off.

"Let's move through, quick and quiet—grab a car and a weapon, and then get back on the road."

She stepped back from the church door as if suddenly realizing that something dangerous might be inside.

"Right."

Across from the church was a large brick building with massive white columns. At the top of the pillars was a sign that read *Bland County Court House*. There was a flagpole out front, but nothing flew on it. The building itself looked to be in relatively good shape, with its doors and windows intact. The same white symbol was painted on a large granite marker resting beside the walkway.

"Why would they mark a court—"

She was interrupted when the church door suddenly opened. Before either of them could decide what to do, people began spilling out. When they saw Tanner and Samantha, they stopped and huddled together, as if afraid of the strangers. They seemed especially surprised to see Samantha, perhaps because she now looked rugged enough to be the daughter of Crocodile Dundee.

After some hushed deliberation, a heavyset man, wearing dirty white pants and a blue suit coat turned and hurried back into the church.

"So much for quick and quiet," Samantha mumbled under her breath.

Seconds later, a tall gaunt man clad in a black suit and top hat gently threaded his way through the parishioners.

"Hello there, strangers," he said, walking toward them with a hand extended.

"He looks like Abraham Lincoln," whispered Samantha.

Tanner stepped forward. He shifted the gaff to his left hand, which would enable him to shake the man's hand or hook him through the eye, depending on what the situation dictated.

The remaining parishioners reluctantly stepped from the church, slowly fanning out into a large semicircle facing the town's visitors. There were at least two dozen of them.

"I'm Brother Bill Lands," the tall man said, shaking Tanner's hand. The man's grip was soft, and his skin cold and clammy, like he had spent the night digging in a graveyard.

Tanner offered what he hoped looked like a friendly smile.

"Tanner Raines, and this is my daughter Samantha."

Samantha looked up at him, not at all surprised by his lie. Tanner had used such introductions in the past, explaining that it kept questions to a minimum.

"Are you folks from around here?" Lands asked, smiling with teeth that seemed impossibly big for his mouth.

"Just passing through. Our car broke down yesterday, and we've been forced to hoof it."

"Oh my, that's awful. I hope you'll allow what's left of the good people of Bland to help you in some small way."

Tanner shrugged. "What we really need is a car."

Brother Lands smiled. "I believe we can help you with that. We've moved all the cars that still run over to the transformer plant." He looked over at the fat man who had fetched him from the church. "Brother Carl, would you see what you can find for these good people? And put a little extra gas in it too."

The man nodded, offering a nervous smile.

"It'll take me an hour or so to get over there and back."

Lands turned back to Tanner.

"Can you suffer our company that long?"

"We'll take an hour of waiting over a day of walking, anytime."

Lands chuckled and motioned for Brother Carl to go ahead and retrieve the car.

"Would you care to come inside and wait for a spell?" A nervous murmur sounded from the crowd of worshippers behind him. "Across the street in the courthouse would probably be most comfortable place," he clarified.

Tanner glanced at the huge T-shaped brick building off to his left. He couldn't remember a single occasion when anything good had ever happened to him inside of a courthouse. On the other hand, he could find no logical reason to decline the invitation and risk insulting someone who was trying to help get them back on the road.

"Sure," he said. "Why not?"

CHAPTER 11

Something warm and wet slid across Mason's face. He jerked forward and reached for his Supergrade. Bowie stared at him, smacking his lips together, as if trying to decode what flavor of dirt and sweat had collected on his master's face.

Mason yawned and rubbed the sleep from his eyes. He hadn't meant to fall asleep, and the sun was already starting to show in the eastern sky. Whether or not Bowie had slept or kept watch, he couldn't say. All he knew for sure was that nothing had found them in the night, and for that, he was thankful. Unfortunately, Nakai was still no closer to being caught.

He studied the highway below. Even at a distance, he could see the bright red stains of blood covering the cars and asphalt. It had been a massacre, plain and simple.

"What do you say?" he said, scratching Bowie under his chin. "Should we go and have a look?"

Bowie yawned loudly.

Mason stood up and slowly worked the kinks out of his back. He had slept on the ground more times than he cared to count, but the older he got, the more his bones reminded him of the benefits of a mattress. He took a moment to stretch his shoulders, arms, and hands. Then he pumped his legs up and down a few times to get the blood flowing. Bowie stood watching him with his head tilted.

"I realize I must look like I'm getting ready for an early morning jog. But I'm not going down into that mess at anything less than one hundred percent."

He practiced drawing his Supergrade a couple of dozen times, making sure that the entire motion was fluid and once again ingrained in his muscle memory. Mason could put a single round on target in less than half a second, but that only held true when nothing went wrong. And as he had told his students at Glynco many times, the key to nothing going wrong was practice. He smiled, remembering a student's question on the subject.

"Do you have to practice every day?"

"No," Mason assured him. "Only on the days you want to live."

Mason had gone on to explain that, if a lawman were lucky, he might only have to draw his firearm a few times in his entire career. Of those, he might discharge it once. But the outcome of that one encounter would likely be dictated by the hundreds of hours he had spent preparing for it.

When Mason was satisfied with his warm-up, he picked up his M4, checked it, and started slowly descending the steep slope toward the interstate. Bowie walked beside him, occasionally stopping to sniff traces of gunpowder still swirling in the air.

❧ ❧

Daylight brought with it a disturbing clarity to the carnage. Bodies were strewn in every direction with gallons upon gallons of blood spattered on the cars, asphalt, and concrete dividers. Arms had been torn off. Heads had been bashed in with such brutality that brains had been expelled through the ears. Bodies had been eviscerated, with long cords of guts strewn about like strings of Christmas garland. It was as if bloodthirsty Vikings had decided to prove that, with enough brutality, hand axes could win out over modern weaponry.

Mason had witnessed the horrors of war before, both in Iraq and Afghanistan, and he had found that the only way to keep from being overwhelmed by the gore was to develop an almost clinical detachment from those who had suffered. They were dead and gone. The piece parts that remained were no different than meat in a butcher's shop. That rationalization only went so far, though, when he found himself slipping on entrails and tripping over severed heads. Butcher shop or not, it was an unsightly mess.

As he arrived at the far end of the bridge, he spotted two figures dressed in black fatigues cautiously working their way up the on-ramp. One was a short, dark-skinned man, Hispanic or perhaps American Indian, and the other a giant African American who looked meaner than Kimbo Slice. No doubt this must be Nakai and his fearsome partner, Jeb.

Mason ducked behind one of the tractor-trailers and quickly surveyed the area. There were plenty of places to hide, but hiding wasn't what he had in mind. The odds had greatly improved, thanks to a horde of maniacal zombie-like monsters, and the interstate was as good a place as any to make a stand. But even if he could win a ranged firefight with two trained mercenaries, which he doubted, it wouldn't get him what he needed. He sought more than justice for his fellow marshals; he sought information.

And that was something that couldn't be extracted when trading bullets.

An idea came to him, and he turned to Bowie.

"Stay here."

The dog looked at him and squinted, like a child testing to see how serious a parent really was.

"I mean it. Don't you move."

Bowie reluctantly lay down and flopped his head on his front paws.

Mason rose to a crouch and hurried down the freeway until he got to the first of the two HMMWVs equipped with a .50 caliber machine gun. Two soldiers lay nearby, one a lieutenant and the other a corporal. Both looked like they had been put through a blender.

Mason climbed up into position behind the heavy weapon. It had been more than ten years since he had last stood behind a Browning M2, and it took him a moment to remember the ins and outs of operating the weapon. The M2HB was by all accounts one of the finest heavy machine guns in the world, air cooled and able to put out nearly six hundred rounds per minute.

The ammunition had been torn away from the weapon during the melee, so he would need to ready it for operation. He checked that the feed tray cover was down and the bolt forward. Quietly lifting a long string of .50 BMG ammunition, he inserted it into the feed tray until the pawl engaged the first round. Then he pulled the retracting slide handle rearward and released it. It made a distinctive *clunk* as it flew forward. He cycled it a second time to chamber the first round. He double-checked that the gun was set in automatic mode and locked down the bolt-latch release. Ma Deuce was ready to rock and roll.

Mason swung the M2 in the direction of the on-ramp. The two men were not yet visible, so he squatted down and stared out through the broken windshield of the HMMWV. Less than three minutes later, he saw them. Nakai and Jeb moved carefully from one point of cover to the next, one man bounding ahead and then waving the other on. Professionals, he thought. Not to be underestimated.

He waited until they were about halfway across the overpass, too far along to retreat back down the ramp but not close enough to pose a serious threat. When they had just come up alongside the Greyhound bus, he stood up and gripped the handles of the Browning. He gave the butterfly triggers a quick press with both thumbs. The gun bucked back and forth, and a short burst of .50 caliber slugs smashed into the grill of the bus. The hood flipped up, and pieces of its fender tore away.

Nakai and Jeb immediately dove to the ground, using the wheels of the bus to shield them. Both men no doubt knew that the Browning would make short work of any such cover, but their options were limited.

Mason leaned over from behind the gun and shouted to them.

"Toss the weapons!"

Neither man moved.

"Okay," he muttered under his breath, "if you need a little persuasion..."

He sent another burst toward them, this time smashing out the bus windows and chewing through the metal that held the roof in place. The entire top of the bus caved in.

"Last chance!" he shouted.

One of the men tossed something about thirty yards in front of them, and a cloud of thick gray smoke billowed out. Within seconds, the wall of smoke completely concealed the bus and everything around it. The smoke didn't reach all the way to Mason, but it did a fine job of obscuring everything else.

He started to squeeze off another burst, planning to sweep from left to right, when he heard Bowie growl. The dog was now completely enveloped in the smoke, and Mason had no way of knowing whether he had moved. More likely than not, Bowie was already making his way toward the enemy.

"So much for this bright idea," grumbled Mason. Throwing his feet over the side of the HMMWV, he dropped to the ground.

༛ ༝

When the first volley of .50 caliber rounds hammered into the bus, Nakai and Jeb instinctively dove behind the bus. It not only minimized their silhouette, it also put something solid between them and the heavy weapon.

"He'll cut us to pieces," Jeb said, high-crawling forward a couple of feet and peeking around one of the huge bus tires.

They heard a man shout for them to toss out their weapons.

"He thinks we're pinned down," said Nakai.

"We're not?"

Another burst of gunfire tore into the bus. When the shooting stopped, the roof started to collapse in on itself, like it had become the victim of giant metal-eating termites.

"I'll pop smoke," said Nakai. "You go right, and I'll go straight up the middle, fast and hard."

Jeb nodded.

Nakai pulled the pin and tossed the smoke grenade as far as he could from a prone position. A cloud of gray smoke poured out, quickly filling the roadway.

Jeb rolled all the way to the right side of the road, scrambled to his feet, and followed the concrete divider forward. He let his AK-47 hang across his chest, freeing his hands to feel his way through the thick smoke. He came to the back end of a car but managed to squeeze past it. The smoke was incredibly thick, and he began to cough. He fought off the panicked feeling of not getting enough oxygen and continued his careful advance. If he could come out along the wall when the man's attention was on Nakai, he could end things with a careful shot to the head, quick and easy.

Something growled in front of him. Or had it been to the side? He spun left and then back to the right, unable to pinpoint its direction. Jeb grabbed his rifle and swung it up in front of him. If he fired, he would give away his position and almost certainly be cut down by the .50 caliber machine gun. Reluctantly, he released the rifle and slowly slid out his machete. The fat heavy blade could cut through anything, living or dead.

Another growl vibrated ominously through the thick smoke, this time from behind him. He spun to face it, slashing out with his knife. The blade found nothing but air. To his right, he heard a slight scratching sound, like claws dragging on the pavement. What the hell was out there?

Something huge slammed into him, knocking him backwards. Jeb tried to slash it with his machete, but the creature was already in too close. He stumbled over a broken headlight and fell as the beast used its weight to drive him down to the ground. He felt a warm wet mouth engulf his throat. Teeth locked down, piercing his jugular on one side and his airway on the other.

The blade clattered to the ground as Jeb fought against the beast, struggling to pull its mighty jaws open. His fingers bled as they pulled against sharp teeth. For a moment, he thought he might actually free himself. But then the beast shook its head from side to side, ripping his throat out and sending a fountain of blood spraying into the air.

ও ও

Nakai's legs were stiff from a fitful night of being on the run, but they didn't fail him as he barreled out of the smoke, his Aug pressed tightly against his shoulder. He fired short three-round bursts at the .50 caliber position, closing the distance as quickly as possible. Sparks flew as the rounds pelted the HMMWV's armor plating that protected the machine gun nest. It took him a moment too long to realize that no one was returning fire.

He scanned left and right. Nothing. He started to wheel around when he heard a voice from behind him.

"Freeze!"

He froze.

"Drop the rifle."

Nakai quickly calculated his chances of dropping to a knee and firing the Aug as he turned. Not good. He lowered the Aug to the ground and lifted both hands to shoulder level. He left the Sig Sauer P226 in its holster at his side.

"Walk forward ten steps, then turn slowly."

He did as instructed. When he turned, he saw a man wearing civilian clothes, a blazer and blue jeans, and a belt with a badge clipped on it. He pointed a 1911 pistol at Nakai's head, and from the way he held the weapon, there was no doubt he knew how to use it.

❞ ❟

Mason looked down his sights at the man who had callously murdered so many of his fellow marshals. He was tempted to squeeze the trigger, forever putting an end to him. But he stayed his hand, knowing that this would be his only chance to get answers.

"You and I are going to talk," he said.

Nakai nodded slowly. "Okay."

"I'm Deputy Marshal Mason Raines. I'm assuming that you're Nakai?"

"I am." Nakai's eyes darted left and right, looking for Jeb.

A shape slowly emerged from the smoke, but it was not his trusted lieutenant. It was a giant dog, and the animal's mouth was covered in bright red blood. Mason motioned for Bowie to come to his side, and he quickly obeyed, never taking his eyes off Nakai.

"If you're expecting your big friend, I think that's a train that won't come."

"Impressive animal," he said.

"Bowie can hold his own."

"You said you had questions."

Mason nodded. "I do."

"You want to know why we killed the marshals."

"That and other things."

"And I suppose you're going to offer me my life in return."

Mason stared hard into his eyes.

"No. Judgment day is here for you. Nothing you say is going to change that."

"Then why should I cooperate?"

"Because if you tell me the truth, I'll give you a chance to go for that piece at your side."

Nakai bit at his lip. "A fair fight?"

Mason nodded.

"All right. What do you want to know?"

"Why did you bomb FLETC?"

"We were hired to retrieve a large batch of rifles. The chemical bombs were provided to help us complete the mission." He motioned to the tractor-trailers around them. "You can check our cargo if you like."

"No need."

Nakai smiled. "You already knew that much."

"One of your men told me."

"All right. What else then?"

"Who hired you?"

Nakai thought about the question before answering. Normally, he would never betray a customer, but this situation was a little different. Either he or the marshal would be dead in less than a minute. If the marshal died, so would his betrayal of confidence. And if he died, he could forgive himself a final transgression for a chance at survival.

"An old friend of mine from the service, Major General William Hood."

Mason had never heard of him.

"Why would a US general hire you to steal rifles?"

"He wanted them delivered to a man named Lenny Bruce. He runs a militia up near Lexington."

Mason nodded again. The facts jived with what Van Gogh had told him.

"For what purpose?"

"That I don't know. My best guess is that he wants Lenny to stir up some trouble."

"Was he trying to enable a coup of some sort?"

Nakai shook his head. "Nothing that ambitious. I think it was a distraction or maybe a statement of some kind. I can't say for sure."

Mason thought for a moment, trying to put the pieces together.

"General Hood's not at the top of this, is he?"

"I wouldn't think so."

"Who, then? Give me a name, and I'll give you your chance."

"I have your word?"

"You do."

"The truth is I don't know for sure. What I do know is that Hood has been working closely with another man for the better part of ten years. My guess is that he's the one running things. But as I said, it's only a guess."

"Give me a name."

Nakai hesitated. "His name is Lincoln Pike."

Mason shook his head. "You're lying."

"No. Everything I told you is true. The question is whether or not your word means anything."

Mason heard his father's voice in his head. *You don't owe this dirtbag a damn thing. Put a bullet in his head and move on.*

Despite the warning, Mason lowered his Supergrade and shoved it into its holster.

The corners of Nakai's mouth twitched with a satisfied little smile as he slowly brought his hands down to hang at his side.

Bowie growled, not at all comfortable with the way things were proceeding.

"You ready?" asked Nakai.

Mason nodded.

Both men went for their guns at the exactly same time, neither waiting for the other to move first. Nakai's P226 cleared his holster a millisecond before Mason's Supergrade. But rather than raise his weapon, Mason immediately flipped the muzzle up and fired from the hip. The 230-grain jacketed hollow point punched through Nakai's sternum, nicking his heart before smashing against his backbone. He fell to his knees, teetered for a moment, and then pitched forward on the bloodstained asphalt.

Bowie slowly walked over and nudged Nakai's lifeless body. When he didn't move, the dog turned back to face Mason.

"Believe me," he said, holstering his firearm, "he had it coming."

CHAPTER 12

The sheriff's office in Bland's courthouse looked like it had been taken right from the set of Mayberry. A small jail cell lined one wall, bare except for two bunks with neatly folded blankets, and a five-gallon potty bucket. An empty rifle rack sat behind the sheriff's desk, as did a cradle for handheld radios. The entire place had been picked clean. The only things left were the battered furniture and a few sheets of paper scattered on the floor.

Tanner and Samantha sat in heavy wooden chairs, worn smooth from years of use. Brother Lands sat across from them, leaning back in a swivel chair that squeaked every time he moved. He had an excited look about him, as if waiting for a piece of good news.

The room's only window was open, and a cool breeze filtered in through a thick metal grating. Three men from the congregation were stationed around the office, shifting from foot to foot like they were wearing new shoes. One was short and bald, another other had a bad haircut that hung down in front of his eyes, and the third had a nose that looked like it had been stuck in a pencil sharpener. Of the Three Stooges, only Curly looked like a serious contender. Even so, Tanner was confident that they wouldn't be a problem, should it come to that.

"You folks lose many to the outbreak?" he asked.

"Nearly everyone," replied Lands. "Of the county's nearly seven thousand residents, only thirty-seven of us remain."

Tanner was stunned. "The virus killed all but thirty seven of you?"

"Sadly, no. The virus did its part, to be sure, but we did the rest. Those who became infected were systematically killed to prevent the spread. The few who survived took vengeance when they were well enough." He sighed. "In the end, the town killed as many as the sickness."

"That sounds like a bloodbath. How'd you folks manage to survive?"

"We discovered the source for our salvation, the way people always do when put in impossible situations."

"Religion?"

He nodded. "We took a hard look at our faith and realized that God was punishing us."

"Why would God do that?" As a Buddhist, Tanner put no credence in such notions, but he figured it didn't hurt to better understand the situation at hand.

"Because God is vindictive," Lands said without the slightest hesitation.

"Okay," Tanner said, tentatively. "And so—what? You decided to live a more righteous life to get off His shit list?"

"Let's just say we learned to live differently. And when we started to trust in Him, really trust, He began to care for us again."

Tanner studied him, trying to read what was behind the man's dark eyes. Something wasn't quite right. A return to religion was to be expected, given what had happened, but that didn't account for his alarm bells going off the way they were.

"If there's only thirty-seven of you left, darn near everyone must have been at the church."

"Indeed. Everyone who remains is part of our fold."

"Everyone? Not a single Jew, Catholic, or atheist remains?"

"Everyone came to understand that we're here to do His work." Land's eyes settled on Samantha.

The voice of caution that had been whispering in Tanner's ear for the past ten minutes now rose to a level that couldn't be ignored. He stood and walked to the open window to look out. The metal grating looked stout enough to prevent prisoners from skedaddling. He could see a patch of overgrown grass and weeds at the back of the courthouse. Beyond that, there were a few houses as well as a couple of old cars parked across the street.

"You get many travelers passing through?"

"No, not many," answered Lands. "Certainly not people traveling with children."

Tanner nodded. The threat had something to do with Samantha.

The room fell silent for nearly a minute, broken only by the squeak of Brother Land's chair.

Growing more and more uncomfortable with the silence, Samantha turned to Brother Lands and said, "Can I ask you something?"

"Of course, child."

"Why is there a white 'S' painted on all the doors?"

"Who says it's an S?"

"It looks like an S. I guess it could be a worm or a snake, but that would be even weirder than an S."

Lands seemed a little miffed by her comment.

"It's a symbol of our faith. Nothing more."

She thought about it for a moment.

"What? Like the snake from the Garden of Eden?"

He squinted at her.

"Yes, child, something like that."

From the window, Tanner glimpsed two men coming up from the back of the courthouse. Both were hunched over, shuffling from corner to corner as they worked their way around to the front of the building. One man carried a deer rifle, and the other a long-barreled shotgun.

Tanner turned and quickly surveyed the room. His fishing gaff was sitting in the coat rack beside the front door. It wasn't particularly useful against men with rifles but enough for a few unarmed men confined to a sheriff's office. He walked to the office door and threw the deadbolt. Then he shoved in the anchor bolts at the top and bottom of the frame. It was a heavy fiberglass door, and having been secured at three points, it would all but require an axe to break through.

When he turned around, everyone was staring at him, uncertainty in their eyes.

Brother Lands stood up, an indignant expression on his face.

"What do you think you're doing?" he demanded.

Tanner said nothing as he reached over and slid the gaff from the coat rack.

"I asked you what you're doing." Brother Lands' voice betrayed the kind of frustration that someone feels when a plan suddenly goes sideways.

"I could ask you the same thing."

The knob on the door behind Tanner rattled as someone tried to enter.

He sidestepped a few feet in case they decided to try to shoot out the deadbolt or, worse, blindly fire through the meat of the door.

Seeing that nothing was going according to plan, Larry, Moe, and Curly slowly came together in the center of the room, eyeing Tanner.

Mistake, he thought. They would have done better to come at him from different angles.

Without saying a word, Curly rushed forward, bent over and arms outstretched. When he got to within about five feet, Tanner swung the gaff up with both hands, like he was trying to land a six-hundred pound marlin. The pointed metal tip caught the man under his chin, poking through his mouth and up into his sinus cavity before finding its way out through one of his nostrils. The result was absolutely horrific. The man clutched the hook and screamed, struggling with the impossible task of freeing himself.

Tanner stiff-armed him with the fiberglass handle, never taking his eyes off the other two henchmen. Neither of them took a step forward. After a few agonizing seconds, Curly collapsed to the floor in shock. He lay there unconscious, blood bubbling from his mouth and nose.

Tanner stepped forward, tilted the gaff, and slid the bloody hook from his mouth. Then he turned to face Brother Lands and the other two men.

"I know what you're thinking," he said in a calm voice. "That was terrible, right? Maybe the most awful thing you've ever seen."

They said nothing as they stared at the dark red pool of blood slowly spreading across the wooden floor.

"See, here's the thing," he continued, taking a step toward them. "Your friend got off easy. You three won't be so lucky." He swung the gaff to the side, and a long streak of blood spattered against the wall.

Lands suddenly lunged forward, grabbed a handful of Samantha's hair, and jerked her to his chest. She screamed and struggled to get away.

"Drop the weapon, or I'll kill the girl."

Tanner felt his face warming as his heart began doing overtime.

"You couldn't even imagine the consequences of that," he said, staring into the man's eyes.

Lands seemed to lose his nerve.

"Please," he pleaded, "she's important. We've been waiting for this—for her!"

"Not gonna happen." Tanner looked back at Larry and Moe. Both looked like they had stepped in wet cement, afraid to move one way or the other.

"What are you waiting for?" barked Lands. "Do something!"

Tanner slid the metal end of the gaff across the wooden floorboards. It made a dry scraping sound.

"You boys sure you wanna dance with me?"

The two men looked from Tanner to Lands and then back again, desperately trying to find a way out. Clearly, this wasn't what they had signed up for.

A loud bang sounded behind Tanner as someone hit the door with the butt of a rifle. It didn't budge.

Tanner took another step forward, and Larry and Moe both took a step back. He pointed to the jail cell.

"That's your only chance of ever seeing the light of day again."

They looked over at the cell and seemed to genuinely consider the option. Then without warning, Larry changed his mind and lunged forward with a front kick aimed at Tanner's gut.

Tanner saw it coming, stepped back a half-step, and hooked the man's back foot with the gaff. Larry fell flat on his back with a loud *umph*. Tanner immediately shuffled forward and stomped down on the man's groin. Larry moaned and curled into a tight ball, clutching his crotch with both hands.

Stepping around to one side, Tanner put his boot to the back of the man's head. The blow caught him in the mastoid, and he immediately lost consciousness. Just to make sure it was lights out, Tanner kicked him again, this time squarely on the ear. Larry jerked once and lay still.

Moe raised both hands and began to back away.

"Not me, man," he said.

Samantha stopped struggling and twisted her head to look up at Brother Lands.

"You should let me go," she said. "He'll kill all of you. Believe me. He will."

Lands slowly loosened his painful grip. When she felt his hands come free from her hair, she pulled away and ran to Tanner. Lands looked utterly defeated.

Tanner pointed to the jail cell.

"Both of you, inside. Now."

Moe and Brother Lands reluctantly walked over to the cell and stepped inside. Tanner swung the door closed. He had no way to lock it, so he slid the sheriff's desk across the room to brace the jail cell door. Moe eyed the questionable setup.

"I know," said Tanner. "If you really want out, you'll get out. But I'm operating on the honor system here. I'm trusting that you'll be smart and choose to sit in there rather than face what will be waiting for you out here."

Moe looked down at the bunk, unfolded the blanket, and sat down. After a moment, Brother Lands took a seat on the opposite end of the bunk, leaned his head back against the concrete wall, and closed his eyes.

"They'll never let her leave," he said. "The town's very salvation depends on her."

Tanner ignored him and walked to the far side of the room to talk privately with Samantha.

"What's he talking about?" she whispered.

He shrugged. "All I know is that when a nut job wants a young girl, it's never for anything good."

She looked over at Lands and shook her head.

"I'll be glad when I'm finally a woman and better able to take care of myself."

"Don't rush it. When you're a woman, there will be all new dangers. Besides," he said with a smile, "you're getting to be pretty scrappy as it is."

"Scrappy? Is that supposed to be a compliment?"

"Always."

She shrugged. "Okay, so what do we do now?"

"We need to get you out of here. You're the gasoline in all this. If you're gone, this will die out."

They both turned back to study the room, as if expecting to suddenly see a secret hatch or, better yet, a crate full of heavy armament left behind by the National Guard. They saw neither.

"Ideas?" he asked.

As if on cue, there was another bang on the door, this time with something heavier than a rifle. Once again, the door held.

"We're obviously not going out that way," she said.

Tanner pointed to the window.

"Think you could fit through there?"

"Not with those bars. Besides, even without the bars, you'd never get your enormous body through that hole."

"Enormous body?" Tanner pretended to be hurt. "Was that meant to be a compliment?"

"Always," she said, grinning.

Tanner walked to the window and studied it. The hole measured about fourteen inches square, definitely too small for him to squeeze through. Fortunately, the metal grating wasn't as big a problem as Samantha had thought. On one side of the grating were hinges and on the other, a small lockable pin that held the apparatus closed. Perhaps it had been installed that way for fire safety, or perhaps it was just cheaper than drilling into the brick and mortar. Either way, it made it much easier to get open from the inside.

He hurried to the desk and dug through the drawers. At the back of a shallow pencil drawer, he found a small manila envelope. Inside was a silver key that looked like it might fit a bicycle lock. He snatched it up and raced back to the window. Even before he inserted the key, he knew it would fit. A few seconds later, the grate was swinging open.

He leaned his head out. No one was at the back of the courthouse. He turned to Samantha and pointed to two broken-down cars in front of a shabby white house across the street.

"Head for the cars. Then circle around to the back of the house and get out of sight."

"But where should I go from there?"

He lowered his voice. "You remember that burned-out school we passed coming in?"

"Yeah."

"Think you can find it?"

"It's only a few blocks away. Of course, I can find it."

"All right, then here's the plan. You sneak out. Get yourself over to that school and wait for me."

She looked doubtful. "But how will you get out?"

He used the gaff to point toward Brother Lands.

"He'll be my ticket out of here."

"You're going to use him as a hostage?"

"A bargaining chip."

She looked over at her Savage .22 rifle leaning against the chair.

"Should I take my rifle?"

He shook his head. "Without ammunition, it's only going to slow you down. I'll bring it with me."

After a moment, she pressed her lips together and nodded.

"Okay, but if you don't show..." She let the words go unfinished.

Something bludgeoned the door again. This time it sounded like some kind of makeshift battering ram.

"Go," he said. "Now. Before they start catapulting cows."

She grabbed a chair and slid it under the window. Then she stepped onto the seat and started to lean out. Something occurred to her, and she ducked back in and gave him a quick hug.

"Just in case," she said.

"In case what?"

"In case they shoot you to pieces."

Without another word, she shimmied out the window and dropped to the ground outside.

ॐ ॐ

Samantha bolted across a thick carpet of grass and ducked behind the nearest parked car. She pressed her back against the cold sheet metal and surveyed the street. No one was in sight. Apparently what remained of the town was busy congregating either at the church or the front of the courthouse.

Fortunately, getting back to the school wouldn't require going by either one. All she needed to do was travel south, following the two-lane road back to where it forked off Highway 656. The total distance was probably only a few hundred yards, but traveling even that far without being seen was going to be tricky. She would need to get off the road first.

About fifty feet away was a two-story white house with a tall brick chimney that was leaning over so far that it looked like it might tip over at any minute. Beyond the house was a thick line of trees.

Perfect, she thought. I'll hide in the trees and follow the road back to the intersection. She took a deep breath and ran for her next position, a thick bush sitting at the front corner of the house. Twenty-three steps later, she skidded in behind it like a baseball player sliding into home plate. A branch stabbed into her forehead, adding to her growing number of scratches.

She rose to a crouch and shuffled around to the side of the house. The paint on the old building was dried and flaking off in large white sheets. She hurried on, hopping over the hoses of an air conditioning unit and dodging a rain barrel that smelled like sewage. When she came to the rear corner of the house, she poked her head around to make sure there wasn't a dog that might give away her position. As soon as she did, she knew she was in trouble.

Not twenty feet from her, sat a woman in dirty blue jeans and a maroon Virginia Tech Hokies sweatshirt. Before Samantha could duck back around the corner, the woman looked up, and their eyes met.

૎ ્

Tanner watched as Samantha raced across the street and ducked out of sight behind the large white house.

"Good girl," he muttered. "Go for the trees."

He waited for two long minutes, staring out the window to make sure that things went as planned. Samantha never came back into view.

Another thunderous strike shook the sheriff's door. The center of the door split, and the frame began to pull away from the wall. A few more hits like that one and they would be in.

"Keep hammering!" he shouted. "If it comes down, bad things are going to happen to Brother Lands."

The pounding stopped. After a long moment of silence, a man spoke with a slight Hispanic accent.

"If you kill him, you son-of-a-bitch, I'll cut you to pieces myself."

"Maybe so. But you'll be digging two graves. You got my word on that."

There was another pause. "What do you want?"

Tanner smiled. The situation was looking up.

"Have everyone but you get the hell out of the courthouse. Once that's done, I'll come out, and we'll have us a little talk."

"What's to keep me from shooting you?"

"Oh, I don't know—love for your fellow man?"

The man thought for a moment.

"How about you let me come in and see for myself?" he said in a tentative voice. "Make sure you haven't already killed him."

"I could. But if you come in, there's a good chance I'll end up snapping your neck. You sure you want to take that chance?"

The man hesitated. "Fine. Just you and me, out here in the hall."

Tanner heard hushed talking followed by the sound of men moving out of the courthouse. A single set of footsteps came back to the door.

"We're alone."

"All right," said Tanner. "Give me a minute."

"What for?"

"Because I'm trying to teach you some patience."

The man snarled.

Tanner walked over and picked up Samantha's rifle. He adjusted the sling, and hung it muzzle down across his back. Then he walked over to the jail cell and pushed the desk aside.

Lands and Moe both stood up, unsure of what would happen next.

Tanner pointed to Lands. "Just you."

Moe started to sit back down and then hesitated.

Tanner stared hard at him.

"The honor system, remember?"

He sat.

Brother Lands stepped out from the cell.

"We're not bad men," he said.

"Men who do bad things are bad men."

Lands started to argue the point, but was interrupted when Tanner grabbed his hair and pulled him around front.

"Hey," he said, "what do you think—" He was cut short by the bloody metal gaff being hooked into his open mouth. The sharp tip pressed against the back of his throat, causing him to gag.

Tanner stood behind him, one hand gripping Lands' hair, the other choked up on the handle of the gaff.

"The time for talking is over," he said, pushing Lands ahead of him. "If you cause me even the slightest grief, I'll trout you in front of God and everyone."

ℜ ℝ

Samantha stood motionless, like a rabbit refusing to accept that it had been seen, even as a hawk swooped in for the kill. Without standing up from the porch swing, Hokies waved for her to come closer. It was a soft beckoning, like she was calling over a neighbor to share a cup of iced tea.

Samantha turned and looked back over her shoulder toward the side of the house. Going that way wasn't an option now that she had been seen. If the woman sounded the alarm, she would be running right into the thick of them. She turned around and weighed her chances of getting to the trees. They weren't that far, a couple of hundred feet maybe.

"I can make it," she whispered. "I can."

She broke away from the house and ran.

Hokies was on her feet and giving chase before she had even taken five steps. Samantha had never won a race in her entire life, not even on track and field day against kids who were a grade behind her. She had always chalked the losses up to being small for her age, but the truth was she never really believed that she could win. Today was different. Today she had no choice.

She sprinted with a strength she had never felt before, her legs pumping up and down and her arms swinging back and forth. Even though Hokies was easily a foot taller, she beat the woman to the trees by nearly two full seconds.

As soon as he entered the tree line, Samantha ducked under a large briar, spun around a pine tree, and plowed through waist high bushes. Hokies was right behind her but ran neck first into the hanging briar. The sharp barbs pierced her skin, and she nearly fell backward as she stopped dead in her tracks, screaming in pain.

"Come back here!" she shrieked.

Samantha never looked back, ducking and dodging her way through the intricate maze of trees and brush.

Carefully pulling the briars away from her skin, Hokies turned back toward her house.

"Come quick!" she shouted. "The girl! She's over here!"

&ed; &ec;

Tanner pushed Brother Lands out of the sheriff's office, one hand on the gaff, and the other gripping the crown of the man's hair. A tall Mexican man stood a few feet away, his back facing the door to the courthouse. He held a Remington 1100, 12-gauge shotgun and wore bandolier of ammunition hanging diagonally across his chest like Pancho Villa. With a thirty-inch barrel and a total length of almost five feet, the shotgun seemed enormous in the confines of the building's entryway.

As soon as they stepped out, Pancho said, "What the hell do you have in his mouth?"

Tanner pulled lightly on the hook.

"This is what I call 'life insurance.'"

The man suddenly seemed uncertain. He hadn't expected to see Lands come out of the room, and certainly not with a giant hook in his mouth.

"What do you want?"

Tanner shrugged. "Nothing really. I came out to tell you that the girl's gone."

"Bullshit. She's inside."

Tanner eased the hook forward about an inch, and pulled back on Lands' hair, like he was a talking puppet.

"Tell him."

"She's gone," he gurgled. "Out the window."

Pancho leaned around, trying to peer into the sheriff's office.

"It's true," said Tanner. "Now the question is what do we do next?"

Before Pancho could answer, a bony man with a mop of red hair burst through the courthouse door.

"She's running..." He struggled to catch his breath and get the words out. "Through the trees behind the courthouse."

Tanner immediately drove Brother Lands forward, the gaff cutting into the back of his throat. They slammed into Pancho, pressing him against the courthouse wall and pushing the shotgun barrel high into the air.

The red-haired man came up behind Tanner, but he hesitated with his arms outstretched, unsure of exactly what to do with a man who was twice his size. Tanner answered the question for him by spinning around with an elbow strike to the side of the man's head. The single blow took his legs out from under him, and he collapsed onto the floor.

Pancho shouted for Brother Lands to get off him, but the gaff was still cutting into his mouth, and he couldn't move in any direction without it slicing deeper into his throat.

Tanner whipped the handle end of the gaff around like a pugil stick, catching Pancho in the eye. The torqueing motion poked the hook through Lands' cheek, and his protests turned into painful shrieks. Tanner continued leaning into both men, pinning them against the wall. But the exertion was taking it out of him, and he knew that, sooner or later, one of them would manage to slip out from his three-man wall sandwich.

Deciding that it was better to control the situation, he shoved the gaff sideways, driving Lands away on his tiptoes as he followed the metal hook out into the room. Before Pancho could take advantage of the space, Tanner immediately closed the gap and slammed back up against him.

Realizing that holding onto the shotgun was doing nothing more than tying up his hands, Pancho finally dropped the weapon. Shifting to one side, he managed to drive a knee up between them. That put enough space to enable him to slide sideways along the wall and finally free himself.

Tanner pressed ahead, firing a quick jab with his left hand, which immediately bloodied the man's nose. Before he could deliver a more powerful cross, Pancho brought up a short, but effective uppercut. The blow caught Tanner under the chin, and it rocked his head back a few inches. Rather than retreat, Tanner whipped his head forward, head-butting Pancho on the bridge of his nose. More blood began to flow down the Mexican's face, and he stepped back, trying to collect himself.

Tanner shot out a roundhouse kick, his shin landing solidly against the side of Pancho's knee. The leg buckled and ligaments tore free. To his credit, the man didn't fall. Instead, he reached forward with both hands, hoping to change the fight from a standing one to one on the ground. Tanner parried his hands away and sliced up with an elbow strike to the man's face. The blow knocked out Pancho's two front teeth and split his upper lip all the way to the tip of his nose.

Refusing to give up, he pummeled Tanner with everything he had. Tanner reached forward with both hands, popped his thumbs into

Pancho's eyes, and pulled his head down into a tremendous knee strike. The blow instantly broke the man's neck and sent blood spraying all the way up to the ceiling. Tanner tossed him aside and turned back to face the other two men.

The skinny redhead was still on the ground, conscious now, but unable, or perhaps just unwilling, to stand back up. Lands had managed to finally free himself from the gaff, but he was moaning, holding both hands over the hole in the side of his face.

Tanner reached down and picked up the shotgun. It weighed almost nine pounds and felt absolutely enormous. He pressed his thumb up into the ammunition tube. It was tight, which meant that it contained four shells. He eased back the operating handle and saw a fifth shell in the pipe.

Five wouldn't be enough. He walked to Pancho and yanked the bandolier up over his head. There were easily thirty rounds in it. Enough for what had to be done.

Without saying a word, he walked over and beaned the skinny man with the butt of the shotgun. When he turned around, Lands was staring at him with venom in his eyes. Tanner lowered the business end of the shotgun toward him.

"On your feet, asshole."

"You poked a hole in my cheek," he said in a garbled voice.

Tanner motioned with the shotgun.

"Up."

Lands slowly got to his feet.

Tanner moved closer and grabbed him by the throat.

"What did you want the girl for?"

Lands didn't answer.

Tanner squeezed until he felt the man's windpipe starting to collapse. Tears poured down Lands' face, and he finally motioned for him to stop.

"She's—" He stopped and swallowed, trying to get his voice to work. "She's the one," he choked.

"The one what?"

"The one our Lord told me was coming. The one He demands we give to him."

"Demands as in what—kills?"

"She's the one," he pleaded. "He saved us. Without another offering, we'll be afflicted like all the others. He told me this is the only way to ensure our salvation."

"Then I guess you're all in for one hell of a disappointment."

Tanner squeezed Lands' throat again, but this time, he didn't let go until he no longer felt the soft thudding of the man's pulse.

కా ఇ

Samantha was no stranger to fear. She had been afraid almost her entire life. Whether it was being called on in class or humiliated by school bullies, fear never left her. She would have thought that an apocalypse would only have made it worse, but surprisingly, it didn't. Instead, it had turned fear into a more cyclical event. Sometimes it was so close that she felt unable to move, petrified as if Medusa had cast eyes upon her. But other times, like when she and Tanner were cutting wisecracks or enjoying the warmth of a fire, there came a welcome relief from the fear.

This understanding came to her as she hid in the nook of a huge oak tree, desperately trying to catch her breath. She had run directly west, deeper into the woods and away from the townspeople. Unfortunately, that meant she now needed to turn south to get to the burned-out school. If she did that, though, she might give up the small lead she had built over those chasing her.

She could no longer see or hear the woman with the Hokies sweatshirt, but Samantha had no doubt that she was still behind her somewhere. In the distance, she heard the sounds of dogs barking. They seemed to be coming in her direction.

"I can't outrun a dog," she said, looking around for a place to hide. There were plenty of trees, bushes, and rocks, but nothing that would keep a dog from finding her.

She had an idea. Dogs track by smell, right? she thought. If there's a strong smell, they'd go to it rather than to her.

She stepped away from the tree, moved to a small bush, and pulled down her pants. She let a few drops of urine fall on the ground beside the bush and then quickly shuffled over to another bush. She did this to half a dozen spots in the area before pulling her pants back up. She took a quick whiff of the air. It could have been her imagination, but she thought she detected a faint ammonia-like odor.

Satisfied, she turned and started running south.

కా ఇ

Tanner peeked out through the partially open courthouse door. Other than a single unarmed man standing across the street in front of the church, no one else was in sight. He didn't know how much time he had before they caught Samantha. Perhaps they already had. Perhaps they were inside the church about to plunge a dagger into her heart to satisfy their bloodthirsty deity.

He stepped from the courthouse with the shotgun raised to his shoulder.

"You there!" he shouted to the man across the street. "On your knees!"

The man whipped his head around and started to shout for help.

Tanner squeezed the trigger, and a load of buckshot knocked the man off his feet. With the shotgun still up, he swept left and right. The street was empty.

He brought the weapon down and ran to the church. The bright red door was closed. Without checking to see if it was locked, he kicked to the right of the handle. The door flew open as the jamb gave way. He swung the giant shotgun up and stepped into the church.

The room was dark and slightly smoky. A dozen empty pews had been pushed up against the walls. In the center of the room was a long foldout card table covered with a blood-soaked white sheet. An ornate menorah sat at one end of the table, all seven candles freshly lit, and a bloodstained butcher knife sat at the other. Behind the altar, a full-sized crucifix had been flipped over and duct-taped in place so the corpus of Christ was hanging upside down. Encircling everything was a huge white pentagram painted on the wooden floor, the bucket of paint still sitting in a corner.

Tanner stood there for a moment, coming to grips with what he was seeing. He wasn't sure exactly what he had expected, but the crude sacrificial altar was not only revolting—it was amateurish. Devil worshippers were bad enough, but even they were expected to have some measure of professional pride.

Without even thinking about it, he walked over to the altar and toppled the candelabra. Flames licked the wooden crucifix, and within seconds, it was ablaze. When he turned back around, a man with a scruffy beard and a woman wearing a Hokies sweatshirt were standing in the doorway. They hurried into the church, screaming for him to stop.

Holding the shotgun at waist level, Tanner shot them both. Blood sprayed onto the walls as buckshot ripped into them. All of it combined—the blood, the huge pentagram, and the heat of the burning inverted crucifix—made him feel like he was standing at the gates of Hell, striking down demons as they tried to cross over.

He pulled three rounds from the bandolier and shoved them into the weapon. Stepping over the bodies, he moved out into the street. He was in a killing mood, and God help anyone who got in his way.

∾ ∿

From the edge of the trees, Samantha saw the burned-out school up ahead. Whether the fire had been intentional or accidental, she couldn't tell. However it had happened, it had done a number on the building. The roof was almost completely missing, only the scorched rafters remaining.

She ducked down and rushed across the open grassy field. She had to cross in front of two small brick houses, but fortunately, neither appeared to be occupied. She continued on past the long gymnasium. The building was made of sheet metal, and the paint had blistered from the heat of the fire. One of the basketball goals still hung from the ceiling, its rim charred and black.

She made her way around to the back of the school and entered through a burned-out doorway. The inside of the building had been gutted by the fire, and the burnt smell was nearly overpowering. What remained of the walls was covered with thick black soot. The ceiling was completely missing in most places, and every window had burst from the intense heat. Fortunately, the floor was set on concrete and seemed safe enough to walk across.

She stepped carefully around nails, broken desks, and parts of the collapsing structure. A badly burned body lay in one corner, curled up, like the person was trying to hide from the fire. Samantha bent down and picked up the partially burned cover of a book. *Charlotte's Web*. She smiled, remembering the story of a pig and a spider that became the best of friends.

Her mind turned to Tanner. She grinned. Surely he was the pig.

She gently put the cover back down and continued picking her way through the school. She came to a classroom that hadn't been as badly burned as the rest of the building. Small desks were still arranged in neat rows, facing a melted pull-down projector screen. She moved to one of the chairs and sat, expecting it to comfort her. Strangely, it felt only small and confining.

Samantha ran her hands along the top of the desk, wondering if she'd ever go to school again. She liked school. Liked learning. It was something she was good at. But like Tanner had said, studying pilgrims, long division, and igneous rocks didn't seem so important anymore.

Things were different now. She and Tanner were living in a different world, at least until she got back to her mother. She closed her eyes and imagined her mom's face. It was still clear in her mind. She missed her mom's smile, her soft kiss at night. Tanner would never do that. Well, probably not.

What would her mom think of him? She covered a smile and started to giggle. The giggle turned into a warm laugh, which was cut short by the sound of gunshots in the distance.

๛ ๙

Tanner walked west on Fairground Street, heading toward the house behind which Samantha had disappeared. Fifty or sixty yards ahead, three men emerged from the tree line. One carried a rifle, and the other two had handguns. Samantha was not with them.

Tanner stopped, brought the shotgun to his shoulder and fired. The nine double-aught pellets spread about four feet apart, peppering the man holding the rifle and winging the man to his right. Both men fell to the ground. The third man brought up a small semi-automatic handgun and began to fire wildly in Tanner's direction. Nothing even came close to hitting him.

Tanner fired again, knocking the man off his feet. He continued toward them, feeding fresh rounds into the belly of the shotgun. The man who had been winged was still alive and fumbling with bloody fingers to get a revolver out of its holster.

"Hands!" yelled Tanner, pointing the massive shotgun barrel at him.

The man raised his bloody hands into the air.

"Don't shoot me," he begged, blood seeping out from his neck and shoulder.

"Where's the girl?"

"She got away." He motioned with his head toward the trees. "In there." The man caught sight of a plume of gray smoke rising up from behind the courthouse. "You're burning our church!"

"I may burn the whole goddamn town."

The man reached for his pistol, surely knowing that he would never get to it in time.

Tanner shot him in the chest, and he bounced nearly a foot off the ground.

When he was satisfied that all three men were dead, Tanner bent over and searched their bodies. The first man had a bolt-action deer rifle. Unfortunately, the stock had been split in two by a couple of double-aught pellets. The second man carried a Kahr PM9, a quality pistol that was two sizes too small for Tanner's hands. He took it anyway, shoving it into his back pocket. He could find no spare magazines or ammunition for the weapon. The final man had a Ruger Bearcat .22 single-action revolver. Another small gun, this one built for younger shooters. He took it too with the notion of passing it on to Samantha. A quick search of the man's pockets revealed an unopened box of fifty .22LR rounds. They would come in handy.

He did a quick count of those either dead or out of the fight. Six in the courthouse, if he counted Moe, who was presumably still sitting tight, one outside the church, two inside, and now, three more at the tree line. That made twelve. Lands had said the entire town was down to thirty-seven people.

He nodded, pressing his lips together. Twenty-five more to go.

❧ ❦

Samantha stood next to the burned-out window sill, watching as a faded red Chevrolet pickup pulled up in front of the school. Tanner was sitting in the driver's seat. She wheeled around and raced out of the building, rushing toward him. He stepped from the truck, leaving the engine running and the door open. She jumped up and hugged him, and he held her in the air for a moment before lowering her to the ground.

"Did they hurt you?" he asked.

"No. But they wanted to."

"What went wrong with our plan?"

"A woman saw me almost as soon as I left the courthouse."

"So much for your ninja training."

She grinned. "At least they didn't catch me. I ran so fast. You should've seen me." She raised her arms up like she was sprinting.

"You did good, Sam," he said with a broad, warm smile.

She looked up into his eyes.

"Did you kill them all?"

"No."

"Good," she said softly.

"Why good? They're the vilest people to ever walk the Earth."

"Maybe so, but my mom always said I should walk away from a fight whenever possible."

He nodded again. "She's right. We should both walk away anytime we can."

"And when we can't?"

"When we can't, we'll make damn sure they don't walk away."

CHAPTER

13

President Glass stared at the paper, still uncertain why General Carr had felt it important enough to request a private meeting in the dilapidated conference room. It was a simple bill of lading, showing a shipment originating from the naval station in Everett, Washington, and delivered to the one in Norfolk, Virginia. The bill of lading was dated October 24, 1969, and the payload was described as a shipping container with contents weighing 6,431 pounds.

"I don't get it," she said, flipping the paper over to see if anything was written on the back. "What am I looking at?"

General Carr's voice was even and firm.

"It's a clue, Madam President."

"All right, but a clue to what?"

"If I'm right, that bill shows someone taking possession of the bombs, before they were even declared missing."

"In 1969?"

He nodded.

"What makes you so sure it's the bombs?" she asked.

"Look at the note the receiving officer made when it was inspected."

She studied the page. In the corner was a small indiscriminate note. Only four words were scribbled. *Twelve crates marked Weteye.*

"What in the world is a Weteye?"

"Weteye was the military's nickname for the Mk-116 bomb."

She rubbed her fingers across the aged ink as if trying to divine what the receiving officer had seen that day so many years ago.

"This is really it? You've found them?"

"I found how and where they first arrived. That's all."

She looked at the signature at the bottom of the page. Delivery was accepted by a Lieutenant Pete Vickers.

"Do you think Lieutenant Vickers is the one who bombed the law enforcement center?"

"No."

"Why not? He apparently took possession of the bombs. He could have—"

"The lieutenant died four days after signing that paper."

"Four days? How?"

"Apparently, he jumped to his death from his high-rise apartment."

She looked at him with doubt in her eyes.

"That sounds more like someone tying up a loose end."

"I agree."

She slid her fingers down to touch the page where Vickers' signature had been penned.

"Who was he, this Vickers fellow?"

"A career sailor. Solid by all accounts." Carr brought out a large folder and put it on the table. A color photo of a man with short red hair was clipped to the front.

"You got his personnel file?"

He nodded. "Thumb through it. See if anything stands out."

She opened it up. Inside were the usual military papers: enlistment information, duty stations, assignments, training, qualifications, insurance policies, promotions, and awards. A few pages had black marks on them where a permanent marker had been used to blot out information.

"Part of his file is redacted?"

"Yes, but why? Look at what's missing."

She read a page of orders that contained several of the black marks. Vickers assignment and a description of his duties were both redacted. The duty station and dates of service, however, were not. *USS John F. Kennedy, 7 September 1968 – 28 October 1969.*

"He was aboard Big John when it was first commissioned?"

The general smiled. "You know your ships."

"You forget my father was a commander. He talked about the *John F. Kennedy* with great admiration."

"Did he also mention that the ship briefly carried more than one hundred chemical weapons?"

She looked up at him, startled.

"It did?"

"When the vessel was first commissioned, a special holding area was set up to house chemical and biological weapons. Their existence was highly classified, and even the sailors onboard had no idea what they were carrying."

"The captain would have known. A captain is required to know every square inch of his vessel. My father did teach me that."

"I agree."

"So, he knew?"

"He did."

"And who commanded the aircraft carrier in '69?"

"Captain Frank Monroe. Classified documents show that he was the one who first reported the twelve bombs missing. But that didn't occur until 1970, when the remaining payload was being transferred to the Rocky Mountain Arsenal in Colorado. In his report, he mentions a young lieutenant assigned to safeguard and monitor the weapons while they were onboard the vessel, a young man who fell to his death while away on leave."

"Vickers?"

The general nodded.

President Glass set the personnel file on the desk.

"That means Lieutenant Vickers stole the bombs."

"It would seem so."

"But why?"

"I think the better question is for whom," he said.

"You think he was acting as a middleman."

"It's the only thing that makes sense. I think someone got to him."

"Got to him? As in bribed?"

"Not exactly. Two weeks before Vickers signed that paper, his four-year-old daughter was taken from a playground a block from his home."

"My God," President Glass said, covering her mouth.

"Her older sister saw the whole thing happen. She told police that two well-dressed men with short haircuts took the little girl."

"And was she ever found?"

"The day after Vickers took the swan dive, his daughter was discovered playing unattended in a McDonald's jungle gym, nearly fifty miles away."

"They let her go?"

"Thankfully, yes."

The president picked up the folder and stared at the man's face.

"They forced Vickers to steal the weapons, and then they murdered him for his troubles."

"That, or maybe they had him kill himself to save his daughter."

"And could the little girl tell the authorities anything?"

He shrugged. "I can't say for sure. I wasn't able to get the files detailing the investigation. But I do know that no arrests were ever made."

"In other words, they got away with it."

"It would seem so."

She set the file back down.

"While this is all fascinating, it doesn't get us any closer to the people who killed the marshals at Glynco."

General Carr looked over his shoulder to make sure that the conference room door was securely closed.

"What?" she asked. "What do you know?"

He slid his chair around to the side of the table and leaned in. Since her husband's passing, President Glass was unaccustomed to having someone so close to her. It felt private. Intimate even. And it was not entirely unwelcome. She had always drawn strength from Carr's presence.

"Tell me," she whispered.

"Lieutenant Vickers had unique access to the bombs. Probably less than a handful of people in the country could have done what he did."

"And?"

"And very few people knew what his mission really was. Officially, no one on the *USS John F. Kennedy*, other than Captain Monroe, knew about it."

"Unless the captain was in on it, someone else had to know."

"Exactly. Not only know, but they had to have a way to get to him."

"And to watch him to make sure he did as instructed," she added.

"That's right."

"Okay, so Vickers or Monroe must have told the wrong person."

General Carr smiled and held up a finger.

"Now, we're getting to the interesting part. According to Captain Monroe, the entire time Vickers was onboard the carrier, he had only one close friend."

"Who?"

"Another young lieutenant, a man who Monroe described as a charismatic officer destined to lead men."

She tilted her head.

"Who?"

He leaned in so close that she could feel his breath on her ear.

"Lieutenant Lincoln Pike."

President Glass went deathly still. They sat motionless for several seconds, neither of them saying anything. Finally, she turned and looked in his eyes.

"What are you saying?" she whispered.

"Madam President, you know what I know," he said, dodging the question.

"General, what are you saying?" she repeated.

He leaned back and stared at the folder, his confidence shaken by the directness of her question.

"I... I don't know anything for sure."

This time she leaned toward him, and he could smell the perfume that she dabbed on her neck every morning.

"Please, Kent," she whispered, realizing that it was the first time she had ever called him by his first name, "I don't care what you know. Tell me what you think."

He looked at her, their faces only a few inches apart.

"I think he's involved."

"But why would he do something like that? Steal the bombs all those years ago—use them now to kill hundreds of law enforcement officers. It doesn't make any sense."

"Don't you see? He wants to undermine you, your presidency."

"No," she said. "Lincoln can be a pain in the ass, but surely he's not capable of this."

"What about your daughter?"

President Glass felt her throat seize up at the mere mention of her missing child.

"What about her?"

General Carr reached out and took her hands in his own. It was a breach of personal space that could not be justified or later explained away. A line had been crossed.

"Samantha was going to be taken just like Lieutenant Vickers' daughter."

"No," she said, shaking her head. "What happened to Samantha was an accident."

"Was it? Are you sure?"

She stared at him, waiting for him to say more.

"Madam President, things just don't add up."

"What kind of things?" She felt her heart pounding. Could Lincoln really be behind her daughter's disappearance? Was it even possible?

"Think about it," he said. "What are the odds that a UH-60, checked just prior to takeoff, would abruptly crash while flying less than four hundred miles over friendly airspace? And if it was a malfunction, why didn't the operator put out a distress call? Furthermore, why was Samantha reported dead by site inspectors?"

"The wreckage was burned. It could have been a mistake."

General Carr shook his head.

"I don't buy it. Remember, General Hood was running the recovery operation, and he's one of Pike's men. You know that. They wanted you to think she was dead. Hell, they might have been trying to kill her from the very beginning."

Tears started to well at the corners of her eyes.

"Why would they do something like that?"

"Leverage, Madam President."

She wiped a tear from her cheek but immediately returned her hand to his.

"Do you think General Hood or some of his people have her?"

"No," he said, shaking his head. "I think things went wrong. Somehow, she got away. And now she's in the wind, causing them all kinds of grief."

She tightened her grip on General Carr's hands.

"That's my Samantha," she choked, swallowing hard. "But if you're right about this—"

"If I'm right, you're in danger. You can't afford to trust anyone. Not anyone."

She reached up and touched the side of his face.

"I trust you."

He smiled. "Thank you, Madam President. I would do anything for you. I hope you know that."

She nodded. "What are we going to do now?"

"You're going to lie low. Keep your head down, and don't let anyone know that you suspect something."

"And what will you do?"

His jaw tensed, and his eyes hardened.

"I'm going to see how deep this thing goes."

"This isn't over yet," Mason said, thinking out loud as he poured water into one hand and used it to wash the fur around Bowie's mouth.

The dog looked up at him and blinked, obviously enjoying the attention.

Mason poured some of the water into a bowl and set it down beside him. Bowie immediately began slurping it up, drinking for nearly a full minute without stopping. With Bowie taken care of, Mason soaked a couple of rags and used them to clean himself up. When he finished, he felt a couple of years younger, not to mention a whole lot cleaner.

He opened a package of beef jerky and tossed a piece to Bowie. He pulled out another for himself and chewed on it, considering his next move. If Nakai was to be believed, and Mason had no reason to think otherwise, General Hood was the one who had orchestrated the attack on Glynco. For that, he would have to be held accountable.

Mason's first step would be to do some digging. He needed to find out as much as possible about the man. Who was General Hood? Why would he have ordered the murder of hundreds of lawmen? And why was he working to undermine the country's recovery by arming a violent militia in Lexington?

An even bigger question was whether the Vice President of the United States was indeed pulling the strings. The only way to find that out was with the help of General Hood. Mason was reasonably confident that, if he could get to Hood, he would be able to convince him to divulge the names of those involved. And titles be damned, if it ended up that Lincoln Pike was involved, he would face the same cold hand of justice.

In ordinary times, things would have been much simpler. Mason could have simply reported his suspicions to the authorities. Powers with a reach greater than his would have ensured that the facts came to light, even if they were never disclosed to the public. But the world no longer had those checks and balances. There weren't attorneys general or special prosecutors who could be appointed. Neither were there investigative reporters or nightly news specials waiting for a juicy story. No one was watching anyone, and that was a dangerous thing.

"If this country is to have any chance at a future," he said, looking down at Bowie, "we're going to have to see this through. We can't allow anyone who was involved in what happened at Glynco to remain in power. No one is above the law. No one."

Bowie devoured the jerky and looked up expectantly for a second piece. Mason tossed him another chunk of the dried meat.

"If Pike's involved, we'll need President Glass on our side." He hesitated. "Assuming, of course, that she isn't tangled up in this mess too."

It occurred to him that reaching out to President Glass might be harder than it sounded. He had no idea where she was located. Was she still in Washington, DC? He doubted it. The city would be a mess with mountains of dead bodies, not to mention hordes of infected survivors. Even if he could find her, there was the issue of how to make contact in a way that wouldn't end up getting him killed. If Vice President Pike was involved, he could probably find a way to intercept Mason before he made his way up through the chain of command.

"I tell you what," he said, giving Bowie the last piece of jerky. "Let's get back to the cabin and see if we can use the radio to find out more about General Hood. If we're lucky, we might even be able to get a bead on President Glass."

He swung open the driver's side door of his truck, and Bowie hopped in, pacing from one side to the other, obviously excited to be getting back on the road. Mason climbed in beside him and started it up. It was nearly four hundred miles back to Boone, and making it before nightfall would be difficult.

"Believe me," he said, "I'm ready to leave this place too. But we still have one more thing to do."

He eased the truck up the on-ramp, following the path the infected mob had taken during the night. When he got to the top, he carefully inched past the Greyhound bus and parked in the middle of the convoy.

"Sit tight," he said. "This won't take long."

He walked over and picked up Nakai's Steyr Aug. He had no good reason for taking it, other than to gain a little experience with the Austrian firearm. Having carried an M4 in combat, he preferred it over any other rifle, but Mason wasn't above learning to use new weapons. Besides, he had always lived by the motto that one gun was enough, but two were better. The Aug would make a fine backup rifle, and it used the same 5.56 mm ammunition as his M4.

He checked several of the HMMWVs, retrieving both water and fuel. He took only the regular gasoline, leaving behind several jerry cans filled with diesel fuel. He also found a pair of Steiner M22 binoculars, which he stuffed in his glove box. Next, he took two ammo cans filled with NATO M855 steel-tipped 5.56 mm ammunition and a third packed full of Federal Hydra-Shok .45 ammunition. It was no surprise that the mercenaries carried some pretty deadly hardware.

He stared up at the .50 caliber machine gun mounted atop the lead HMMWV.

"I wonder," he mused, climbing up to check it out.

The weapon was attached to the hardtop using a standard M36 ring mount. The gun sat on a roller carriage that swung freely around a circular track, enabling it to fire in any direction. Equipping his F150 with the same ring would require modifications worthy of the experts at the Gas Monkey Garage. And without some way to steady the weapon, it was all but useless.

He searched the HMMWV's cargo area and almost whooped with joy when he found an M3 tripod folded up in the back. The M3 was a versatile ground mount with telescoping legs, and a traversing and elevating mechanism that enabled the operator to dial in shots when visibility was limited or when shooting at long range. He hauled the forty-four-pound tripod over to his truck and set it in the bed. Then he turned back and looked over at the Browning machine gun. Removing the eighty-four-pound weapon from a mount six feet off the ground was not going to be easy.

He started by unloading it and removing the pin that secured it to the ring mount. The weight of the gun made it impossible for him to simply hoist it up onto a shoulder. Instead, he climbed out onto the hood of the HMMWV and carefully lifted the weapon off the mount. He slid it down the windshield and lowered it to the hood as gently as his back would allow. Then he jumped down to the ground and got a good grip on it. Getting the gun from the hood of the HMMWV to the bed of his truck was more straightforward, and the whole transfer only took about four minutes.

He took all the .50 BMG ammunition that he could find—six cans in total, each containing 100 rounds and weighing thirty-five pounds apiece. By the time he was finished, he had added more than three hundred pounds of gear to his truck's payload. Still, he thought, having an M2 in the back might very well come in handy one day.

Unable to resist the temptation to see how well it worked, he cleared space in the bed of his truck, set up the tripod, and lifted the machine gun into place. He secured the pintel and inspected his handiwork. The weapon was enormous, measuring more than five feet in length. He set an ammo can next to the gun and loaded it exactly as he had done earlier in the day. Lowering the tailgate, he swung the weapon around to face one of the tractor-trailers. He pressed the butterfly triggers, and a burst of six slugs tore ragged holes through the side of the truck.

Bowie poked his head through the cab window and started barking.

"It's all right, boy," Mason said, leaning over and patting him on the neck. "I'm done."

He tied down the barrel with a bungee cord and draped a canvas tarp over the weapon. It was ready for use, should the need ever arise.

Mason looked over at the six tractor-trailers. He couldn't in good conscience leave them behind for a militia to find. The worst of the infected seemed incapable of operating firearms, but there were still plenty of dangerous men who could wreak havoc with an arsenal of automatic weapons.

He pulled his truck down the interstate a few hundred feet and climbed out again. Bowie started to ease out of the truck, but Mason stopped him.

"Sit tight. It's going to get hot."

He gathered up a few rags, soaked them in gasoline, and went from one tractor-trailer to the next, stuffing them in the gas tanks. Then he hurried down the line, lighting them one at a time. Unlike Hollywood movies, the vehicles didn't explode. Instead, the tanks made loud *puff* sounds as the gasoline ignited. The fires slowly spread, starting first with the cabs and then moving back to the cargos. Tires melted, metal warped, and windshields burst as the flames took hold.

Bowie seemed fascinated by the fire, staring out through the windshield with wide eyes and occasionally sounding off with a short *woof.* Mason watched to make sure that every tractor-trailer burned completely, leaving nothing serviceable behind. When he was satisfied, he started up his truck and put it in gear.

Bowie turned to him with excitement in his eyes.

"Yeah," he said, "it's time to go home."

ॐ ॐ

The most direct route back to Boone was to follow I-95 as far as I-26 and then turn north toward Columbia. Caution, however, dictated taking a slightly more circuitous route, first skirting Savannah, and then following the much smaller Highway 321 all the way up. The only point at which Mason thought he might have to detour off the highway was near Columbia, but he wouldn't know that until he saw the condition of the roads.

The first thirty miles passed without incident. The drive was so quiet, in fact, that Mason began to think that the trip home might be entirely uneventful. It was only as he entered the outskirts of Hardeeville, South Carolina, that things took a surprising turn.

As he carefully steered around an overturned school bus, he saw a large shape lying up ahead in the road. A pack of feral dogs was circling and biting at it. At first, Mason thought it might be a bloated cadaver of some type, but as he got closer, he saw that it was actually a large black horse. The animal struggled to get up, but both its back legs were badly chewed and unable to support its weight. The dogs were relentless, biting at its neck, legs, and face.

Mason hit the brakes hard, grabbed his M4, and jumped out of the truck. He brought the weapon to his shoulder and fired a shot over the animals' heads. The dogs scattered, and Bowie leapt from the truck, chasing after them. Mason whistled, and Bowie stopped and looked back over his shoulder with a pleading in his eyes to let him give chase.

"Oh, go on," he said.

Bowie raced after the dogs, barking wildly.

Mason slowly approached the injured horse. The poor creature was in terrible pain. Its body was covered in a white foamy sweat from nearly running itself to death. Worse yet were the puncture bites and ripped flesh covering the animal's legs and face. It tried to raise its head and sit up, but simply didn't have the strength. It would die, of that Mason was certain, but death would not come quickly. He squatted down and patted the horse on its thick neck, and when he did, the animal laid its head back on the pavement.

"I'm afraid this is the end of the line," he said, stroking the beautiful creature.

It stared up at him with a huge dark eye, strangely peaceful for being in such awful pain.

Mason slowly stood back up and raised his rifle, accepting that it was his responsibility to end the animal's suffering. He placed the muzzle perpendicular to its forehead, aiming for the intersection of an imaginary line that that went from each eye to the opposite ear. The horse lay still, looking up at him, as if resolved to its fate. Mason nodded his farewell and pulled the trigger. The shot was true, and the animal no longer moved. He squatted back down and gently pushed on the cornea of one of its eyes. The horse didn't blink. It was dead.

That was when Mason noticed a second bullet wound, this one behind the horse's front leg. He pressed a finger into the hole. By the size of it, he thought it was probably a 30.06, which helped to explain how the dogs had been able to bring down such a strong animal.

He stood up and stared down at the horse for a long time. It was a gorgeous creature, and why anyone would shoot it was beyond him. The only explanation was that someone had shot it for food. The bullet must have missed anything vital, and it had managed to run off—a shame for both the horse and the hunter.

Bowie came trotting back up, his head held high.

"Did you give it to 'em, boy?"

Bowie walked over and sniffed the horse. He circled it once and then went over and stood quietly by the truck, as if waiting for Mason to say his final goodbyes.

Mason took one last look at the horse, shook his head, and headed back to his truck.

ॐ ॐ

Three miles up the road, Mason could hardly believe his eyes. There in the middle of the lane was a second horse. This one was very much dead. Fortunately, the dogs had yet to find it. He pulled up alongside the animal and studied it from his window. It was a brown and white Quarter Horse, probably no more than a couple of years old. The only signs of injury were two bullet holes, one through its neck and the other through a hindquarter. A huge pool of blood lay under the animal.

"Son of a bitch," he said, clenching his teeth. This wasn't about hunting at all.

The crack of a gunshot sounded from further up the interstate. Then another.

Mason sped ahead, driving as fast as he dared. After about half a mile, he saw them—two men in a bright red Dodge Ram pickup. One man drove while the second rode in the bed, leaning over the roof of the cab with a rifle in his hands. They were weaving through cars, trying to get off another shot at a horse galloping down the median.

Mason pressed hard on his horn, and both men spun around to see who was closing in on them. After a few seconds, they gave up the chase and swung to a stop in the middle of the road. The man standing in back turned and hopped down from the bed, hunting rifle in hand. The other man climbed out of the cab, apparently unarmed.

Mason stopped about fifty yards behind them, turning his truck at a slight angle in case he had to take cover behind the engine compartment. Bowie tried to press by him to get at them, but Mason held him back.

"Stay with me," he said, looking into the dog's eyes.

Bowie hopped down and looked back at him, whining impatiently.

The two men were already approaching fast. The one with the rifle was easily six-foot-three and sported long blonde hair, reminding Mason of the Italian fashion model, Fabio. The other was a few inches shorter and walked with a slight limp as he hurried to keep up.

Mason stepped around to the front corner of his truck and waited for them. They reminded him of college baseball players, strong and youthful, filled with an almost playful energy. Young men out having fun, he thought. But that in no way gave them a pass for what they were doing.

"What the hell, mister!" shouted Fabio.

"Hold it right there," Mason said, sliding his jacket open and placing his hand on the butt of the Supergrade.

"What are you, some kind of undercover cop?"

"I'm Deputy Marshal Mason Raines. And you are?"

"I'm none of your goddamn business," he said, forcing a confident smile. "And that's my boyfriend, Jeremy."

Jeremy's face tightened. "Knock it off."

Fabio reached over and pushed him.

"Or what?"

Jeremy looked to the ground.

"Just quit saying stuff like that. It ain't nice."

Fabio took a step toward Mason.

"I'll tell you what isn't nice," he said. "It's the marshal here going and honking at us like that. We'll probably never catch up to that damn pony now."

Mason tried to keep his temper in check. He reminded himself that they were killing animals, not people. It helped, but only a little.

"You got something against horses?"

"No," Fabio said, making an exaggerated face. "How could I have anything but love for those giant sacks of shit?"

Mason shook his head, sensing that things were quickly heading toward violence.

"Let me ask you something, Marshal. You ever shoveled horse shit? No? Well, I have. Hundreds of pounds of that green stinky crap."

"You sound like an expert."

Fabio tipped his head forward as if he couldn't believe what he was hearing.

"Are you insulting me, Marshal?"

"Not at all. I'm glad that a fellow like you could find gainful employment."

Fabio's eyes narrowed, and he gripped his rifle.

"The horses aren't your property. We let them go from a riding school east of Hardeeville. I figure that, since we let them go, we can do damn well whatever we please to them."

"Is that how you figure it?"

"You see it different?"

"I do."

Sensing the growing tension, Bowie began to move sideways around the men, growling.

Jeremy stepped forward and pulled at Fabio's arm.

"There ain't no call for this," he pleaded. "Shooting the horses was dumb if you really think about it."

Fabio jerked his arm free.

"Get your hands off me."

"You should listen to him," Mason said in a firm voice.

"Or what?"

Mason didn't answer.

"Maybe we should chase you down the highway a bit. See if you fare any better than the horses. I've never hunted a man before."

Mason gave him a cold smile.

"I have. Plenty of times. And believe me, it's a hell of a lot different than running down a horse."

That seemed to give Fabio pause, but only for a moment.

"You don't have any jurisdiction here."

"Wrong. The Marshal Service is a federal law enforcement agency. And even if it wasn't, common law allows any citizen to stop another from committing a violent crime." He looked over at Jeremy. "You sure you want to be a part of this?"

"Not me, Marshal," blurted Jeremy. "I've never been in trouble with the law. Not once."

Fabio looked over at him and shook his head.

"You've got to be the biggest pussy to ever survive an apocalypse."

Jeremy looked at the ground again and started to back away.

"Maybe so," he said. "But my momma wouldn't want me dying over some stupid horses."

Bowie kept pace with Jeremy, advancing for every step he retreated.

Fabio looked at Mason and shrugged.

"I guess it's just us men."

Mason shook his head.

"Not hardly. Men don't shoot defenseless animals for fun. You're still a boy."

"You think so?"

"I do. And for that reason, I'm going to cut you a break."

"How's that?" he sneered.

"I'm not going to kill you."

"That's mighty nice of you, Marshal," he taunted.

Mason smiled. "I'm feeling generous on account of all the shit you've had to shovel."

Fabio's face burned a bright red.

"I'll count to three," he said. "Then we'll see who's the boy. How about that, Marshal?"

Mason took a deep breath and let it out. He could feel the beat of his heart slowly accelerating, providing extra oxygen.

"No need. I'll shoot you when I'm ready."

"You sure talk big for—"

Fabio never saw Mason pull the Supergrade, nor did he hear the crack of the firearm. He simply fell, clutching his side, overwhelmed by the pain of a hollow point bullet punching through his side. He screamed in agony, shoving his rifle away as if it had suddenly caught fire.

Bowie started to move on Jeremy, but the man immediately threw his hands up.

"Help, Marshal!" he shrieked.

"Bowie!"

The dog stopped and looked back at him, licking his lips.

Mason shook his head.

Bowie turned and eyed the man but didn't advance any further.

"Get in your truck and go," Mason said, pointing toward the Dodge.

Jeremy nodded and ran for the pickup. A few seconds later, he was speeding down the highway, dodging abandoned cars and other debris.

Mason stepped forward and kicked the rifle away from Fabio. The man was pressing his hand against the bullet hole, dark blood oozing from between his fingers. His entire body was covered in sweat.

"Jeezus," he cried, "you shot me."

Mason squatted down and studied the wound. It was a through and through, but there was the distinct smell of urine. That meant the bullet had punctured one of the man's kidneys—painful, but not necessarily a death sentence.

"You gotta help me, Marshal."

Mason ignored him. He had learned the hard way not to administer first aid to those he shot. The last man he gave bandages to later tried to kill him for a case of gold coins.

"Listen up," he said. "I've got some good news and some bad news. Which do you want first?"

Sweat trickled down Fabio's cheeks.

"Give me the good news."

Mason nodded. "The good news is that the bullet didn't hit anything you can't live without."

"Oh, thank God," he groaned, sitting up and sliding over to prop himself against the tire of a nearby car.

Without saying anything more, Mason stood up and called for Bowie. The dog hurried over, sniffing Fabio as he passed. Together, they started back toward his truck.

"Hey, Marshal," shouted Fabio. "You never did tell me. What's the bad news?"

Without turning around, Mason pointed off toward the tree line. There in the shadows stood four large German Shepherds.

chapter 15

Tanner followed the North Scenic Highway out of Bland, thankful to see the town disappear in his rearview mirror. Samantha seemed to pick up on his train of thought and turned to look over her shoulder.

"Let's not go there again," she said. "Not ever."

"Agreed."

She turned back around and began searching the cab of the truck. It was empty except for a few registration papers in the glove box and a tire iron behind the seat.

Tanner dug something out of his pocket.

"Here," he said, handing her a small box of ammunition.

She opened it up and carefully reloaded the Savage .22 rifle. As she put the rifle back on the floor, her stomach growled loudly.

"You hungry?" he said.

She nodded. "My mom always said it's important to start the day with a healthy breakfast."

"Like Froot Loops?"

"Exactly."

He smiled and pointed up ahead to a house with a large detached garage.

"Want to see if there's anything left in the cupboards?"

She looked back over her shoulder again, double-checking that Bland was indeed officially out of sight.

"Okay, but if there's a snake on the door, we don't stop."

He nodded. "Fair enough."

Tanner pulled up into the gravel driveway, grabbed his newfound shotgun from the bed, and stepped out. Samantha followed after him with her rifle in hand. They approached the house carefully, their eyes scanning from left to right, looking for anything that didn't belong. The place looked abandoned. The front door was kicked in, and two large windows were smashed.

"I think we're okay," he said, stepping up onto the porch.

She moved up beside him and cautiously leaned her head inside the door.

"Anyone in there?" she hollered.

No one answered.

Tanner pushed what was left of the door out of the way, and they stepped inside. It opened up into a living room, with a hallway going off to the right and an eat-in kitchen to the left. It smelled damp and unlived in.

They quickly searched the entire house, making sure that it was indeed unoccupied. When they were satisfied, they returned to the kitchen and began rummaging through the cupboards. The entire place had been picked clean. The only thing that remained was a small bag of cat food.

"How hungry are you?" he asked, pointing to the bag.

She wrinkled her nose. "Not *that* hungry."

"Come on then, let's find another house down the road."

They stepped back out onto the porch, empty-handed and twice as hungry as when they had gone in. Tanner glanced over at the detached garage. It looked like a workshop.

"Let's check that out," he said, heading down the porch steps.

She shrugged and followed along.

The building was locked up tight, the door deadbolted, and the garage secured with slide latches from the inside.

"It looks like we'll have to—" she started.

Tanner gave the door a savage kick, and it tore free from the jamb, long wooden splinters splitting off the frame.

She rolled her eyes. "Never mind."

The shop was cold and dark, and rank with the smell of grease and sweat. Tanner went over and slid the two garage doors up to let in some sunlight. Whoever had lived in the house had obviously done some auto mechanic work, either as a hobby or profession. A black '67 Pontiac GTO sat surrounded by three rolling tool chests. The hood of the car stood open, and the engine was partially disassembled.

"Someone left their baby behind," he said, looking inside the windows of the car.

"It's pretty."

"Bite your tongue, girl. A '67 GTO isn't pretty."

"No?"

"This was a car built for manly men. And manly men don't drive pretty cars."

She rolled her eyes again.

"And what, may I ask, is a manly man?"

"A manly man…" He searched for the right words. "A manly man is someone who not only knows how to live, but also knows how to die." He nodded, satisfied with his answer.

"And I suppose you're one of these manly men?"

"Well, now that you bring it up… "

She scoffed. "Seriously, give me an example of a manly man. Other than you, I mean."

He thought about it a moment.

"All right, I got one. How about Kit Carson?"

She laughed. "That sounds like a candy bar."

He shook his head.

"Go ahead," she said, stifling another laugh. "Really, I want to know."

"Kit Carson was a trapper and frontiersman, a real tough old bird. He lived with the Arapaho and Cheyenne tribes, and led a regiment during the Civil War. You know what his final words were?"

"I don't know what any of his words were. I don't even know who he was."

Tanner ignored her. "The last thing old Kit ever said was, 'I just wish I had time for one more bowl of chili.' Now that, darlin', is a manly man."

She laughed. "That's a good one all right. What are *your* last words going to be?"

"I'm going with, 'Someone get me another beer.'"

She snickered. "I can see that."

Tanner turned and began digging through one of the tool chests.

"What are you looking for?"

"This," he said, lifting out a pipe cutter. He rummaged a little more and found a long metal file and a sheet of emery cloth. "And these."

"What's all that for?"

"You'll see," he said, carrying everything over to a large cast iron vise mounted to a workbench. He unloaded the shotgun and clamped it in place, using two pieces of wood to keep the vise from marring the weapon.

"You're going to cut the barrel off, aren't you?"

"I can't very well carry this thing around."

"It is awfully big."

"It's a friggin' pole vaulting stick."

He slipped the pipe cutter around the barrel and positioned it about two inches beyond the end of the magazine tube.

"Wow, that much?"

"I figure I'll cut it down to about sixteen inches. Any shorter than that and it'll kick like a donkey with a hard—." He cleared his throat. "—a toothache."

He tightened the pipe cutter and began sliding it around the barrel, occasionally retightening it to keep the cutting wheel pressed into the metal. After a couple of minutes, the end of the barrel cut free and fell to the floor with a loud *clang*.

"Now, we dress it up a little to get rid of any burrs or sharp edges." He ran the file around the lip a couple of times and then spent a few minutes with the emery cloth smoothing everything out. When he was finished, he loosened up the vise and lifted out the shotgun.

"What do you think?" he asked, holding it up.

"Very manly."

He grinned. "Come closer and I'll show you how this gun works."

"I already have a gun," she said, stepping closer.

"I know, and the .22 rifle is perfect for you, as you've already proven. But there may come a time when you need a little more stopping power."

She surprised him by not arguing the point.

"We load it exactly like we did the other shotgun, only this one has a button underneath that needs to be pressed when you insert the shells. See?" He pressed a large silver button beside the feed ramp.

She nodded.

"Once you load it, pull the bolt handle back, and let it fly forward. That moves the first shell into the chamber."

"Seems easy enough."

"Show me." He handed her the sawed-off shotgun.

"It's heavy," she said, hefting it with both hands.

"Yes, and it will probably knock you on your butt if you ever have to fire it. But it'll also get the attention of whatever you're shooting at."

He handed her the shotgun shells one at a time, and she loaded four. The last one was hard for her to push up the feed ramp, but she finally got it. She pulled the bolt handle back and let it slide forward.

"Now, top it off," he said.

She slid one more into the magazine tube.

"The difference between this weapon and the one I had before is that this one feeds the next shell automatically. That means that when you pull the trigger, it automatically ejects and chambers a new shell."

"You don't pump it?"

"Nope."

"Why wouldn't they make every shotgun like that? Isn't it faster?"

"You bet it is. But autoloaders are more likely to jam than pump shotguns."

"Ah," she said. "Makes sense."

"Come on," he said. "Let's take it outside and shoot a few shells. While we're at it, I'll let you try out the Bearcat too. If you're going to stay alive, you'll need to know your way around guns."

As they turned to leave the garage, Samantha noticed a pillowcase sitting on the floor beside one of the garage doors. It was stuffed full and tied closed with a bright orange ribbon.

"What do you think that is?"

Tanner nudged the makeshift sack with his boot. It felt heavy. He untied the ribbon and saw that there were dozens of cans of food inside, as well as several bottles of water. He lifted out a can of chicken noodle soup and held it up for her to see.

"It's not Froot Loops, but it'll fill your belly."

Samantha came over and started rummaging through the pillowcase. She pulled out a can of yellow peaches.

"This wouldn't be too bad," she said. "Should I go back inside and see if I can find a can opener?"

"No need," he said. "There are plenty of ways to open a can."

She looked around the shop.

"Like how? With tools?"

"Sure, tools would cut the cans open. But I'll show you another method that doesn't require anything more than a little concrete." He squatted down and placed the can of soup, top-side down, on the concrete floor. "The edge of a can is nothing more than a flap of rolled steel. If you rub it against concrete or a smooth rock, you can abrade it away and get into the can."

"Is this another one of your survival tricks?" she asked, her face coming alive.

He shrugged. "If you want to call it that."

"Okay, show me. I want to learn all the tricks."

"Here goes." He started scrubbing the can back and forth on the floor, sending dust up into the air. After about thirty seconds, liquid started leaking out onto the concrete. "When you see the liquid, you're getting close."

He continued for another few seconds, and then slipped his finger under the can and turned it right side up. He gave the sides of the can a gentle squeeze, and part of the metal lid popped up.

"Wow!" she exclaimed. "You did it!"

He pulled the lid the rest of the way off, and the smell of salty chicken immediately began to permeate the garage. Tanner tipped the can and dumped some of the soup into his mouth.

"Now you try," he said, talking through a mouthful of noodles.

"Okay, but I probably won't be able to do it."

"So says the girl who shot four men and outran an army of satanic worshippers."

She set the can on the floor and began sliding it around, imitating what Tanner had done. It took about a minute before liquid started seeping out.

"Hey, I'm getting it."

"Give it a little longer, and then use your fingers to make sure the lid doesn't fall off."

She did exactly as he said, and when she flipped the can back up, the lid had drooped down into the can. She tipped the can forward and gave it a little shake to get the lid to pop out. Then she pulled it the rest of the way off and smiled as she looked down at a can full of tender yellow cling peaches.

Breakfast was served.

෧ ๙

With a pillowcase full of canned food and bottled water, Tanner and Samantha were able to turn their attention to putting miles behind them. They decided to steer clear of the interstates, except when absolutely necessary. Instead, they stayed on the North Scenic Highway, paralleling I-77, all the way to the East River Mountain Tunnel.

The huge gray and white concrete structure reached forty feet into the air and had two lanes going east and two others going west, with a thick dividing wall between them. All four lanes were jam-packed with cars, many of them crashed into one another. A few had caught fire and were nothing more than blackened metal shells.

"Please tell me we're not going in there," she said.

"What? You mean you don't want to crawl around cars filled with dead bodies in a pitch-black tunnel?" he asked, grinning.

"Uh, no."

"Me neither. What do you say we double-back and pick up Highway 598?"

As he started to wheel the truck around, he caught sight of a long string of motorcycle headlights approaching from behind.

"You've got to be kidding me," he sighed.

"What?" She spun around. "Oh no, it's them again."

Tanner grabbed his shotgun and the bandolier of ammunition. He stuck the Bearcat in the back of his waistband and the Kahr PM9 in his front pocket.

"Come on," he said. "We've got to get out of sight."

"But where?" Samantha asked, scrambling out of the truck with her rifle, and staring up at the steep slopes that rose along both sides of the road.

Tanner looked toward the tunnel.

"Please, no," she pleaded. "It's so dark."

"I'd rather take my chance in the dark than with twenty pissed-off bikers. Come on."

He took off for the tunnel, and after hesitating for a moment, Samantha followed. They ran about thirty yards into the tunnel and took cover behind a car.

"It smells awful in here," she said, trying to talk without breathing through her nose.

He took a deep sniff.

"It's not so bad."

She wrinkled her nose up.

"It smells like—"

"Dead bodies?"

She nodded. "Lots and lots of them."

He couldn't argue the point. There were several hundred cars in the tunnel, most of which had bodies either in or near them. There were enough cadavers to fill a small graveyard.

The sound of engines grew louder, and they peeked up over the top of the car to get a better look. The gang came to stop a few feet outside the tunnel. Once again, they started revving their engines for a little fun. The noise echoed down the tunnel, vibrating windows. When they finally tired of the game, they killed their engines and pulled off their helmets to enjoy a few cigarettes.

Samantha pointed toward the man wearing the distinctive Predator helmet.

"It's him," she whispered.

Tanner nodded. "He and I have unfinished business."

"Do you think they'll come in after us?"

"Nah. They probably didn't even see us."

Predator slipped off his helmet and set it on the seat behind him. The man's huge mustache and sideburns were almost as distinctive as his helmet. He glanced around, and his eyes settled on the old pickup that Tanner had been driving.

"It's just an old truck," whispered Tanner. "Let it be."

Ignoring his silent suggestion, Predator dismounted, walked over to it, and placed a hand on the hood. Alarmed, he slowly spun in a full circle, searching the area, his eyes finally settling on the tunnel. He shouted something to his men, and they scrambled for their weapons.

"They know we're here," Tanner said softly.

A horrific scream suddenly sounded from deep inside the tunnel. It was inhuman, like the sound a grizzly might make if its foot had been caught in a steel jaw-trap.

Samantha flinched and grabbed Tanner's arm.

"What was that?" she whispered.

He looked over his shoulder, peering into the darkness.

"I think they woke something up."

"*Something?* Not someone?"

He shrugged. "It sounded more like a something."

Still clutching his arm, she said, "When I was little, my mom used to read stories to me—Curious George, Pippi Longstocking, Winnie the Pooh—kid's stuff, you know?"

"And?"

"And I remember that, in one story, there was a creature so terrible that even its name made everyone shake with fear. It was called the Backson." She shivered, pointing down into the dark tunnel. "That scream is what I imagine a Backson would sound like."

"Whatever it is, I agree that it's probably trouble. But that," he said, pointing at the bandits who were slowly approaching the tunnel, "is most definitely trouble."

She sighed. "We're between a rock and a hard place."

"A what?"

"A rock and a hard place. It means both options are bad."

"I know what it means," he said, grinning. "I was just surprised that you got it right."

She cut her eyes at him.

"So? What are we going to do?"

"We do like we always do," he said. "We pick the hard place."

⸱ ⸩

The tunnel was so dark that it was more like an abandoned iron mine than a passage for interstate travelers. The floor sloped down, and until they got to the bottom, it would be impossible to see the proverbial light at the end of the tunnel.

A thunderous boom sounded from inside the tunnel entrance. They glanced back and saw Predator standing on the hood of an abandoned car. He held Tanner's .44 Magnum revolver above his head like a sign of his manhood.

"Come on out, or we're coming in to get you."

Tanner considered taking a shot at him but decided he was probably out of range of the sawed-off shotgun, and most certainly out of range of either pistol. He could use Samantha's rifle, but it didn't seem worth the risk of giving away their position. Right now, Predator only suspected that someone was in the tunnel. Besides, thought Tanner, he was probably bluffing about coming in after them. Better to heed Samantha's advice and walk away whenever possible.

Daylight shone in from the entrance, but it only reached twenty or thirty yards into the tunnel. Tanner figured that he and Samantha had already disappeared into the darkness, but just to be sure, he continued another twenty yards in before standing up to give his legs a rest.

"We're clear," he said softly.

Samantha slowly stood up.

"Do you think they'll come in after us?"

He was about to reassure her that they wouldn't when he saw Predator and three of his men enter the tunnel.

"Don't worry about it," he said. "They'll never find us in here."

He turned around to look deeper into the tunnel. It was complete and total darkness. If they were to have any hope of making it to the other side, they would need to feel their way forward. His biggest concern was losing Samantha.

Tanner looked around and saw the body of a man crumpled against the wall of the tunnel. He hurried over and unlaced one of the dead man's boots.

"What are you doing?" she whispered.

He tied one end of the shoestring to his belt loop and the other end to one of hers.

"Keep the string taut, and don't lose your pants."

"Lose my pants?"

"Just stating the obvious."

"You are so weird sometimes."

"It's why we get along so well. Now, come on."

Samantha stayed a few feet behind him as they slowly delved deeper into the tunnel. Before long, they were no longer able to see one other. They could hear each other breathe, or bump into a car, or stumble over a dead body, but everything was now surrounded by impenetrable darkness.

"I can't see my hand in front of my face," she said, her voice trembling.

"What do you need to see your hand for? You planning on doing your nails?"

She chuckled. "Now, that's funny."

They heard Predator stumble and fall. He cursed loudly and fired a shot down the tunnel.

"We aren't giving up!" he yelled. "My men are already on their way to the other side. Even if you do get out, they'll be waiting."

"We're trapped," she said, pulling lightly on the string between them.

"Not hardly."

"But he said—"

"Don't sweat it. Even a one-legged Viet Cong with cataracts could set up an ambush in this tunnel. If he follows us down to the bottom, I'll deal with him."

She seemed to gain strength from his confidence.

"Okay."

Tanner extended his hands about a foot in front of his face and took small, careful steps, as he proceeded ahead. He could live with knocking a shin against a bumper but didn't want to whack his nose into a side view mirror. Whenever he felt the cold metal of a car or truck, he moved sideways along the body, alternating going left and right with each vehicle, in the hopes that it kept him moving forward. Even so, traversing through a pitch-black tunnel filled with vehicles facing in every possible direction was a very slow process. He estimated that it would take them at least two hours to get to the other side of the mile-long tunnel. His only consolation was that once they got to where they could see the light shining in from the exit, it should go a little faster.

Tanner heard something move ahead of them. It sounded like a roll of carpet being dragged across the ground. He stopped, and Samantha bumped into him.

"What is it?" she whispered.

"Shh." He reached around and pushed her down, squatting beside her with his shotgun pointing in the direction of the sound.

A large shape moved past them in the dark. It was on the other side of the tunnel, close to the wall, but it stunk like the walking dead.

After it passed, she whispered, "Was that a Backson?"

He felt of her face and leaned in, putting his mouth close to her ear.

"I don't think we want to find out. Let's keep moving, real quiet like. No more talking."

He felt her head nod gently up and down. Turning, he continued ahead, hurrying as fast as he dared.

Less than a minute later, horrible screams sounded from behind them— men being torn apart, shrieking like children who had awoken to discover that Dracula was not only real, but leaning over their bed. The boom of Predator's pistol sounded once, and then… nothing.

Tanner felt the string pull taut as Samantha stopped in her tracks. He was afraid to pull it too hard for fear of it coming free of one of their belt loops.

"Come on," he whispered, his impatience growing. What was she doing? They had to move!

"It'll come for us too," she said. There was a finality to her words. "We can't outrun it. Not in this darkness. It'll catch us."

He started to argue with her, to explain that he couldn't fight something he couldn't see. Then, as hard as it was to accept, he realized that she was right. It would catch them. And it would kill them.

"You know what?" he said, turning around. "You're right."

"I don't want to be right."

"I know you don't. But let's deal with what we've got."

"How? We can't see!"

Neither of them saw a reason to whisper any longer, and their voices were slowly rising.

"All right," he said. "Let's change that."

Tanner felt around for the nearest car and ripped open the door. A cloud of blowflies buzzed across his face, and he batted them aside as he leaned in. He felt around until he found the knob that turned on the headlights. As soon he pulled the knob, bright beams blasted out through the darkness.

Samantha covered her eyes, blinded.

"It'll see us!" she cried.

"It already sees us. This way we can see it too. Ready yourself."

Samantha turned her back to the lights and brought up her rifle.

Tanner yanked the shoe lace from his belt loop, raced to another car, and clicked on its headlights. They were much dimmer than the first but still added some light to the mix.

They both saw a large shadowy figure shuffling toward them. It was huge and indistinguishable, like some mythical Shambling Mound that had crawled out of the swamp.

Tanner leaned through the window of a utility truck and turned on its lights too. The entire area was now lit up, and the light felt protective, like a campfire on a starless night.

"To me!" he shouted to Samantha.

She backed toward him, her eyes never leaving the creature that was approaching. It was maybe fifty yards away and moving steadily through the blockade of cars toward them.

"It's coming!" she shouted.

"Let it come," he said, bringing the shotgun to his shoulder. He had five shots. There would be no reloading. Either he would kill it or he wouldn't.

When it was about thirty yards away, the Backson entered the light. What they saw had two arms, two legs, and a head. But it was not human. Not anymore, it wasn't. The creature was more like an ogre or a troll, if such things really existed. It was impossibly large, easily weighing five hundred pounds and standing nearly seven feet tall. It had an enormous bald head covered in bulbous blisters, and arms and legs swollen with thick cords of muscles.

The Backson stopped and stared at them with shiny black eyes, each drizzling long streaks of inky goo. Then it took a step toward them, dragging its feet across the asphalt, as if they were too heavy to lift.

Tanner pointed the shotgun center mass and squeezed the trigger. The gun belched fire, and a handful of buckshot slammed into the creature's chest. It screamed in pain and raced forward at a speed he would have never thought possible for something so big. Tanner brought the weapon back down and fired a second burst. It hit the Backson in the left shoulder, blood and skin spraying onto the car behind it. He was just bringing the shotgun back on target for a third shot when it reached him.

The monster slammed into Tanner, knocking him over the hood of a car and sending the shotgun flying away. The blow was so powerful that he briefly blacked out, and when he awoke, he felt a giant hand pulling him up by his hair.

There was a small crack of a gunshot. Then another. And another. The creature jerked with each sound. Samantha stood about ten feet behind it, popping .22 slugs into the meat of its back as fast as she could cycle the bolt of her rifle.

The Backson turned to face her, pulling Tanner around like he was its favorite stuffed animal. Samantha stepped back and lowered her rifle, her face becoming pale.

"Oh, no, you don't!" Tanner snarled, tightening his right hand into a fist and punching up into the creature's groin. Knuckles met nuts, and it shrieked in pain.

He hit it again, and the Backson flung him toward Samantha.

Tanner landed near her feet and rolled onto his back.

"Go for the eyes!" he shouted.

Samantha suddenly felt like a toddler trying to lift a car. Fear and panic weighed on her arms and legs, making every action feel like she was trying to move through chewing gum. Her only thought was to drop the gun and run. Just run! But even that seemed impossible. She found herself standing motionless, unable to act, staring at a creature that should only belong in storybooks.

Tanner pulled the Kahr compact pistol from his front pocket, lined it up, and shot the creature in the face. The bullet hit two inches below its right eye, popping a clean hole in the middle of its cheek.

It charged, screaming with mindless fury. Tanner pumped two more rounds into it in quick procession, and then it was upon him. The Backson's huge hands beat down on him, cracking a rib and pummeling his left eye. He rolled away barely in time to avoid a tremendous two-handed strike that would surely have killed him.

The monster chased after him, but it slowed, blood seeping from a dozen wounds. Tanner pushed to his feet and hurled himself forward, driving his shoulder up into the creature's ribs. It grabbed him, wrapping both hands around his neck. Tanner instinctively did the same, and two struggled to choke the life out of one another.

Behind the beast, Tanner saw Samantha standing paralyzed, watching their life and death struggle. As tears dripped from his eyes, he desperately wanted to tell her that everything was going to be okay, that there was nothing to be afraid of, that he would kill anything that came for her.

Tanner drove his thumbs deep into the creature's windpipe even as he pressed his own chin down to prevent it from doing the same. He felt the Backson's grip weakening, but he also felt his own faltering. A ring of darkness began to close in around him, and he pinpointed on the creature's eyes—two inky black pools of pure hate. He squeezed with every ounce of strength he had left. And that was enough.

His thumbs punched through the Backson's windpipe, and its grip immediately fell away from his throat. The creature's legs buckled, and Tanner followed it to the ground. He crouched there for a full minute, choking the beast. When he was sure it was dead, he retrieved his shotgun and shot it once through each eye.

When it was all over, he helped Samantha to sit down, and they both settled back against the door of the utility truck. He put his arm around her and pulled her close.

"It's over," he said, his voice hoarse.

She seemed unable to speak as tears dripped down her face.

Tanner held her for several minutes, resting and collecting himself. He hurt from a dozen places, but the worst were his ribs. He touched them to make sure that nothing was poking out that shouldn't be. There wasn't.

"I'm sorry," she said, choking on the words.

"For what?"

"For freezing up. I couldn't move."

"Wasn't that you who shot it in the back?"

She nodded. "Yes, but—"

"If you hadn't gotten its attention, it would have broken my neck."

She stared at the ground, not at all convinced.

"Sam, we do what we can. Every single time."

"I could have done more."

"Okay. So, next time, do more."

She swallowed and nodded.

He squeezed her shoulder, and she leaned against him.

"How can something like that even exist?" she asked.

Tanner looked over at the beast lying in a huge pool of blood.

"The virus is changing people. Making them bigger and stronger. This one lived in a dark tunnel and had plenty to eat. Ideal conditions, I suppose."

"He doesn't look human anymore."

"No, he doesn't."

"Do you think there are more of them in here?" she asked, looking around.

"No," he answered quickly.

"How can you be sure?"

"If there were, they would have already come for us."

"Right." She looked over at him. "What about you? Are you okay?"

"I'm fine. He barely even scratched me."

"Let me see."

He pulled away and let her have a look at him, acting as his field medic like she had on many occasions.

"Your eye looks terrible," she said, grimacing. "It's huge and purple."

"It'll heal."

"What about here?" She pressed against his ribs, and he had to bite his lip to keep from screaming.

"Can't feel a thing," he said through clenched teeth.

"Okay," she said, standing up.

"Okay what?"

"Okay, we should get going. If we hurry, maybe we can get through the tunnel before the motorcycle riders show up."

He smiled and slowly pulled himself to his feet.

"Glad you're back."

Mason spent the rest of the day driving north on Highway 321, his thoughts repeatedly drifting back to the dying horse. The pointless cruelty reminded him of when soldiers became traumatized or bored and took to tormenting the locals in occupied territories. Whether it was Nazis raping young French farm girls, or the Imperial Japanese Army brutalizing prisoners of war, people with violent authority could quickly forget their decency. When finally confronted, they would justify their barbarism, but it always came down to one simple truth. Some people lacked the moral strength to keep their humanity when they believed they would no longer be held accountable.

While leaving Fabio as dog bait was perhaps unduly harsh, it struck Mason as poetic justice. Perhaps he would get to his rifle in time and manage to kill the dogs. Even if he did, Mason hoped that their confrontation would forever serve as a reminder that actions had consequences.

Without thinking about it, he flipped on the radio and spun the dial. He didn't know what he was hoping to pick up, maybe a news announcement, maybe an old-timer transmitting a little big band music from an antenna set up on the roof of his garage—anything to help take his mind off dead horses and the jackasses who shot them. What he found on several stations was a short government broadcast that looped over and over.

Citizens of the United States should not give up hope. Emergency supplies are being distributed as infrastructures are slowly being rebuilt. The cities of Norfolk, Virginia, Denver, Colorado, and Olympia, Washington have been designated as the first of the New Colonies. These cities, much like the nation's founding colonies, will serve as places where people can live in safety, businesses can be established, and basic human needs can be met. Future broadcasts will indicate when citizens should move to these locations. For now, everyone is encouraged to join together with family and friends, sharing supplies and skills, in order to survive this most difficult time.

Mason listened to the broadcast several times before shutting off the radio. He hadn't seen any evidence of supplies being distributed, but that didn't necessarily mean they weren't, only that they hadn't yet reached the areas through which he had traveled. The concept of establishing New

Colonies seemed like a step in the right direction. If the government was able to create viable city-states, they could serve as the building blocks of a new nation.

Encouraged by what he had heard, Mason popped in a little Steely Dan and sang along with the music as he worked to put miles behind him. He made it all the way past Columbia without difficulty. He passed a few travelers scavenging for food and water, but none paid him any attention.

As the sun slowly set to his left, he entered the outskirts of Chester, South Carolina. The town was barely a mile across, and he thought he could probably get from one side to the other in less than five minutes. He had driven through Chester years before, but his only memory was of a family-run restaurant that served homemade barbeque pork sandwiches. Like Pavlov's dog, even the mere thought of the moist meat caused his mouth to water.

At the edge of town, the highway changed names to Columbia Road. Mason slowed his truck and turned his full attention to the road. Anywhere survivors congregated, whether in towns or on interstates, there existed a greater potential for danger. Several small houses were on the left side of the street, and a billboard for Henry the Hammer, attorney-at-law, was on the right. He pressed on a little further, hoping to find a suitable place to rest for the evening.

As he passed a mechanic's garage, a sheriff's car pulled out behind him and hurried to catch up. Mason quickly pulled to the side of the road and shut off his engine. Bowie stood up in the bed, leaning out over the tailgate, eager to see who was behind them.

Mason slid out of his truck and moved around to stand in front of the engine compartment. While such an action would have been considered foolhardy under normal circumstances, he couldn't take the chance of getting caught in the cab.

A man stepped from the cruiser, wearing a wrinkled sheriff's uniform. He was thick around the middle, but strong too, like he had baled hay and fixed tractors his entire life. He carried a pump-action shotgun in both hands and had a Glock G22 holstered at his side. As he approached Mason's truck, Bowie gave a short *woof.*

He smiled at the dog but said nothing.

Mason put a hand on his Supergrade and called out to the man.

"I'm Deputy Marshal Mason Raines. Identify yourself."

The man stopped and lowered the shotgun.

"Howdy Marshal. I'm Sheriff Billings. Don't worry now, I don't mean you or your dog no harm." He turned back to Bowie and said, "You're a good boy, aren't you? Yes."

To Mason's surprise, Bowie danced around, whining for affection from the stranger.

Mason stepped from behind the truck and took his hand off the Supergrade. Bowie had proven himself a pretty good judge of character in the past.

"Good to meet you, Sheriff," he said, shaking the man's hand.

Billings nodded and then looked over at Bowie.

"May I?"

"If you don't, he will."

The sheriff stepped over to the bed of the truck and gently wrestled with Bowie, talking to him in a soft, loving voice. The dog licked and scrubbed against him like he had known the man his entire life.

Mason smiled. He had always considered himself a 'dog person,' but Sheriff Billings was a true dog whisperer.

"I'm surprised that a town the size of Chester still has a sheriff's department."

Billings kissed Bowie on the nose and then turned back to face Mason.

"Well, there's not many of us left. That's for sure. What about you, Marshal? You outa Glynco?"

Mason nodded. "I taught at the law enforcement center."

Sheriff Billings smiled, spitting on his hand and slicking his hair down.

"Being a federal marshal and all, you probably take me for some dumb redneck, and you'd be right enough. But please don't take me for soft, okay, Marshal?"

Mason met the man's eyes.

"That I won't do."

Billings smiled and nodded.

"We folks in Chester have always been a tough lot."

"I can't say I know much about the town, but I have no reason to doubt it."

"About the only thing we're famous for is what happened to Aaron Burr back in 1806." He pointed down the street. "Stories have it that, on his way back to be tried for treason, the vice president jumped off his horse and begged the good folks of Chester to help him get away." Billings laughed as he imagined how the scene probably played out. "Didn't do him no good though. They hog-tied him and sent him on his way. That's Chester for you."

Mason smiled. "Sounds like an interesting story."

"You hear it told from time to time." He looked back over at Bowie. "What's your dog's name?"

"That's Bowie. He seems to have taken a liking to you."

Hearing his name, Bowie propped up on the tailgate and whined for more attention.

"I've always had a way with animals." Seemingly unable to resist Bowie's call, the sheriff stepped a little closer and began rubbing behind the dog's ears.

"Is there a place we could bunk for the night?" asked Mason. "We've been driving all day."

"Sure," said Billings, his face lighting up, "I know the perfect place. Bowie will have to sleep outside though. They have their rules."

Mason nodded. "As long as he's safe."

"Oh, he'll be fine. I'll look after him personally. Nobody around here's gonna harm a dog like Bowie. Not while I'm alive, anyway."

k⁁

Mason followed Sheriff Billings' cruiser down a long winding road that paralleled a set of train tracks. They passed a little grocery mart, a small junkyard for farm equipment, a real estate office, and a feed-and-seed store. Most places were empty, but the feed-and-seed had a small crowd gathered out front. The people were talking amongst themselves, exchanging goods, and generally seemed to be doing well enough.

Another half-mile up they came to a church, across from which was a two story Holiday Inn. The church was completely abandoned, except for a single black hearse parked under the awning. The hotel's parking lot, however, had a dozen cars neatly parked in front. The cruiser pulled into the driveway of the hotel and stopped. Billings climbed out with a smile on his face.

"You're gonna like this, Marshal," he said.

Mason looked around at the cars.

"All these people are visitors to Chester?"

"What can I say? We have what they want."

"And what's that exactly?"

"Come on, I'll show you."

Mason told Bowie to sit tight and followed Sheriff Billings into the hotel. As soon as he stepped through the door, everything became clear. Six women, three white and three black, sat on two long couches. A third couch remained empty, except for a giant of a man with a shiny gold badge pinned to his shirt and an AR15 lying across his lap.

The women ranged in age from perhaps twenty to well over fifty, but none were hard on the eyes. They wore tight-fitting pants and bright blouses, or thigh-length dresses with fishnet stockings.

"Ladies," Billings said with a nod, "say hello to Marshal Raines."

Each woman said hello in her own way, either with a wink, a pursing of her lips, or a simple wave. One of them, a petite young lady with short black hair, seemed to study Mason more carefully than the others.

Mason turned to the sheriff.

"Is this what I think it is?"

"It depends. What do you think it is?"

He turned away and lowered his voice so that the women wouldn't hear.

"It looks like a house of ill repute to me."

Billings wrinkled his brow.

"A whorehouse," clarified Mason.

The sheriff grinned. "Then it's exactly what you think it is."

Mason gently grabbed the sheriff's arm and led him back outside.

"You're running a whorehouse?"

"Of course not. I'm the sheriff. It's my job to make sure the women stay safe. That's all. I'm a peacekeeper, same as yourself."

"And the town's okay with this?"

"Are you kidding? It's one of our most successful businesses. Sex is like sugar. People can do without it for a few days, but much longer than that can leave you craving a candy bar in a bad way."

"And what about you? Are you okay with pimping out these women?"

"Marshal, you got it all wrong. These girls don't work for the town. They work for themselves. They choose to trade their services for goods. Usually food, water, and necessities, but it's always up to them. Most of the girls are only doing this for a while to keep their kids or husbands fed."

"Husbands?" laughed Mason. "You're kidding me, right?"

He shrugged. "Nowadays, people do what they have to. When things get better, I'm sure they'll quit and do other things. Right now, it's this or work the fields. And believe me, the fields are harder on the back. The way I see it, at least these women are safe, and they can bring supplies home to their families."

"And what does the town get out of it?"

"The tax is set at twenty percent. That was voted on too. The girls grumble about it, of course, but I think most of them agree it's fair. If you feel like we're doing something illegal here, Marshal, you can take it up with the council. They're reasonable enough folks. Every man and woman has a voice here in Chester."

Mason scratched his head, not quite sure what to make of the situation.

"You said this was one of the town's businesses. What else is there?"

"Paper money isn't worth anything, so it all comes down to bartering. We trade water, gasoline, food, medical care, and," he pointed to the hotel, "sex."

Mason shook his head but said nothing.

"We figured this kind of thing was gonna go on anyway," the sheriff continued. "So, the town council thought we might as well at least keep the girls safe."

"And take your cut," added Mason.

Billings nodded. "And take our cut."

∂ ∂

Sheriff Billings put Mason up in one of the hotel rooms without charge, saying that it was the least he could do for a fellow lawman. Neither Billings nor the girls seemed to understand why he insisted on sleeping alone, but no one objected or pushed their wares. Bowie slept in the back of the truck, which Mason suspected might help to keep curious fingers away from his supplies.

Mason lay in the bed for a long time, staring up at the ceiling, thinking about the small town of Chester. They were making their own way in the world, and he couldn't muster up the outrage necessary to stand in their way. Who was he to dictate other people's morals? If the women of Chester wanted to trade their bodies to improve their lot in the new world, that was their business. Prostitution had been around since the dawn of time for one good reason. It was marketable.

A headboard bumped against the wall in the room next to his. Then again. And again. It started picking up the pace. *Bump, bump, bump.*

Mason began to laugh. It started off as a soft chuckle, but before long, he was as loud as the couple in the adjacent room. He couldn't explain why, but the absurdity of the situation struck him as incredibly funny.

∂ ∂

Mason awoke to a soft knock on his door. He slid his feet over the edge of the bed and grabbed his Supergrade. Trouble didn't usually knock, but there was a first time for everything. He moved to stand beside the door.

"Who is it?" he said.

"It's Trish." The woman's voice was soft, like she was trying to keep from waking his neighbors. "Can I talk with you, Marshal?"

Mason covered the peephole with his hand to make sure no one was standing ready to plug him through the eye. Nothing happened. He chanced a quick peek and saw a beautiful woman with short brown hair standing in front of the door. He recognized her as the woman who had been studying him earlier in the lobby.

He opened the door a few inches but left the swing bar guard in place. "What is it?"

"Can I come in for a second?" she asked.

He hesitated.

"I promise I won't bite," she said with a wink.

He unhooked the lock and held open the door. She stepped inside tentatively, as if it were her first time in a hotel room alone with a man.

"I already told—"

She moved close and put her fingers to his lips.

"Marshal, I need your help."

He felt the heat of her body warming his bare chest.

"With what?"

"I think my sister's in trouble."

"What kind of trouble?"

She looked down at the floor.

"I don't know exactly. All I know is that she's missing."

"And you need someone to go with you to check on her?"

She nodded, looking back up at him.

"Does she live here in Chester?" he asked.

"No. She's about five miles west of town."

Mason started to turn away and put a little distance between them, but she reached out and touched his arm.

"Please, Marshal. I don't have anyone else to ask. Most of us don't have cars anymore because of the gas shortage. Those who do are too afraid to leave town unless it's absolutely necessary. Helping out a—well, you know—a working girl, isn't seen as worth the risk."

"Why don't you ask the sheriff? He seems okay."

"He is okay. But Sheriff Billings won't take me either."

"Why not?"

She shrugged. "Partly because he thinks it's his job to stay here and protect the town. Mostly because he thinks I'm worrying over nothing." She leaned up against him. "Please, Marshal."

Trish's beautiful brown eyes were intoxicating, and Mason felt his legs growing weak.

"Fine," he said. "I'll run you out there in the morning."

"Really?"

"Sure, why not?" He turned and walked back over to the bed and flopped down, not trusting himself to overcome the lust growing in his belly. "Pull the door shut on your way out. I'll meet you in the lobby once I get up and moving."

But Trish didn't leave. Instead, she locked the door and then came and stood beside his bed.

"I want to thank you for your troubles," she said, standing with her arms at her side so that he could get a good look at her petite body.

Mason knew what she was getting at, but he also knew he couldn't accept that kind of thanks.

"I can't," he said, his voice breaking slightly.

"Why? Are you gay?"

He laughed. "No."

"You have a wife then?"

"A girlfriend, over in Boone."

"And you want to remain faithful to her?"

"I do."

Her lips turned up into an understanding, but incredibly seductive, smile.

"Then I'll give you as much as you want and nothing more."

He started to protest but found himself without words as she untied the strings of her dress and let it fall to the floor.

જી ∞

When Mason awoke, Trish was lying beside him. Both of them were naked, and he could smell the delicious musk of her body. He closed his eyes and laid his head back against the pillow, replaying the night. Strictly speaking, he hadn't betrayed Ava, but there was little doubt that she would scratch his eyes out if she were ever to see him lying in bed with a naked woman. Mason loved Ava, but he also accepted the fact that he was imperfect. In the end, Trish had helped him to sleep better than he had in weeks, and for that, he was thankful.

Sensing that he was awake, she leaned over and kissed his shoulder.

"Good morning, cowboy," she said.

He rolled over and kissed her softly. The situation wasn't her fault, and he sure as hell wasn't going to make her feel unappreciated.

"Morning."

"That was nice."

"Yeah, it was." He smiled and touched her face. "You're very beautiful, Trish."

"You're not so bad yourself, Marshal."

He flopped back on the pillow.

"You're feeling guilty," she said. "Don't."

"I'm good."

She placed a hand on his chest.

"You kept your vows."

He turned back to her and smiled.

"More or less."

She leaned in and nibbled his ear.

"More or less."

ॐ ॐ

Mason turned his F150 west on Pinckney Street. Trish sat beside him, and Bowie rode in the back. It was still early enough that most of what remained of Chester was still asleep in their beds.

"How long has your sister been out of touch?" he asked.

"She rode into town on her bicycle last week to pick up a few things. That's the last time I saw her."

"Is there someone who might have needed her attention? A husband? Kids?"

"No. She lives alone in a small house that our mom left us."

"Could she have met a man?"

Trish shook her head.

"Tracy's always been sort of a wallflower. I can't imagine anything like that happening so quickly."

They drove past a pack of wild dogs fighting over a cadaver.

"Let's hope those mongrels didn't give her trouble when she was riding home."

Trish stared out at the animals, and they stared back.

"I read there were eighty-five million dogs in the US," she said. "That means they outnumber us now, something like ten to one."

Mason gestured back toward Bowie.

"They're not all bad."

"No, of course not," she said, glancing back at Bowie. "Has he been with you a long time?"

"Since the beginning."

She nodded, not asking what he meant by that.

"The house is up ahead on the left," she said, pointing. "There."

Mason pulled into the dirt driveway but stopped well away from the small wood house. A black Harley-Davidson motorcycle was parked up near the porch.

"I'm guessing that's not the bike you were talking about."

"No," she answered, her voice trembling.

"All right. Stay here while I check it out."

As he started to open the door, she reached over and put her hand on his arm.

"Be careful, Marshal."

He climbed out and motioned for Bowie to join him. The house was dark and quiet. The front windows were slightly open, probably to get a little airflow into the home. Spring was getting into full swing, and it could get stuffy by midday.

"Go check around back," he said, gesturing for Bowie to circle the house.

The dog took off, eager to stretch its legs and maybe find something worthy of an early morning adventure.

Mason stepped up onto the porch and glanced in through one of the partially open windows. A fat man with a thick white beard and dressed in a red union suit lay on the couch, snoring. He looked like Santa might after a particularly rough night of hitting the hooch. Mason didn't see anyone else in the living room.

Bowie came around from the other side of the house, and Mason motioned for him to stay put. The dog stopped and looked around, obviously uncertain of the situation.

Mason bumped the screen door with his foot a few times, watching to see what the man on the couch would do.

Santa scratched his balls, stretched, and sat up, yawning.

"Who the hell?" he mumbled, reaching down between the couch

cushions to retrieve a large revolver. He stood up and stumbled toward the door.

Mason stepped back off the porch and put his hand on his Supergrade.

The door swung open, and Santa stared out through the screen door.

"What do you want?" he said, licking something dry and crusty off his lips.

"I'm a Deputy Marshal. Step out on the porch."

Santa took a moment to consider his next move.

Mason gripped the Supergrade but said nothing more.

The big man finally stepped out, the pistol hanging loosely in his left hand. He had a heavy black boot on one foot, but the other was completely bare.

"Did I do somethin' wrong, Marshal?"

"I don't know yet. But if that gun comes up, it'll be the last thing you ever do. Are we clear?"

He shrugged. "I ain't got no reason to shoot you. Not unless you're gonna try to pin somethin' on me I didn't do."

"I'm looking for the young woman who lives here."

"Ain't nobody lives here anymore. I stopped to find some grub and a bed, and found the place empty. You got my God's honest word on it."

"How long have you been here?"

"Just since dark. That's it. I ain't squattin' or nothin'."

Mason thought for a moment.

"All right. Here's what we're going to do. First, you're going to set the pistol down on the porch, and then you and I are going inside to take a look around. You okay with that?"

Santa hesitated. "Sure thing, Marshal. I got nothin' to hide." He bent over and set the revolver on the porch, sliding it away with his bare foot. "See, Marshal, I ain't gonna be no trouble."

Mason stepped up on the porch and the two of them went inside with Santa leading the way. Mason left the screen door propped open in case Bowie was needed. The home was quite small, consisting of a living room, eat-in kitchen, and a hallway that led off to a bathroom and bedroom. A back door was at the far side of the kitchen. There was enough light coming in through the windows that Mason was reasonably sure that no one was hiding in the living room or kitchen. The house was a bit messy, but there weren't any obvious signs of a struggle.

"She ain't here. You wanna check the bedroom and crapper too?"

Never moving his hand from the Supergrade, he nodded and motioned for the big man to lead the way. They walked down the small hallway and Mason peered into the bathroom. It was empty. Next came the bedroom. It probably only measured twelve feet on a side and contained a double bed, a dresser, a small nightstand, and a closet with an accordion style door. The covers were pulled up on the bed, not neatly by any means, but some effort had been made to put it back together.

"I told you," he said with a big smile, "ain't nobody here but me."

Mason squeezed by the big man and walked around the room. Nothing obvious stood out. Turning, so that he could keep one eye on Santa, he swung open the closet. Other than some clothes hanging up and a few shoes on the floor, it too was empty. Mason started back toward the door when something occurred to him. He turned back around and gave the covers a quick tug. There, in the center of the bed was a fresh bloodstain, still wet in the middle.

Before he could turn back around, Santa barreled into him, slamming Mason into the bedroom wall. His head punched through the sheetrock, but his right shoulder wasn't as lucky as it pounded against a wooden stud. He screamed as his shoulder popped out of joint. Before Mason could pull free of the wall, Santa hit him with a solid punch behind his ear. His legs buckled, and he fell to his knees.

The world started to go black as Mason struggled to get his arm working well enough to draw his pistol. The big man swung his foot back, but before he could kick it forward, something grabbed him from behind.

Santa let out a thunderous shout as Bowie clamped down on his calf.

"Get offa me!" he yelled, hopping on his one free leg.

Bowie snarled and shook his leg from side to side, ripping muscle away from bone.

Santa screamed in pain, windmilling his arms as he fought desperately to keep his balance.

Bowie jerked him back toward the door, and despite his best efforts, the three hundred pound man fell flat on his back. In the time it took for him to raise his hands, Bowie was on him, first biting Santa in the groin, and then moving up to his face.

Mason heard the big man's screams but made no effort to call off Bowie. Instead, he struggled to his feet, his head finally clearing enough to enable him to remain standing. He took a deep breath, tears of pain rolling down his face, and slammed his shoulder against the wall. The ball went back into the socket, and almost immediately, his arm became usable again, albeit sore as all hell.

When he turned back around, Bowie stood looking up at him, drops of blood dripping from the fur around his mouth. Santa lay dead behind him, the man's throat ripped out. Mason leaned back against the wall and slowly lowered himself to sit on the floor. Bowie immediately came over and lay across his lap.

"That definitely did not go as planned," he said, grimacing.

Bowie glanced over at the dead man as if to argue the point.

Mason quickly checked the dog for any injuries. The cut on Bowie's leg that he had suffered the previous week at the hands of a few backwoods cannibals was still tightly sutured.

"I think you fared better than I did," he said, touching the tender spot behind his own ear.

Bowie smacked his lips together a few times.

"Come on," he said, struggling to get to his feet. "Let's see what's what around here."

They walked through the house a second time, looking in every cabinet and closet big enough to hide a woman. Nothing. Tracy was nowhere to be found.

"If she's here, she's got to be outside somewhere, which means she's probably dead and buried."

They went through the back door to stand on a small cement slab. The yard was overgrown with weeds, and there was an old lawnmower and a few odd tractor parts scattered about. At the back corner was a grass-covered mound that stood about three feet above ground level. Mason walked toward it, slowly getting his strength back. As he got closer, he saw that there were pullout doors on one side of the small hill. It was an old-time storm shelter.

Bowie sniffed the doors and began to growl. The handles were tied shut from the outside with baling wire. Mason untwisted the wire and swung open the door, prepared to find the worst. To his surprise, a young woman was seated inside on a small cot. She was naked, except for a blanket wrapped around her shoulders. One of her eyes was swollen shut, and streaks of dried blood were smeared on her thighs.

"Tracy?"

She scrambled away from him, curling into a small ball in the corner of the underground room.

"I'm a US Marshal. I'm here to help."

She looked up at him but said nothing.

"Your sister, Trish, sent me to find you."

She began to sob. "Trish?"

"She's here. Come on, dear," he said, extending his hand. "You're safe now."

ॐ ॐ

Mason rolled to a stop in front of the Holiday Inn. There were even more cars in the parking lot than when he had left earlier in the morning. Sex really was a thriving business.

"I can't thank you enough, Marshal," Trish said, helping her sister out of the truck.

"I'm sorry I couldn't do more."

She pressed her lips together and nodded.

"Tracy's alive, and that's all that matters."

Sheriff Billings pulled up behind Mason's truck, and Trish waved for him to come over.

"Are you going to be okay?" asked Mason.

She slid back inside the truck and gave him a long warm hug, pressing her body against his.

"Don't worry about me. I'm good." She smiled and touched him on the cheek. "Promise you'll come see me anytime you're out this way."

He smiled but said nothing. It was a promise he couldn't make.

She nodded and kissed him softly.

"Just know that I'm here, cowboy," she said with a wink.

He nodded. "Thanks."

They heard Sheriff Billings' approach and ask Tracy what had happened. Trish slid back out of the cab and gave Mason one final wave.

"Take care, Marshal."

"You too, Trish."

Mason put the truck in gear and turned north onto Highway 321. It was still about a hundred and thirty miles to Boone, but if he was lucky, he might be there in time for lunch.

CHAPTER
17

When Tanner and Samantha finally exited the East River Mountain Tunnel, there was no sign of Predator's men. They didn't know whether he had been bluffing about some of his men lying in wait, or whether they had run into trouble of their own. All they could say for certain was that they were thankful to find a quiet freeway waiting for them.

They found a Nissan Maxima with a full tank of gas and keys in the ignition parked only a few feet outside the tunnel. Why the owner had abandoned the car was anyone's guess. Maybe he had thought he would fare better on foot, or maybe he'd been dragged from the vehicle by the beast in the tunnel. Either way, he'd left behind a car that should get them all the way up to Salamanca, and in some measure of comfort too.

Tanner drove down the road, enjoying the feel of the soft black leather against his back. Samantha sat quietly beside him, looking out the window. After a few miles, he was able to steer them onto Highway 19, which would take them all the way up to Pittsburgh, nearly three hundred miles.

Samantha glanced over at him.

"Your eye isn't as big anymore, but it's turning black. Does it hurt?"

He gently touched it with his fingers. The soft tissue was sore, but nothing felt broken.

"Nah."

"I think that's the first black eye I've ever seen," she said, moving her head from side to side to get a better look.

"A shiner is meant to be worn like a badge of honor." He slid his fingers up to gently scratch the fishing line used to stitch a wound on his forehead. "At least he didn't tear my stitches."

"They look ready to come out," she said. "The skin's all puckered around the strings."

"It's been nearly a week since that cranky old grandma sewed me up, so I guess it's probably time."

"You want me to take them out?"

"Of course."

"I'll need some small scissors and maybe some tweezers."

"We can find those."

"You sure do get hurt a lot."

"It's the life I live," he said, grinning.

She paused. "Delivering this note was a mistake, wasn't it?"

The question caught him by surprise.

"Why do you say that?"

"Because of all the trouble we've run into—the snake people, those motorcyclists, the creature in the tunnel. It's been bad from the very beginning."

"We'd have run into other dangers if we'd gone straight to Virginia."

She shrugged. "Maybe."

"Sometimes, you turn left on life's road; sometimes, you turn right. But once you've made that decision, you have to march ahead and push through anything in your way. Never waste time thinking about what it would have been like if you'd taken the other path."

"Why not?"

"Because it'll keep you from enjoying the one you're on."

"You're saying that I should focus on where I'm at now?"

"Wise men would call it 'being in the moment.'"

"And what do *you* call it?" she asked, grinning.

He smiled. "I call it enjoying life."

"You think we can really enjoy life, even now?"

He looked over at her.

"I don't know about you, but I've had worse days."

"How can you even say that? You were nearly ripped apart by a... a Backson."

"Maybe, but it still beats being stuck in a jail cell."

She sat quietly for a moment.

"I've had worse days too," she said. "One day I went to school with two different shoes on."

He chuckled. "Now that would be a bad day."

"You can't imagine," she said under her breath.

He looked off to the west. They had maybe two hours of daylight left.

"I'm beat. What do you say we find somewhere to bunk for the night?"

She yawned. "Sure, if you need to rest, that's fine."

Up ahead was a sign for the Summersville Lake Retreat and Lighthouse.

"You ever seen a lighthouse?"

"Nope."

"Want to?"

She shrugged. "I guess."

He eased off Highway 19 and onto Route 129. Almost immediately, they saw a two-story log cabin gift shop on the right side of the road. A large green canoe sat atop a sign that read, *Cabins, Camping, and Boat Rentals*. Beside the gift shop was a dirt parking lot filled with a long line of boats and camper trailers, and behind those, stood a tall white lighthouse.

Tanner turned into the gravel driveway, pulled past the gift shop, and swung around to park beside the lighthouse. They climbed out and took a look around.

"Pretty cool," he said, looking up at the tower.

"Very cool."

Tanner went over and bumped on a small metal door that led inside. It looked barely big enough for him to fit through.

Samantha studied a large metal plaque that sat out front.

"It says here that this is West Virginia's only working lighthouse."

He laughed. "Last time I checked, West Virginia doesn't butt up against any major body of water, so, I'm guessing one is probably enough."

She read the sign aloud.

"This steel tower stands one hundred and four feet tall, measures twelve feet across at the base, and weighs seventy-seven thousand pounds." She looked over at him. "Is that heavy for a lighthouse?"

He shrugged. "Don't know. You want to go up inside?" He thumped the door again, wondering how hard it would be to open.

"It also says that you have to climb one hundred and twenty-two steps to get to the top."

"Like I said, if you want to go up, I'm happy to wait here for you."

She grinned. "Too many stairs for you?"

"About a hundred and twenty-two too many. What do you say we go check out that store instead?"

She nodded, and they climbed back in the Nissan.

Like nearly every other business in the country, the gift store looked abandoned. The door was splintered along its edge, and there were prybar marks from where someone had forced it open. A set of log stairs led up into the store, and a bulletin board sat out front that showed a map of the campsites, RV parking, and cabins.

"Fewer steps," she said, grinning.

He cut his eyes at her.

"Come on."

They grabbed their guns and headed up the stairs. One of the hinges had come loose, and the door leaned out at an angle. Tanner poked his head into the store. It looked empty but stunk something awful. He pulled the door out of the way, and they stepped inside.

Inside, it looked like the aftermath of an earthquake. Racks of supplies were overturned, and packets of freeze-dried food, bottles of water and sports drinks, hiking gear, and an assortment of toiletries were scattered all around the large room. The only thing that spoiled the find was the bloated corpse of a young woman lying on the floor of the store's small bathroom.

"Lots of good stuff in here," he said, picking up a backpack. "We should resupply."

She nodded, holding her nose until she could get used to the stink.

They began rummaging through the piles of supplies. By the time they had finished, they had backpacks stuffed with food, drinks, flashlights, medicine, fresh socks and underwear, toothbrushes and toothpaste, and even some toilet paper. Samantha also found a small fixed-blade knife in a leather sheath, which she quickly attached to her belt.

Perhaps her most useful find, though, was a pair of fingernail clippers, which she used to remove the stitches from Tanner's forehead. As she snipped and pulled out the last stitch, she sat back and inspected her handiwork.

"Well?" he asked.

"You have little holes in your skin, but at least there's nothing disgusting oozing out of them."

He rubbed the scabs with the tips of his fingers.

"Thank you. It feels good to have those out."

"I'm no expert on head butting, but I don't think you're supposed to hit them in the mouth."

"I'll keep that in mind the next time I'm fighting for my life."

"Good."

He shook his head.

"Do we have to stay here for the night?" she asked, looking over at the corpse.

He studied the store. There were two doors and a dozen windows from which he could see the highway. Unfortunately, that meant that travelers could also see them.

"It's probably better if we get off the main road a bit," he said.

"Where should we go? The tower?"

"That would be kind of cool, but being trapped in a narrow metal tube doesn't sound very tactical. How about we head around to one of the cabins?"

"Camping again?" she moaned.

He lifted his backpack and started for the door.

"One day, you're gonna remember this as having been the time of your life."

She followed him out, shaking her head.

"I'm pretty sure that's not going to happen."

☙ ❧

The Summersville Lake Retreat only had three cabins, and each was nearly indistinguishable from the others. They were built using modern plank siding designed to look like weathered cedar, and topped with green sheet-metal roofs. Long ramps led up to the rustic buildings, making it possible for even those in wheelchairs to easily gain access. All three structures looked new, surely built within the last few years.

Tanner checked all three cabins to make sure they were empty. He didn't want chainsaw-wielding neighbors paying them a visit in the middle of the night. Samantha insisted that they stay in the cabin furthest in the woods because it was the only one without dead bodies inside.

The cabin had three bedrooms, two with bunk beds and the third with a large, but lumpy, queen-sized mattress. There was also a pullout couch in the main living area. The kitchen and two bathrooms were empty and of little use without electricity or running water. There were, however, several fuel-burning lanterns in the living room, which allowed them to get settled in and enjoy dinner even after dark.

After finishing a meal of potted meat and freeze-dried vegetable soup, Samantha climbed in the bunk bed and fell asleep even before Tanner had time to check the doors and windows. Once he was certain that everything was buttoned up tight, he braced the door shut with a chair and pulled out the couch in the living room. It didn't take him long to nod off.

When Tanner finally awoke, it was to the sound of Samantha brushing her teeth.

"Are you awake?" she called out, hearing him stirring.

"Unh," he grunted.

"It's a beautiful day outside."

He glanced at the front door. The chair was missing, but the door was still locked.

"You go outside?" he asked, getting up and walking toward the bathroom.

She splashed some water from a bowl onto her face.

"I did."

"You take your rifle?"

She cut her eyes at him in the mirror.

"What do you think?"

He held back a smile. She was learning.

Tanner pressed around on his ribs with his fingertips. One was very tender, probably cracked. But it wasn't his first cracked rib and surely wouldn't be his last. His eye was feeling better, and the swelling was already coming down. He dug out his toothbrush and stood behind her so they could share the mirror.

"You sleep okay?" he mumbled with the brush in his mouth.

"Honestly, I feel like I slept for a week."

"Good for you." He spat the foamy paste into the sink and slurped up some of the water that she had poured in the bowl.

"Do you think we'll make it to Salamanca today?"

"We'll try."

"I can almost see that little girl's face when we tell her how brave her father was. Things like that are important to kids, you know?"

"Uh-huh," he said, not at all convinced that things would go as well as she hoped.

She gave him a questioning look.

"You don't think so?"

"In case you haven't noticed, things never go as planned."

She pushed by him, a sour expression on her face.

"You're what my mom would call a eunuch."

Tanner whipped around. "Bite your tongue, girl."

"What? It's a person who always thinks the worst of everything."

"You sure you got the right word?"

"Yep," she said, stowing her toothbrush, "and you're definitely one of them."

CHAPTER 18

The more President Glass thought about Lincoln Pike's treachery, the more it felt like a tapeworm was trying to eat its way out of her gut. If General Carr was right, her vice president was not only a traitor, he was also a mass murderer. His deed rivaled those of Saddam Hussein and Bashar al-Assad, massacring his own people using weapons of mass destruction. And for what purpose? To instigate a bloody coup, overthrowing her presidency? She would gladly have traded her post to save even one of those poor souls who had perished.

She was tempted to simply have Pike arrested, immediately, and with as much public fanfare as she could muster. There would be questions of legality, of course, but she could likely pull it off with General Carr's backing. Whether the arrest would ultimately hold up, however, was another matter. Without hard proof, the vice president might find enough support to force his release and return to power. Hell, he might even have her impeached for what he asserted was an illegal arrest.

The more prudent path was to bide her time until they had gathered enough evidence to build an airtight case. They could set up taps on Pike's phone, search his computer files, and listen in on private conversations with his close confidant, General Hood. Something would eventually implicate the vice president in his treasonous activity, of that, she was certain. However, despite what General Carr asserted, they couldn't do it alone. She would need to bring in a few trusted advisors.

She would start with her Chief of Staff, Yumi Tanaka. Next would be the Director of the Secret Service, Jim Robards. She trusted both implicitly, but even more important was the fact that they were in the business of keeping secrets. Robards would undoubtedly have reservations about spying on the vice president, but she felt certain that she could convince him to participate. As for Yumi, she was already privy to a host of sensitive information. President Glass was confident that she wouldn't object too loudly to helping to coordinate the clandestine activities.

Even just deciding what to do next made her feel better, like she was taking concrete steps to end the madness. It would be Yumi, Robards, and

General Carr for now. No one else. She couldn't afford to take a chance that Pike might get wind of the investigation.

She would need to brief them separately so that she could tailor her delivery. President Glass had learned a long time ago that everyone responded to different stimuli. In Yumi's case, she thought it would likely be loyalty, and in Robards', duty. She would also need to let General Carr know of the change in plans.

She picked up her phone and dialed Yumi Tanaka.

Yumi answered on the first ring.

"Yes?"

"I need to meet with you."

"Yes, ma'am. When?"

"Now, please."

Yumi seemed surprised. "Is everything all right?"

"Not over the phone. Let's meet in our special conference room in say, ten minutes?"

"Of course, Madam President. I'll be there."

"And Yumi..."

"Yes, ma'am?"

"Don't mention our meeting to anyone—not anyone, okay?"

"I won't. Are you sure you're all right?"

"I'm fine," President Glass said, heartened by her concern. "But we have something difficult ahead of us, and I can't afford for anyone to get wind of it."

"Yes, ma'am. I'll be right there, and don't worry, I won't mention the meeting to anyone."

President Glass's next call was to General Carr. After a quick discussion, he too agreed to meet her in the conference room. However, he seemed overly concerned about her decision to include others in their investigation. General Carr was a good man, perhaps a great man, she thought, but he needed to learn to trust.

❧ ❧

Yumi Tanaka felt sweat begin to bead along the top of her forehead. What the hell was President Glass up to? Did she know about Yumi and the vice president? No, of course not. She wouldn't have called to set up a private meeting if she had. What was it then? She was up to something that required secrecy. The fact that Yumi was being called in on it was a good thing. But that inclusion might not be enough to stop events from unfolding in a most unfavorable direction. She had to be prepared for the worst.

Yumi opened the desk drawer and withdrew a small fixed-blade tanto knife. It was wrapped in a piece of colorful rice paper and was designed to look like an exotic gift, easily mistaken as a ceremonial trinket collected during her travels overseas. But the knife was much more than a novelty. The three-inch blade was forged entirely from zirconium dioxide, a ceramic that was harder than steel and invisible to metal detectors. Both edges had been ground with a diamond-dust-coated wheel until they were razor-sharp.

While it was certainly not in her personnel file, Yumi was no stranger to knives. Having spent two years in the Philippines as a teenager, she had learned the right way to handle a blade. She had only cut a person once, and that was a would-be suitor who had forced his hand down her pants. When she opened up his inner thigh, he had come to appreciate the error of his ways.

Yumi carefully slid the paper-wrapped knife into the side pocket of her jacket. She could have it in hand in the blink of an eye. She had no idea what President Glass had in mind, but one thing she knew for certain— she wouldn't allow any harm to come to Lincoln. Not today. Not ever.

⇛ ⇚

Yumi was already waiting when President Glass entered the conference room. Two Secret Service agents moved past her and carefully searched the room. Once they were satisfied that the President's Chief of Staff was the only occupant, they left to stand outside the door.

President Glass sat down and pulled her chair close to the table.

"Thank you for coming so quickly."

Yumi smiled, thinking that President Glass looked tired and old, like a bag lady who begged for quarters outside the subway station.

"Of course, Madam President," she said. "Please tell me what's happening."

"I'm afraid it's serious."

Yumi leaned forward, resting her hands on the table.

"It's also very sensitive," added the president.

"Ma'am, you can trust me with anything."

President Glass smiled and patted her on the hand.

"I know that." She paused for a moment, deciding on how start. "General Carr and I have been investigating a terrible attack on a law enforcement center in Glynco, Georgia."

Yumi suppressed a smile. This was old news. Lincoln had already told her about the chemical attack, and with great pride. Still, perhaps there was something to be learned. If not, she might at least be able to provide a little misdirection.

"What kind of attack?" she asked.

"Someone bombed the center with sarin gas. They killed hundreds of US Marshals."

"Why would anyone do that?" Yumi gasped. "For that matter, who would even have access to sarin gas?"

"Those were our questions as well," President Glass said, nodding. "So, we did some digging. What we found was even more troubling than the attack itself."

Yumi didn't like the sound of that. She sat back, slowly withdrawing her hands from the table and placing them in her lap.

"What could possibly be worse than the poisoning of hundreds of peace officers?" she asked.

President Glass looked around the room as if double-checking that they were indeed alone.

"We found a connection between the bombs that were used and someone in the highest levels of our government."

Yumi felt her heart begin to pound violently against her chest. Just how much did President Glass know?

"Who?" she asked, sliding her hand into her coat pocket.

President Glass leaned over the table and whispered, "It's Vice President Pike. We think he may be involved."

Yumi tightened her grip on the knife, pushing the rice paper away from the handle.

"That's impossible," she said. "The vice president? Surely, there's been some kind of mistake. Why would he do something so heinous?"

"General Carr believes his intent is to undermine my presidency."

Yumi shook her head. "And that would lead him to kill hundreds of marshals? I can't believe it."

"I don't know for certain that Pike orchestrated the attack, but I do know that he's connected to it."

"Madam President, I don't like the vice president any more than you, but asserting something like this could backfire. People might think you're trying to suppress him because he's been an outspoken critic of your policies. You could end up looking like a jealous tyrant."

Even as she made her case, Yumi realized that it didn't really matter whether or not she was successful in convincing President Glass to abandon her investigation. The vice president would forever be under suspicion, and that would leave him impotent and ineffective.

President Glass took a deep breath, obviously frustrated by Yumi's unexpected resistance.

"Don't you think I know that? I wouldn't suggest it if we didn't have proof."

"What kind of proof?" she asked, sliding the knife out of her pocket and holding it beneath the edge of the table.

"We traced the delivery of the bombs back to an acquaintance of Pike's. It might not be enough to put him away, but it's too much of a coincidence to ignore. The vice president is involved in this, and by God, I'm going to prove it. That's why—"

Yumi whipped the blade up and sliced through the side of the president's neck. The weapon was as sharp as any samurai's katana, and it slid through her carotid artery with only the slightest resistance. The strike was so quick that, for a moment, President Glass just stared at Yumi in disbelief. Then, with the next beat of her heart, blood sprayed out in a huge fan, covering the table and sprinkling warm drops across Yumi's face. The president fell back against the chair, her hands clapped over the gash as she tried to stop the flow of blood.

Yumi leaned across the table and stabbed her, this time with a quick in-and-out motion that penetrated the gap between her top two ribs. The ceramic blade pierced a lung but missed her heart by an inch.

President Glass weaved from side to side, her eyes slowly closing as her blood pressure plunged. Unable to hang on to consciousness any longer, she pitched forward, her head smacking against the table with a dull *thump*. Blood continued to pump from her neck, spreading out into a pool that raced across the table and dripped off the other side.

Yumi was preparing to stab her one final time when the door swung open. General Carr stood in the doorway, his eyes wide with shock. As he began to shout, Yumi leaped around the table, determined to put an end to the investigation once and for all. She lunged forward, hoping to drive the blade through his eye and into his brain.

But having fought in two wars, General Carr was not an easy man to kill. He sidestepped, brushed the knife away and struck Yumi across the throat with his forearm. The hard edge of his radial bone crunched against her windpipe, and she stumbled back, gasping for air. Before she could recover her balance, he stepped forward and hit her under the chin with his elbow. Her head flew back, and a tooth shot high into the air.

As she started to collapse, General Carr reached out and caught her by the throat. Yumi struggled to stay conscious as she felt his calloused fingers closing around her windpipe. She slashed out with the knife, slicing his upper leg. Blood poured out as his quadriceps pressed their way through the open skin.

But General Carr's grip didn't falter.

She raised the knife again, this time hoping to catch him under the ribs. He batted it away with his free hand, and the knife fell to the floor, breaking the blade into a dozen small black shards. She flailed against his chest with tiny fists, but they grew weaker with every blow.

The last thing Yumi Tanaka ever saw was the piece of decorative rice paper floating through the air like the feathers of a fallen angel.

CHAPTER

19

The remainder of the drive to Boone was smooth sailing. Mason was able to make the final hundred and thirty miles in a little over four hours, which probably counted as a personal best, given the condition of the roads.

As he entered the city limits, he was surprised to see a military UH-60 Blackhawk helicopter rise into the air. Based on its position, he figured that it must have taken off from the Watauga Medical Center's rooftop helipad. As soon as it reached a few hundred feet off the ground, it turned west toward the mountains.

Mason pressed his foot down hard on the accelerator. He could think of no logical reason for the military to be in Boone. Other than border defense, their role had been relegated to guarding supply shipments and screening for the virus. Boone would not have been high on the list for either of those activities.

He whipped right on Deerfield Road and sped up the hill toward the hospital. Father Paul, Dr. Darby, Fran, and a dozen people Mason didn't recognize were huddled outside the hospital's main entrance. They talked and moved about nervously, like school kids who had been evacuated because of a bomb scare.

Mason hopped out of his truck, and Bowie followed, darting past him to get to Father Paul. The portly priest and Bowie had become close friends when they had fought against a band of convicts terrorizing Boone. And while it was clear that Father Paul was not entirely comfortable around large animals, he did his best to give Bowie the love he deserved.

"What's going on?" asked Mason.

Father Paul gently pushed Bowie away, trying to keep the giant dog from knocking him down.

"We don't really know," he said. "A government agent is inside with Ava."

"What type of government agent?"

"He said he was with the Secret Service. He had a badge and a gun, if that means anything. There were three soldiers in uniform with him too."

"Who was in the helicopter that flew away?"

He shrugged. "I guess some of the soldiers. No one came out to let us know that it was okay to go back in."

Mason looked toward the hospital.

"What do they want with Ava?"

Father Paul shrugged. "I can't say for sure. All I know is that after briefly talking with her, they told the rest of us to leave the hospital."

"They forced you out?"

"More or less. One of the nurses just went to get Don and Vince. We figured the town's deputies would know what to do."

"Fine, but I'm not waiting." Mason turned and started for the door.

Father Paul reached out and gently grabbed his arm.

"You should know one other thing." There was worry in his voice. "This might have something to do with the girl your father brought in."

"My father was here?" Oddly, the revelation didn't surprise Mason.

"Less than a week ago."

Hearing that his father was alive should have brought him joy. Instead, it only brought worry. Where Tanner Raines went, trouble followed.

"He had a girl with him?"

The priest leaned in closer and lowered his voice.

"It was the president's daughter, Samantha Glass. Apparently, people are out to get her."

"What?" Mason struggled to put the pieces together. "Why would the president's daughter be with my father?"

"It's a long story best saved for another time. What you need to know is that Ava took a small tracking device out of the girl's arm."

"What did she do with it?"

Father Paul stared at him, his face going white.

"Father," he pressed, "what did she do with the device?"

The priest sighed and shook his head.

"She put it in a drawer in the hospital."

Mason pulled away and hurried toward the emergency room door.

"Stay here," he warned, his voice hard and determined.

☙ ❧

Mason drew his Supergrade as he ran toward the emergency room. He passed through the front doors and found the lobby and waiting rooms both empty. Bowie came running in behind him.

"Find Ava!" he bellowed.

Bowie took off through the waiting room, his nose glued to the ground. Mason ran after him. They entered the treatment area, which was divided into several small mini-rooms, each sectioned off with large curtains that hung from tracks on the ceiling. Most of the curtains were pulled closed, but a few remained open.

Bowie raced to the end of the room and disappeared around a curtain. A few seconds later, Mason heard the dog whimpering and scratching its claws against the white tile floor. Even before he stepped around the curtain, Mason knew what he would find. The air had a discernible heaviness to it, a sense of death that he had felt many times before. He tried to ignore it, telling himself that any kind of sixth sense was nothing more than anxiety. But denying it made it no less real.

Mason whipped back the curtain.

Ava was seated with her wrists duct-taped to the arms of a metal chair. Blood dripped from dozens of small razor cuts on her arms, abdomen, and legs. No single cut was deep enough to have killed her. They had saved that for the thin metal garrote that still hung around her neck like a cowboy's bolo.

Bowie whined and licked the tips of her fingers, unable to understand what he was seeing.

Mason stepped forward, gently pulled the garrote off her neck, and felt for a pulse. Her skin was so warm that, for a brief moment, he held out hope that he would find one. He didn't. He slid his hunting knife free and cut the tape that held her to the chair. She flopped forward into his arms, and he lowered her carefully to the floor. He sat down next to her and lifted her lifeless body into his arms. Bowie sniffed around the room for a moment before coming over to lie down beside them.

Cradling Ava against his chest, Mason began talking softly to her. He told her about everything that had happened since leaving Boone—the militia that had captured him in York, the hotheaded Alexus and her penchant for hanging, the cannibals who had nearly had him for dinner, his grisly findings at Glynco, his discovery and subsequent chase of the mercenaries, the showdown with Nakai—even his indiscretion with Trish, the prostitute in Chester. He told her everything.

And when he finally finished, he told Ava one last thing. He told her that the men who had taken her life would soon be joining her.

ॐ ☙

After another brief conversation with Father Paul, Mason knew as much as he needed to. Agent Sparks was obviously looking for Samantha Glass. He had managed to locate the electronic tracker only to discover that it had been removed from the girl's arm. So, he had turned to torturing Ava to reveal what she knew. Mason suspected that Ava had probably told him everything she knew very quickly, but being professionals, they had continued until they were certain.

He also believed he knew where they were headed. Ava would have told them about his cabin, and they would have assumed that Samantha was hiding there. If his father were indeed still there, they would be in for a hell of a fight. The cabin was very defensible, and Tanner was as tough as any man alive.

"Father Paul, can I trust that you'll take care of Ava?" Mason's words were calm, masking the pain beneath them.

"Of course."

"Do you know that little lovers' lookout to the west of town?"

He nodded. "I do."

"There's a big Northern Red Oak with Ava's name carved on it. I think she'd like to be buried up there."

"Don't worry," he said. "Ava has many friends who will take care of her. You go and do what you must." Father Paul put his arm around Fran, Ava's friend of more than twenty years.

"You kill that sonofabitch," Fran said, wiping tears from her eyes. "You kill him good."

Mason turned and opened the door of his truck. Before he could climb in, a police cruiser rolled up behind him. Vince Tripp and Don Potts scrambled out of the car. Vince had worked for years as a Watauga County Deputy and looked every part the lawman. Don had spent four years as a military policeman and now walked with a prosthetic leg. Both were good men who had stepped up when the town had needed them most.

"What's happened?" asked Vince.

"Those bastards killed Ava," Fran said, choking out the words.

Don looked at Mason. "Who did it, Marshal?"

"Father Paul can fill you in the details. All that matters now is that I'm going after them."

"We're with you," Vince said, patting Mason on the shoulder.

"Damn straight we are," added Don.

Mason shook his head. "These men work for the government. You don't want to be on the wrong side of this."

Vince looked hurt. "After all we've been through, you think there's any chance we'd let you go off and do this by yourself?"

"Not gonna happen, Marshal."

Seeing the determination in both men's eyes, Mason reluctantly nodded.

"All right," he said, looking off toward the mountains. "Let's go get 'em."

ॐ ॐ

Mason and Bowie rode in the truck, and Vince and Don followed closely behind in the police cruiser. They drove as quickly as the road allowed, and twice Mason scraped his truck against abandoned cars in his haste. The only thing that mattered was getting to the cabin before Agent Sparks and his men departed.

He fishtailed onto Buckeye Road, dust flying up behind his truck. Vince and Don dropped back a few car lengths so they wouldn't accidentally end up going off the side of the mountain. Three good men, thought Mason, going out after a handful of bad men. He wondered if the Earp brothers and Doc Holliday had felt the same sense of purpose when facing off against the outlaws at the O.K. Corral. People were going to die today, and there was no guarantee that justice would triumph.

As soon as he saw the turnoff to his cabin, he pulled to the side of the road. Vince and Don swung in behind him and jerked to a stop. Doors flew open as everyone scrambled out.

"Where do you want us?" asked Vince.

"Leave your car here, and come up on foot with your long guns. They'll try to come around and get me from behind. I'd appreciate it if you'd stop them."

Don nodded. "We've got your back, Marshal."

Both men readied their gear: bulletproof vests, AR15 rifles, and plenty of spare magazines. Mason did the same, checking his M4 and slipping on one of the vests he had taken from the dead marshals in Glynco.

"I'll go right," Vince said to Don. "You go left."

Without waiting for additional instructions, they nodded to each other and hurried into the thick woods. Mason smiled. Both men were brave and battle-tested. He trusted them with his life.

Mason climbed back in the truck and headed up the long dirt driveway. When he got to the metal barricade, he swung it open and used the open space to do a quick three-point turn. If his plan was to work, he needed the bed of his truck to face the cabin. He hoped that not having spotted a helicopter in the air meant the men were still on the ground. If that were the case, they had to be in the clearing directly in front of his cabin. It was the only place open enough to land a helicopter.

He backed the truck up the final leg of the driveway, slow and easy, until he reached the edge of the clearing. The cabin sat about fifty yards directly ahead. The black UH-60 helicopter had set down in the tall grass to one side of it. A man sat in the cockpit, but he was watching the cabin and didn't immediately see Mason's truck.

Mason jumped out and vaulted into the bed of his truck. He whipped the tarp off the Browning .50 caliber machine gun and slid into position behind it. Bowie sat beside him, his ears perked up as he watched his master's every move.

As Mason swung the heavy weapon around, the pilot finally spotted him. The man began to frantically fumble with buttons and switches, and the huge rotors started to turn.

Mason double-checked that the Browning was loaded and ready to fire. Carefully adjusting the sights, he lined up on the helicopter. The distance was close enough that he could have hit it with a rock, but he took his time to get it right.

By now, the rotor was spinning up, and the tall grass bent in huge waves. The helicopter tipped forward as the landing skids started to pull away from the ground.

Mason squeezed the trigger.

The UH-60L was specifically designed to be ballistically tolerant, but that in no way meant that it could take repeated close range fire from a .50 caliber machine gun. The huge 706-grain ball ammunition pounded through the windshield, killing the pilot instantly and ripping apart the cockpit. Mason continued peppering the bird until it pitched forward and smashed into the ground. The four rotor blades beat against the dirt, breaking apart to send fragments of titanium and composites in every direction.

Three soldiers and a man dressed in a dark suit raced out of the cabin. Mason swung the gun in their direction. Even as they darted back inside, he knew that he could end it all with a few more presses of the butterfly triggers. As sturdy as the cabin was, it wouldn't withstand the kind of firepower a Browning could put out. Not for long, anyway.

Two things kept him from opening fire. First, he didn't know if his father and the girl were inside. And second, the cabin was important to him, not only as a retreat, but also as the only remaining artifact of his family's presence on the planet.

The man in the suit leaned his head out through the cabin's door.

"Hold your fire!" he shouted.

"Step out with your hands up!"

"We're federal agents! Hold your fire!"

Mason sent a short burst into the dirt in front of the cabin. The agent ducked back inside.

"Step out!" he repeated.

The man stepped cautiously through the doorway and inched out onto the porch. He held a pistol in his right hand, which Mason thought was like bringing scissors to a swordfight.

"Put the gun on the ground, and move away from the cabin!"

The man set the handgun on the porch, walked slowly down the stairs, and knelt in the dirt with his hands on top of his head.

Mason caught a glimpse of two men darting away from the back of the cabin and out into the woods. As he had expected, they were trying to come around him.

He grabbed his M4 and hopped down from the bed of the truck. Bowie stayed close by his side. Gunfire sounded to his left. Mason recognized the quick, *pop, pop, pop* of an AR15. Not fast enough to be automatic fire, but rather, three quick squeezes of the trigger. It was most likely Don bringing down one of the men. Almost immediately, a second burst of gunfire came from his right—maybe ten or twelve shots, followed by a long burst of automatic fire, and then a single shot. Vince had found the other soldier, but it was harder to predict how it had all played out. Was he still alive? Mason had to trust that he had done his job.

He raised his M4 and approached the kneeling man. Even if the last soldier in the cabin had a weapon trained on Mason, he likely wouldn't fire—not if he wanted their leader to continue breathing. Mason stopped about ten feet away.

"Listen," the man blurted, "I'm an agent with the US Secret Service. We're here on official government business. You're making a big—"

"Are you Agent Sparks?"

The man looked startled.

"How do you know my name?"

"I know everything I need to know about you. I know that during your search for Samantha Glass, you murdered the woman I love."

Bowie began circling around behind the man, growling.

"Keep that dog away from me."

"Don't worry. I'm not going to let Bowie kill you. Now, get on your feet."

Agent Sparks pushed himself up and dusted off the knees of his pants.

"Listen, we can work this out," he began.

A soldier suddenly stepped out from the cabin with an M4 pressed to his shoulder.

"Hold it right there!" he shouted. "One move and you die."

Bowie immediately turned toward the soldier. The dog's ears were folded flat, and his lips were curled in a menacing snarl.

"Maybe," Mason said, his finger tightening on the trigger of his own rifle, "but if you pull that trigger, we all die."

"How do you figure?"

"Because," Agent Sparks said, looking over his shoulder, "he'll shoot me, and the dog will tear you to pieces." He glanced back at Mason. "Do I have that about right?"

Mason nodded. "And I wouldn't count on those other two soldiers coming to your rescue either. I'm pretty sure they're lying face down in the woods."

Sparks looked to the trees, searching for any sign of his men. There was none.

"All right," he said, "it seems you've got us at a bit of a disadvantage. The question is what do you want?"

"Let's start by you telling me who killed the doctor in Boone."

Sparks eyes darted toward the man in the doorway.

Without warning, Mason lifted his M4 and shot the soldier in the face. The man dropped his weapon and stumbled out onto the porch. He fell down the steps and lay in the dirt, clutching his face, screaming.

Bowie raced over, latched onto the back of his neck, and gave him a few quick shakes. The screaming stopped as suddenly as it had started.

For the first time, Agent Sparks noticed Mason's badge.

"Congratulations, Marshal, you've just murdered a federal agent."

"If his actions are those of our new government, I'll kill every damn one of you."

Agent Sparks bit his lip and looked off toward the trees, weighing his chances at a possible escape.

"You can run for it if you want," Mason said calmly. "Really, go ahead. Bowie would enjoy the chase."

Hearing his name, Bowie looked over at them and barked.

"Next question. Who are you working for?"

Sparks glared at him. "I work for the Secret Service. I already told you that."

Mason squinted. "No, I think you're like a rat hiding in the shitter. You figure it stinks so bad, no one's going to notice you. Who's really running you?"

Sparks said nothing.

An idea struck Mason.

"It's General Hood, isn't it?"

Sparks eyes betrayed him.

"Ah," said Mason, "it's him again. It seems everywhere I go, that man is killing people I care about."

"Now that you've had your revenge," said Sparks, "you'd be better served by letting me go."

Mason felt emotions swelling up inside him, and it took everything he had not to shoot the man.

"Revenge?" he said through clenched teeth. "You think that's what this is?"

"Isn't it?"

Mason stepped forward and pressed the muzzle of the M4 against Agent Sparks' forehead.

"I'm not a vengeful man, but I am a just one."

"And shooting me like this? That's your idea of justice?"

Mason tightened his finger on the trigger. He wanted to feel the gun buck in his hands, to see the man's head reel back from the shot. But something inside him struggled against it. This was not his way.

He stepped back and lowered his M4, sliding it around to hang across his back.

Agent Sparks said, "We're all just doing our part, Marshal. Surely, you understand that. If you let me go, I can deliver a message to General Hood."

Mason looked over at the man's pistol, lying on the porch.

"Go pick it up."

"I'm not going to have a gunfight with you."

"Then you'll die a coward."

Sweat rolled down the side of Agent Sparks' face.

"That's how it's going to be?"

Mason nodded.

Agent Sparks walked over to the porch and slowly climbed the stairs.

He bent over and carefully lifted the handgun with two fingers. Then, without warning, he swung it up and fired.

The instant that Sparks' hand swung up, Mason drew his Supergrade, sidestepped to the right, and fired a single shot. The bullet passed through the man's mouth, splintering his front teeth before exiting through the base of his neck.

Agent Sparks collapsed to the ground, choking on his own blood.

Mason stepped up on the porch and stood over the man.

"I think you might have been right," he said, raising the pistol. "I am a vengeful man."

CHAPTER 20

After two days filled with all manner of crazy, Tanner and Samantha enjoyed a long day of driving with nothing more exciting than a roadside check by the Viral Defense Corps. By the time they entered the small town of Salamanca, New York, they were tired, but also elated at their progress.

"I can hardly believe it," she said, sitting forward in her seat. "We've had nearly a whole day without a single zombie, Backson, or bandit."

"The day's not over yet," he warned.

Ignoring him, Samantha unfolded the note and read off the dead man's address.

"Do you see 112 Adams Street?"

Keeping one eye on the road, Tanner attempted to study the map that was draped across the steering wheel.

"Here it is, Adams Street," he said, tapping the paper.

She clapped her hands with excitement.

"Let's hope it was worth the drive," he added, feeling a bit like the Man of La Mancha, traipsing off on a fool's errand.

"It will be. I'm sure of it."

They continued on Broad Street, the only significant road other than the expressway to skirt the southern edge of town. The west side of Broad Street sported several stores and restaurants, but from the number of ramshackle buildings and "For Rent" signs hanging in windows, it was clear that Salamanca had not been a vibrant, growing community, even before the pandemic.

When Samantha saw the Seneca Iroquois National Museum on their left, she asked, "Are there actual Indians living here?"

"There sure are. In fact, this whole area is part of the Allegany Reservation. I think the Seneca Nation of Indians own every square inch of it."

"Does that mean everyone who lives here is American Indian?"

He shook his head. "Other people rent the land for businesses and such."

"I see. And that's where the Indians get their money?"

"Along with the casino and bingo parlor."

"Grownups play bingo?"

"Some do."

"For money, right?"

He nodded. "If you like, maybe we can stop on the way out and let you play a few cards."

"Really?" Her eyes grew wide.

He grinned.

"You're pulling my leg," she said. "The people running the bingo game are all dead."

"Maybe, but look on the bright side."

"What's that?"

"You'd probably win."

She rolled her eyes.

"How come you know so much about this place, anyway?"

"Like I said, my ex-wife lives down the road a piece."

"And you came here to visit her?"

"A few times."

"Because you still love her?"

Tanner smiled but didn't answer.

Samantha didn't press the point, saying only, "We should go see her while we're here."

He pointed up ahead.

"There's Adams Street. We're close."

 తు ఆ

Adams Street was a narrow, two-lane road that wound its way through block after block of quaint little houses.

"One-twelve, right?" he said, searching both sides of the street.

"There it is," she cried, pointing to a two-story brick home ahead on their right. The house looked dark, but then so did every other house.

Tanner pulled the Maxima up to the curb and climbed out. By the time he came around to her side of the car, Samantha was already out waiting for him, the note open in one hand and the photo of the little girl in the other. Her rifle was slung diagonally across her back.

"Now listen, Sam," he said, "don't be disappointed if this doesn't go as planned. They might be dead or moved on by now."

She smiled and nodded.

"Sure, sure, I know. Come on, let's go see." She turned and hurried across the lawn and up the porch steps.

Tanner took a quick look up and down the street, and when he didn't see anyone, followed behind her.

"Remember," she said, "you might want to let me do the talking. That way we won't scare her."

"Got it," he said, bumping the butt of the shotgun against the heavy wooden door and then taking a couple of steps back. They heard a second-story window slide open above them.

"What do you want?"

Tanner and Samantha looked up and saw a woman leaning out the window. She was in her late thirties, had long black hair, dark eyes, and was obviously of American Indian descent.

"Are you Isa's mother?" shouted Samantha.

"Yes, I'm Genessee Hill. Who are you?"

"I'm Samantha, and he's Tanner. We've brought something for you." Samantha was smiling from ear to ear.

The woman's eyes opened wide, and her face lit up.

"Oh, my God, you've brought her home!" Genessee disappeared from the window, and a few seconds later, the front door burst open. "Where's my baby?" she asked, looking around the porch and out into the yard. "Is she okay?"

Tanner and Samantha exchanged looks.

"Ma'am, we don't have your daughter," he said.

"What do you mean, you don't have her? You're from the farm, aren't you?"

Tanner wasn't sure how to answer.

Samantha stepped closer and held out the note.

"Miss, we're here to deliver a note from your husband."

Genessee took it tentatively and let her eyes quickly skim the words. Then she read it a second time, much slower. Then a third time, letting her lips move with each word.

If you're reading this note, it means that I'm dead. I've never had much luck in this world, so my end probably wasn't quick or painless. I have no right, but I'm going to ask a favor of you. In my left boot, you'll find a photo of my daughter, Isa. Our address is written on the back. I was away on business when the virus hit, and I've been trying to get home ever since. I wonder if you'd be so kind as to deliver a message for me. Tell my baby girl that daddy did everything he could to make it home and that I'll watch over her from heaven. Please tell her what I couldn't, so that I can rest in peace.

Forever grateful, Booker Hill

Tears formed in the corners of her eyes.

"You found him."

"He was... well, you know, not alive anymore," said Samantha. "But we found the note and your daughter's photo. We drove a long way to bring it here." She held out the photo of Isa, but the woman only glanced at it, unable to pull her eyes away from her late husband's last words.

"Were you able to give him a proper burial?" she asked, choking on the words.

Samantha glanced at Tanner.

"That wasn't possible," he answered.

"I understand," she said, nodding.

"He wanted Isa to know that he loved her, even at the very end," said Samantha.

Genessee starting crying, and her tears fell on the paper.

"Isa's not here," she said.

"Where is she?" asked Samantha.

"At the farm. All our children are at the farm."

"What farm?" asked Tanner.

"The Amish community over in Conewango."

"The Amish took your kids?" asked Samantha.

"No, nothing like that. We sent our children there. The virus was spreading quickly, and we thought that getting them out of town would help keep them safe. The Amish stopped coming around once the virus hit, and hardly any of them became sick."

"And you haven't seen your kids since?"

"No," she said, drying her tears with the sleeve of her blouse. "But the virus is gone now. Nearly everyone who caught it is dead, and it's time for our babies to come home."

"Why doesn't someone just go and get the kids?" asked Samantha.

"We tried. Two women went to get them last week." She shook her head. "The roads are terribly dangerous."

Tanner was confused. "No insult intended, ma'am, but why did you send women? Surely, their fathers or someone like that could go."

Genessee seemed reluctant to answer.

"Hey, it's your business. If you—"

"There aren't any men left," she blurted.

"What?"

"The virus took them."

"All of them?"

"More or less, yes."

Tanner found that hard to believe.

"You're telling me that every last man in this town was killed by the virus?"

"No, I'm saying that all of us who sent our children away have since lost our husbands." She looked down at the paper. "Booker was our last hope. Now there's no one."

"Surely there are other men in the town who would be willing to help."

Genessee looked embarrassed.

"There are, but they ask too much in payment."

Tanner nodded, understanding all too clearly.

Samantha reached out and touched the woman's arm.

"Don't worry," she said. "We'll go get them."

"Sam," warned Tanner.

She cut her eyes at him.

"We were going that way anyway."

"We were?"

She nodded. "You wanted to see your wife, remember?"

"She's my ex-wife, and I don't recall saying I wanted to see her."

"You said it—I remember."

He sighed. "Fine."

"You'll do this for us?" asked Genessee. "You'll go get my Isa? And the other children too?"

He shrugged. "Why not. Apparently we're going that way, anyway."

She reached out and took his hands in hers.

"I'll get the women together to tell them. You're an angel. Bless you. Bless you." She pulled him toward the door. "Now come inside and rest. You and your daughter will stay here for the night."

As they were ushered inside, Tanner leaned down and whispered in Samantha's ear.

"Now see what you've done."

"What?"

"You've gone and turned me into an angel."

❧ ❧

By nightfall, eight women had gathered at Genessee's home. They sat in the living room, holding candles, and it looked more like a séance than a meeting to discuss missing children. Most of the women were American

Indian, but two were white, and one was black. Tanner and Samantha had gone upstairs to clean up and rest from the long drive.

"Listen," Genessee said, standing up and moving to the center of the room, "I have incredibly good news. I found someone willing to go and get our children."

Everyone started talking at once.

"Please," she said, "one at a time."

Ona, an attractive American Indian woman sitting next to the fireplace, raised her hand.

"Who is he, Genie?"

"His name's Tanner. He's not from around here."

The room came alive again, women turning to one another with the same questions. Who was this stranger? Why should they trust him? What did he want in return?

"Please!" Genessee said, raising her voice.

A woman stood up in the back of the room. Peta had a sharp nose and a face that perpetually looked angry, even when she was trying to force a smile.

"How did you happen across this man?"

Genessee put her hand in her pocket and felt the note that Samantha had given her.

"He brought word of my husband's death."

Several of the women immediately voiced their condolences.

"We all knew that Booker was dead," she said quietly. "Nothing else would have kept him away from Isa."

"You know what the men have demanded in return," Peta said to the group. "I, for one, will not—"

"Tanner's different. He's not asking for that."

"What does he want?" asked Ona.

Genessee shrugged. "Apparently nothing."

Peta snickered. "Dear, a man doesn't risk his life for nothing. He's expecting payment. I can promise you that."

"Tanner's not like that. He's traveling with his daughter. They're upstairs cleaning up right now. I'll call them down. You'll see."

Genessee hurried out of the room and up the stairs. When she returned, Tanner was at her side. He was wearing jeans and a plain white t-shirt that had been her husband's. The room came alive as the women turned and spoke to one another in hushed tones, talking about his size, his black eye, and the shotgun that he carried at his side.

Genessee went around the room and introduced each woman. As soon as they finished making the rounds, Peta stood back up.

"Genessee tells us that you're willing to go to Conewango and retrieve our children."

"That's right."

"She also says you'll do it for nothing." Peta made no effort to hide her suspicion.

"She's giving me and my daughter a place to sleep for the night. That's enough."

Ona raised her hand. "Mr. Raines?"

She was a beautiful woman by anyone's measure, and he couldn't help but feel drawn to her.

"Tanner will do just fine."

"Tanner," she said with a smile. "Please forgive our skepticism. Peta and some of the other women are understandably confused about why you would help us. We're strangers. Other men have asked for... well, for favors."

"Favors my foot. They want a pound of flesh," Peta said, pushing her hips to one side. "And we're to believe that you're different."

Tanner chuckled. "Darlin', rest assured I don't want your flesh."

Peta snorted, but said nothing.

"Then why are you helping us?" asked Ona. "And, please, I don't mean any offense by the question."

He smiled. "To be honest, it was my daughter's doing. Samantha's the good-natured one. If it were up to me, I'd never have come here in the first place."

"And where is your little girl?"

He pointed up the stairs.

"Fell asleep almost as soon as her head hit the pillow. We had kind of a rough day."

Before Ona could reply, Peta jumped back in.

"How exactly do you plan to transport fourteen kids?"

He shrugged. "No idea."

"That's not much of an answer."

He yawned. "Like I said, it's been a long day. You ladies figure out the transportation, and I'll drive it over to Conewango. If the kids are there, I'll bring them home. If you want to sit up all night talking about conspiracies or secret agendas, that's your business. As for me, I'm going to bed."

"Before I forget," said Genessee, "any of you who wish to can spend the night here. If you're like me, waiting even one extra minute would be too long."

"If you don't mind, one last question, Mr. Raines," said Peta.

"What is it?" he said, growing annoyed.

"What makes you think you can even get them? I don't know if Genessee told you, but the women who went after them ended up dead."

"We don't know that. And besides," Genessee said, waving her hands in front of him. "Look at him! He's as big as my Booker."

"He's a giant, all right," Ona said with a wink. "I mean that as a compliment of course."

"How else could it be taken," he said, returning her smile.

"Big or not," sneered Peta, "what will you do if you run into trouble?"

Tanner swung the shotgun up to rest across his shoulder.

"Darlin', you obviously don't understand the situation. The question is not what am I gonna do if I run into trouble. It's what's trouble gonna do with me."

ॐ ๙

Tanner stepped gingerly around the women sleeping on the couches and living room floor. He eased open the front door and walked out into the cool night air. The night was incredibly dark, and even navigating his way to the street to take a pee felt like an adventure worthy of Bilbo Baggins.

When he was finished, he returned to the house and quietly closed the door behind him. He stood in the dark room, listening to the women breathe. They were counting on him, and while he played it off like it was just another day, he felt their worry. He took a deep breath and let it out slowly. If their kids were still alive, he would bring them home. It was as simple as that. Sometimes there was no room for failure. Period.

He stepped around the women again and crept up the stairs as quietly as his bulk would allow. Samantha's door was open, and he heard her snoring softly. He crossed the hall and went back to his own room. As soon as he entered, he felt the presence of someone in the room.

"If you're not naked and warming my bed, you've made one hell of a mistake."

"Then I guess I didn't make a mistake," replied a soft voice.

Tanner walked over and saw Ona lying curled up under the covers. Her long black hair was fanned out across the pillow, and in the soft moonlight, she looked incredibly seductive.

"I'd ask what you're doing here, but I've never been one to question a woman who invites herself into my bed."

"What would you say if I told you I was elected to pay you for your troubles?" Her voice was husky and inviting.

He grinned. "I'd say I'm glad the vote turned out the way it did."

She laughed.

"But that's not the case, is it?" he said, sitting on the edge of the bed.

"No." She studied his face, as if trying to decide what type of man was inside. "The truth is I was cold and lonely. Same as every other woman down there."

"Yet only you came up."

"You would have preferred two of us?" she teased.

He smiled. "That wasn't what I meant."

She reached out and touched his hand.

"The truth is I haven't been with a man in a long time."

"What about your husband?"

"He ran out on us three years ago. Won some money at the casino and just disappeared."

"His loss," he said.

Ona lifted the cover a few inches, and he saw that she was completely naked beneath. Her body was trim and her skin rich in color. For a moment, he just stared, speechless.

"I'm sorry," she said, pulling the cover back to her. "This was a mistake."

He reached out and stopped her.

"Darlin' I was just taking a moment to enjoy the view. Now slide over. I'm coming in."

Ona slipped out just before dawn, but Tanner could still smell her on the pillows when Samantha bumped on the door several hours later.

"Are you still alive?" she asked, peeking in at him.

He sat up and stretched.

"Barely."

"It's nearly ten o'clock."

"Thank you for the time check." He started to climb out of bed when he realized that he was naked. "I'll meet you downstairs. You go on ahead."

"Okay, but hurry. Everyone's waiting on you. And guess what?"

"What?"

"They got us a school bus!" She turned and disappeared around the corner.

"Great," he mumbled, crawling out of bed.

Ten minutes later, he walked downstairs, carrying his shotgun in one hand and smoothing his hair down with the other. Last night, he couldn't have cared less what the Chatty Cathys thought of him, but today, he felt like he was reporting for his first day of work.

Genessee hurried over with an excited smile on her face.

"Would you like some coffee, Mr. Tanner?"

"Is it hot?"

"Of course. I just took the water off the fire."

"Then I'd love some. Black is fine."

He looked around the room and gave everyone a once-over. Peta looked even uglier than she had the night before. He passed over her and let his eyes settle on Ona. She was trying to keep a conversation going with the woman sitting beside her, but despite her best efforts, her eyes kept drifting away to look at him.

"Did you sleep well?" Genessee asked, leaning around from the kitchen.

"Better than I thought possible."

Ona covered a smile.

"You must have," Peta said, making it a point to look at the clock on the wall.

Genessee returned from the kitchen and handed him a cup of steaming coffee and a large slice of pound cake.

He took a bite of the cake and immediately nodded his approval.

"Did you eat, Sam?" he asked, crumbs falling from his mouth.

She nodded. "Two pieces."

Tanner took another bite and slurped some of the coffee. When he looked up, everyone in the room was staring at him.

"Okay," he said. "I'll need a list of all of the kids' names."

"We have that," Genessee said, holding up a piece of paper. "Names, ages, general descriptions—it's all here."

"Great. We don't want to leave anyone behind. What about the Amish people who are caring for them? What are their names?"

"The leader's name is Isaac Yoder. His wife is Miriam. They're good people."

He took another bite of cake.

"And do we have an address for Isaac?" he asked.

She flipped over the page, and he saw that a map had been drawn on the back.

"The interstate will take you most of the way. You'll eventually turn north on Highway 62 and then left on Flat Iron Road." She pointed to each of the roads on her makeshift map. "The total distance to the farm is about forty miles."

"Sam tells me you got us a bus?"

Genessee moved the curtains aside, revealing a large orange school bus parked out front.

"There's not a lot of gas in it," she said, "but it should be enough to get you there and back."

"It sounds like you've thought of everything."

"We've done what we can, but it's really all up to you. We're counting on you."

"Don't worry," said Samantha. "Tanner will bring them home."

"And how would you know that?" Peta snapped, looking down her sharp beak of a nose.

Samantha's face burned, but she stayed composed.

"I know because I believe in him. Maybe you should start believing too."

"Mr. Tanner," said Genessee, "please don't take offense. I think Peta's just afraid to get her hopes up again. Having a child of your own, you can understand how hard this is for us."

Peta turned to stare at Tanner. Her face slowly softened and tears began to pool in the corners of her eyes.

"I'll believe you if you tell me you'll bring my boy home," she said, her voice trembling. "But please don't say it if it isn't true. I can't take that. Not again."

Tanner met her eyes and saw not only pain and loss, but also helplessness. He was her last chance.

"One way or another," he said. "I'll bring him home." He looked around the room. "I'll bring them all home."

❧ ❧

Tanner had never driven a school bus in his entire life. Fortunately, the bus they selected was equipped with an Allison automatic transmission and conventional hydraulic brakes, and proved no more difficult to drive than a large U-Haul truck.

Samantha sat in the seat to his right.

"You keep an eye on our starboard," he said. "I'll watch the port."

"Aye-aye, Captain."

She looked out the window and then, hesitating, turned back to him.

"Just so I'm clear—you want me to watch my side, and you'll watch yours, right?"

"Right."

"Got it."

The roads were quiet, and they were out of Salamanca within a few minutes, traveling west on the Southern Tier Expressway. Ten minutes later, they were crossing Quaker Run Road, a scenic route that paralleled the river until it ran down into the Allegany State Park.

"What do you think happened to those two women?" she asked.

"What women?"

"The ones who tried to get their kids back."

He shrugged. "They either ran into trouble on the road or at the farm, I suppose."

"Well, yeah, but I mean do you think it was zombies, bandits, or what exactly?"

"There's no such thing as zombies."

"You keep telling me that, and yet you keep killing them."

He sighed.

"Come on," she said. "You have to admit that thing in the tunnel was definitely not human."

"Maybe not, but he wasn't a zombie either."

"That's what my mom would call arguing over romantics."

Tanner glanced over at her.

"Romantics?"

She nodded. "When you're arguing over romantics, it means you're fussing over something trivial."

He grinned. "Okay, I'll give that one to you."

Tanner looked up and saw an exit ahead for Onoville Road. Without saying a word, he slowed down and headed for the ramp.

"Hey," she said, double-checking the map, "they said to stay on the interstate until we hit Highway 62."

"Maybe so, but you and I know better. What do we say about interstates?"

She thought for a moment.

"I don't know. What?"

"Interstates are filled with murderers, dogs, and dead bodies."

She wrinkled her brow. "We've never said that."

"No, but we should've."

He came to a stop at the end of the ramp and gestured toward the map. "See if you can find Onoville Road."

She ran her finger across the map until she found it.

"Here it is. Steamburg is on our starboard side."

He grinned. "And does that take us toward Conewango?"

"It sure does."

He turned right. Deep cracks split the two-lane road, and the center line had long since worn away. There was a large red barn to the left with two small grain silos sitting beside it. To the right was an old post office with a genuine hitching post out front. He continued ahead.

They came across a huge plot of land on both sides of the road that had been used to grow corn. The stalks of last year's crop still littered the field, and a tractor sat dormant, nearly buried in the tall grass.

A few hundred feet further down the road was a small two-pump gas station. The sign out front boasted about having tax-free gasoline and cigarettes. Three men dressed in denim coveralls stood outside the store, smoking. One carried a double-barrel shotgun, but upon seeing the school bus, offered a friendly wave.

"Are they Amish?" asked Samantha.

"Nope."

"How can you be sure?"

"The gun for one. The Amish reject all forms of violence."

"How do they do that?"

"I guess they turn the other cheek, like it says in the Bible."

"I don't see how they could do that now. Not with all the zombies and criminals out there." She smiled at him. "No offense."

He ignored the slight.

"There's always been violence. Somehow they manage."

She looked down at her rifle.

"Maybe I should become Amish."

Tanner smiled. "Do you know what the difference is between an Amish girl and a water buffalo?"

"No. What?"

"About twelve pounds of hair."

She laughed. "That's mean."

"Maybe, but it's funny."

"Seriously, what else is special about them?"

"You're asking the wrong fella."

"Come on. You said that you'd been here a few times."

"So?"

"So, you must have learned something."

He sighed. "Well let's see... I know that they don't use modern technology. They do everything by hand, like in the old days."

"They don't have cars?"

He shook his head. "No electricity, cell phones, or computers either."

"None of us have those things anymore," she said.

"True. And do you really miss them?"

"You bet."

He laughed. "Yeah, me too."

"Okay, so no electricity or computers. What else?"

"I've heard they have a set of rules called the *ordnung*, or something like that. I don't know if it's ever even been written down."

"If it's not written down, how does anyone know the rules?"

"When was the last time you read a law book?"

"Never."

"And yet you know not to kill or steal."

"Ah, I get it," she said. "What happens if they break the rules?"

"I guess that depends on what they did. If it's too bad, they excommunicate the person."

"What's that mean?"

"They toss him out on his ear."

"But where does he go if he's excom—, you know, if he's tossed out on his ear?"

Tanner shrugged. "I don't know. Maybe there's a big group of ex-Amish partiers out there somewhere, all walking around with their top buttons undone."

"Do you not like the Amish?"

"I got nothing against them."

"But..."

"But nothing. They got their way, and I got mine."

"But your way is the exact opposite of theirs."

He nodded. "I think it's fair to say that I'm made out of Amish antimatter, if there is such a thing."

She thought for a moment.

"I don't think I could do without electricity."

"You are doing without electricity."

"Well, yeah, but you know what I mean. Not for a really long time."

Tanner didn't have the heart to tell her that she would surely be a grown woman before electricity was ever restored.

The next fifteen miles of back roads were more of the same: big red barns, churches, old houses, and acre after acre of farmland. The most threatening thing they encountered was a goat that had strayed out into the road.

As they made the final turn onto Flatiron Road, they saw a horse-drawn buggy blocking the road ahead. Two men wearing black clothes and straw hats stood in front of the buggy with their hands raised.

"Head's up now. Amish or not, let's not take any chances."

"Right," she said, readying her rifle.

Tanner stopped about fifty yards from the Amish men, grabbed his shotgun, and stepped from the bus.

"You want to stay here and cover me?" he asked, looking back at Samantha.

"I'd rather see what they look like."

He shrugged. "Come on then."

As they walked toward the men, Tanner studied them carefully. Neither appeared to have a weapon, and their clothes were the typical Amish fare, handmade black coat and pants, shirts buttoned up to the top, and simple straw hats. They also had healthy beards without mustaches, which was normal for married men. If they weren't genuine Amish, they knew enough to look the part.

When they got to within a few paces, the older of two men stepped forward. He had a weathered face but kind eyes. He glanced at Samantha and then turned to Tanner and extended his hand. The man's grip was strong and his hands calloused. They were real Amish all right.

"I'm Jacob Miller." He gestured toward the younger man. "This is my oldest son, Samuel."

"I'm Tanner, and this is my daughter, Samantha."

Jacob looked at the girl.

"Daughter, you say?"

"That's right."

Jacob met Tanner's eyes but said nothing more about it.

"Unless you're just passing through, you should turn back."

"Why's that?" asked Tanner.

"We have a problem in our community that poses a grave threat to visitors."

Samuel, who looked about thirty years younger than his father, added, "Please, this is for your own safety."

"What kind of threat?" asked Samantha.

"Please," Jacob repeated, ignoring the question, "it's not safe here."

Tanner nodded. "We appreciate the warning, but we're here to pick up some kids."

The old man looked to his son, but he only shook his head.

"What children do you speak of?"

"A few weeks ago, the townspeople in Salamanca sent fourteen kids here to stay with Isaac Yoder. We're here to take them back home."

"Ah," Jacob said, nodding, "yes, I see. You came for the English children."

"That's right."

Jacob looked up at the sun, weighing a decision.

Finally, he said, "Come, then. We must hurry."

જે જે

Tanner followed Jacob and Samuel for the better part of a mile, moving at a pace that their single horse felt was appropriate for the beautiful spring afternoon. They passed several Amish farms that were spread out along Flatiron Road, easily recognizable by their barns, grain towers, and the absence of cars or farm machinery.

When they arrived at a large farmhouse, Jacob turned into the dirt driveway and came to a stop. Tanner pulled in behind them and swung the bus around to make it easier to get back out onto the road.

The two Amish men hopped from their buggy and hurried inside.

Tanner and Samantha stood by the bus, hoping to see a long line of children come pouring out of the farmhouse. Instead of children, however, the two men returned with a middle-aged Amish woman. She looked stout enough to wrestle a pig to the ground, something she had undoubtedly done on more than one occasion. She wore a dark blue dress and had a white apron tied around her waist. Her hair was tucked under a simple white cotton bonnet.

She hurried toward the bus, leaving Jacob and Samuel by their buggy.

"English," she said, adopting the term frequently applied to outsiders.

He walked forward and met her in the middle of the dirt driveway. Samantha stayed close behind him.

"Ma'am," he said.

"I'm Miriam. Jacob says that you've come for the English children."

"That's right."

"And can you provide some sort of proof that you have their parents' permission?"

He pulled out the paper with the descriptions of the children.

"This is all I have."

She looked it over and nodded.

"It's enough." She turned to Jacob and waved. He patted Samuel on the back, and the younger man took off running around the side of the house.

"Where's he going?" asked Tanner.

"The children are all in school. It's across the field about a half-mile away. There is no road access, so he will go on foot and walk the children here. Now, please, come and allow me to fix you and your daughter something to drink."

As everyone walked around to the front of the simple wood house, Tanner was reminded of the times he had visited his ex-wife, Grace. When he had last seen her, she was less than two miles from where he now stood. The world suddenly felt very small indeed.

"Please," offered Miriam, "sit and relax." Without waiting for them to do either, she turned and hurried inside.

Everyone took a seat and looked out at the large farm. An Amish man and his two sons were in the distance, plowing the field with the help of a mule.

Samantha looked over at Jacob.

"Do you mind if I ask you a few things about the Amish?"

He seemed surprised by her directness.

"I suppose not."

"Tanner said you don't drive cars or trucks. Is that true?"

Jacob nodded. "That's right. We are simple people."

She pointed toward the man working in the field.

"But wouldn't a tractor help them to plow the farm faster?"

"Perhaps, but it would also rob a father the chance to share time with his sons."

She nodded. "Okay, but what about electricity? Wouldn't having lights and heating make life easier?"

"Why must life be easier?"

She scratched her head, giving his words some serious consideration.

Miriam came back out on the porch carrying a glass pitcher of milk. She poured them each a small glass, but took none for herself. The entire time they drank, she looked off at the sky, as if expecting a thunderstorm to roll in.

"What happens at nightfall?" asked Tanner.

Miriam shot him a worried look.

"What do you mean?"

Jacob also sat forward, clearly concerned by the question.

"You've been trying to hurry us along since we got here," explained Tanner, "and Jacob warned us on the road that it wasn't safe here. So, I'm guessing something happens at night. What is it?"

She looked to Jacob, waiting to see if he would answer.

"It is an Amish matter and not of your concern," he said.

Tanner lifted the heavy shotgun and laid it across his lap.

"I'd like to be the judge of that for myself."

Jacob would no longer look at him, and Miriam bit nervously at her lip.

They sat for several minutes without anyone speaking. The sun was getting low in the sky, and heavy shadows started to creep over the fields.

Jacob turned to Miriam.

"Where are the children?" he said, unable to hide his agitation.

"It is a long walk, Jacob. They're coming. See? There." She pointed off across the meadow. "It's them."

Everyone stood to get a better look. A few hundred yards away, a procession of young children marched single file across the field. They were garbed in a mix of traditional Amish and modern clothing. Samuel was leading them, and a young woman was bringing up the rear.

As they got closer, Samuel waved, and Jacob waved back. The woman at the back was urging the kids to move more quickly, and the entire procession was nearly at a trot. As soon as they got to the farmhouse, Jacob gathered everyone together.

"Okay, it is time to go now. Please, you must hurry, English."

Tanner counted the kids. Thirteen. He checked again. Same count.

"We're one kid short."

"It's Timothy," the young woman explained. "He was ill and stayed at home with the Hochstetlers. Please, if I don't go now, I won't have time to get home before dark." Without waiting for anyone to reply, she turned and hurried back across the field.

The man who had been plowing the farm passed her as he and his two sons came in for the evening.

"Jacob, what's happening here?" he asked, brushing the dirt from his clothes.

Jacob quickly explained the situation, and the man nodded his understanding. He looked up at the sky.

"If you hurry, you and Samuel can get home in time. Please, go now."

Jacob patted the man on the shoulder as he and Samuel hurried back to their buggy. They climbed in and urged the horse to make haste.

The farmer turned to Tanner and said, "I'm Isaac, and you've already met my wife, Miriam."

Tanner nodded.

"I'm afraid I must insist that you take the children back to Salamanca immediately."

"I can't do that."

"Why not?"

"I'm one short."

Isaac looked to Miriam.

"One of the boys was sick today," she explained. "He's with the Hochstetlers." She could no longer hide the worry in her voice.

"Then you can return for him another day. You must go, now." His words now sounded more like a plea than a firm insistence.

Tanner began calling out the names on his list. The children were all well behaved, and each responded politely when their name was called. Only Timothy Brown was missing. According to the list, he was Peta's boy. Tanner shook his head. If any kid was going to be missing, it was bound to be hers.

He turned to Isaac.

"Tell me where the boy is, and we'll swing by and pick him up on our way out. I can't leave without him."

"You don't understand. There's no time. You must go now."

"No, I think it's you who doesn't understand. I said that I'd come back with fourteen kids, and I'm not leaving without fourteen kids. So, unless you have a spare son you'd like to donate, I'm getting little Timmy."

Miriam leaned over and whispered something in her husband's ear. He nodded.

"Come," he said. "We must get the children inside."

⌘ ⌘

Tanner leaned his shotgun against the wall and helped Isaac lift a heavy wooden shutter. The Amish man nodded his appreciation, and for the next several minutes, they worked together, carefully hanging the shutters over every window of his modest home. When they were finished, both men stepped back and looked at their work. The shutters were constructed from one-inch thick oak planks that were stained from years of exposure to the elements. Whether or not they would hold up would depend on what was coming.

"Thank you, English."

Tanner nodded, picking back up his shotgun.

Isaac slid a chair beside the door and sat, weary from the day's hard labor. Tanner pulled one over next to his. They sat, quietly looking out at the night.

Finally, Isaac said, "I'm sorry for my behavior earlier."

"You're worried. I get it. But maybe it's time you tell me what's going on here."

"Yes, I suppose it's only right." He paused, searching for the right words. "English, are you familiar with our custom of *Rumspringa?*"

"It's a time when you let your teenagers go out and sow their wild oats."

Isaac smiled. "Sow their wild oats—a wonderful idiom indeed. But true enough, I suppose. When our children reach sixteen, the rules for their conduct are somewhat relaxed. Punishments are less severe. They are expected to conduct courting and perhaps even experience non-Amish life to some degree. The purpose of this is to help them make an informed decision of whether or not to stay in the Amish community."

"And do most come back into the fold?"

"Indeed. Almost all do. Young people often think that our customs are somehow holding them back, but when they experience life outside, they feel disconnected from nearly everything they see as important."

"All that's well and good, but what does it have to do with us sitting here in the dark?"

He took a deep breath before answering.

"When the virus first hit, some of our children were away on *Rumspringa*, experiencing life with the English. When we saw how dangerous things had become, we called them home at once."

"Makes sense."

"Yes, but some... some were already infected."

"I'm sorry to hear that."

"We kept them apart from others to keep it from spreading. And in the end, most of them died. It was horrible to see our children die." Tears welled in his eyes, and he pretended to wipe away sweat with the sleeve of his dirty shirt.

"I'm sorry," repeated Tanner.

"That was not the worst of it. The worst came when three boys began to recover. They were hideous to look at, but even worse to be around— unspeakably violent. That is not our way, English. You know that."

"What did you do?"

"At first, we tried a firm hand, threatening *Meidung*, our banishment."

"And did that help?"

"No. It only caused them to grow angrier. Their hearts became filled with vile hate for everyone but their kind."

"Did you cast them out?"

Isaac wiped at his eyes again.

"We did, but not into society. We could not do so in good conscience. So, we built a barn for them to live in. It is forever kept dark because their eyes cannot adjust to the light. They stay in the barn throughout the day and roam freely at night. We leave them food and drink to help them stay alive."

"It sounds like you came to an arrangement with them. That's something, I suppose."

"No," he said, shaking his head. "Ours was but the act of desperate men and women. When they come out at night, they are no longer Amish. They are like wolves on the hunt."

"Why don't you just lock them up?"

"They would not allow it without great violence."

"Let me get this straight. You have a situation where a few murderous teens kill anyone who happens to be out after dark? Is that what we're dealing with?"

Isaac said nothing, but his silence was an answer.

"What will you do about them? Eventually, they'll kill someone you love—a man who is slow coming in from the field, a child who gets distracted on the way home from school. It's bound to happen."

"It has already happened," he said, his voice barely above a whisper. "Two men were killed last week. Their horse injured its leg, and they were forced to travel on foot." He shook his head. "They did not make it home."

"Where are these teens?"

"The second farm to the north. There's a big red barn with an 'X' painted on the side. The house near it was abandoned. The farm past it is the Hochstetlers'."

Tanner thought he heard something unspoken in Isaac's words.

"That's where Timothy is staying?"

Isaac turned and stared into Tanner's eyes.

"Yes."

Tanner nodded. "I understand."

ॐ ∽

"Let me get this straight," Samantha said, ushering Tanner closer to an oil lamp. "You're going out to a barn to fight Amish teenage zombies?"

He shrugged. "It sounds weird when you say it like that."

"It *is* weird!"

"Someone has to do it."

"Then I'm going with you."

He shook his head. "I've never minded doing other people's dirty work, but this isn't for you, Sam."

"But—"

"No buts. You stay here until I get back." He nodded toward one of the girls who had come from the schoolhouse. "Besides, this will give you a chance to talk to Isa. She needs a friend right now."

Samantha looked over at her. Isa sat quietly at the long dinner table, barely touching her food. Instead, she seemed more interested in watching the other children scramble for an extra helping of potatoes or another slice of fresh baked bread.

"I don't have the note anymore. I gave it to her mom."

"That's okay. Keep it simple today. She can deal with that when her mom is around to help."

"Fine, I'll stay here," she sighed. "But be careful. I can't drive a bus, and I'm pretty sure no one else around here can either."

Tanner gave her a quick hug and ushered her off to the kitchen before he quietly stepped out onto the porch. The night air was humid, and the sounds of insects were everywhere.

He walked down the dirt driveway and turned north on Flatiron Road. The road was pitch-black, and only the feel of smooth pavement under his feet kept him from straying into an open field. He regretted not asking Isaac how far it was down to the barn. If he failed to pay attention, he might walk right past it.

His concerns ended up being misplaced. After a few hundred yards, the silhouette of a large structure came into view. He couldn't make out the white 'X' on the side but felt reasonably sure it was the barn in question.

Tanner stopped in the center of the road and began whistling. It was the whistle of a man walking to his favorite fishing hole, carefree and upbeat, guaranteed to draw the ire of evil on the prowl. He whistled for a full minute. Two. Five. Nothing.

Where the hell were they? Out hunting, maybe?

Tanner looked off toward the barn. He was hoping to avoid going into the closed space. Better to shoot them at a distance than have them biting at his face.

"Well, shit," he said. "If you're not coming out, I guess I'm coming in." He doubted that anyone could have heard him, but saying the words made him feel a little better about walking toward a barn filled with The Lost Boys.

He trudged across the dirt path up to a set of heavy wooden doors. One of them was partially open. Half-eaten plates of food were sitting out in the dirt. He kicked the plates aside and swung the door all the way open. Moonlight shone in from behind him to catch a dark shape darting behind a bale of hay.

Tanner stepped in and immediately caught the sour stench of something dead. The sound of flies buzzed angrily from one corner of the room, fighting one another for their midnight snack. The Lost Boys had apparently dragged at least one of their victims into the barn. Maybe they had done so before the kill to have a little fun, or maybe afterward, to have a little dinner. Either way, it smelled pretty rank.

He stood in the doorway and waited to see if his eyes would adjust to the nearly impenetrable darkness. They didn't. The barn was dark, and it was going to stay that way.

"Listen up," he said. "I got no desire to kill a bunch of pimple-faced Amish outcasts. So, if any of you are still human enough to speak, step out and we'll have words."

Nothing moved.

"That's kinda what I figured," he muttered.

After a few more seconds, the young man he had seen dart behind the hay slowly eased out. He was a little over six feet tall and easily weighed two hundred pounds. Another boy dropped down from the loft, landing heavily on his feet. He was shorter, but thick and solid. A third boy stood up from the back of the barn and twisted his head from side to side, like a wrestler might when preparing for a match.

"Oh, my," said Tanner, "you boys are a little bigger than I imagined."

They slowly started toward him.

"I forgot to ask any of your names, so I'm going with..." He pointed his shotgun at the first boy. "... David." He swung the muzzle over to the second. "Marko." He shifted it to the third. "And Dwayne. Don't ask why I chose those names because I'm guessing that, at this point, you couldn't appreciate the movie reference."

Whether it was his confident tone or just mindless rage, something set them off, and all three suddenly charged, whooping like jackals on the hunt.

He flipped the muzzle up and shot Marko at nearly point blank range. The full load of buckshot hit him in the chest, flipping the boy backwards. Tanner swung right and fired a second shot. The blast ripped a chunk out of Dwayne's thigh, but he continued ahead, smashing Tanner against the barn door. Before he could free himself, Dwayne leaned forward and bit savagely at his forearm, forcing him to drop the shotgun.

Tanner ignored the burning pain and hit Dwayne with a rabbit punch to the base of his skull. The blow was short but incredibly powerful, and the young man's legs buckled. Tanner managed to get two good boot stomps to his head before the last of The Lost Boys barreled into him.

They tumbled out onto the dirt road, and Tanner felt his knee twist as he fell. David landed on top and began hammering down with uncontrolled rage. A blow hit Tanner on the cheek and another in his good eye.

Desperate to stop the relentless pounding, he grabbed David by the neck and pulled him in close. The boy struggled, pushing against Tanner's chest as he struggled to get enough space to fight. Tanner reached up with his right hand and grabbed a handful of hair. He braced his left hand under the young man's chin.

Sensing that he had been given a little slack, David started to sit up. When he did, Tanner drove both hands in opposite directions, twisting the young man's neck violently to the side. Vertebrae gave way, and his neck snapped in two. Tanner waited a moment and then jerked a second time, twisting his head nearly all the way around.

❦ ❧

The rest of the walk to the Hochstetlers' farm took Tanner twice as long, even though the distance was about the same. For one thing, his leg hurt from being knocked to the ground, and for another, he didn't feel a pressing need to hurry. Tanner had always felt comfortable in the dark, and without anyone to worry about but himself, he walked at a leisurely pace—albeit with a slight limp.

When he finally arrived at the Hochstetler house, he nearly had to break the door down to convince them to let him in. In the end, they released Timothy to him, but only after the grandfather insisted on using the family buggy to drive them back to the Yoders. His family begged him not to, but he would not be dissuaded. Tanner didn't have the heart to tell him that the bloodthirsty teens were no longer a threat. He had found that, when a man has decided upon a brave deed, it was best not to take that from him.

Early the next morning, Tanner and Samantha loaded the children onto the school bus, checking off their names as they got on board.

"That makes fourteen," Samantha said, as the final youngster climbed aboard.

Isaac walked over, leaving Miriam standing on the porch with their two sons. He shook Tanner's hand.

"I trust you will have a safe drive to Salamanca."

He shrugged. "One can hope."

"I appreciate what you did last night." He paused. "Getting Timothy, I mean."

Tanner nodded. "It's what I do."

Isaac touched Samantha on the head.

"You're lucky to have such a good man as your... father."

"Yeah, he's okay," she said, glancing at Tanner before turning and climbing into the bus.

As Isaac turned to walk back to his wife, Tanner stopped him.

"I wonder if I might ask a favor?"

He turned back. "Anything."

"Do you happen to know an English woman named Grace? I'm not sure what last name she's using now. Could be Raines."

A smile lit up his customarily somber face.

"Indeed, I know her."

"She's alive then?"

"Very much so. She teaches at our school three days a week. By all accounts, she's a hardworking woman, which for the Amish, is about the nicest thing we can say about anyone. It's not far out of your way if you want to stop by and see her."

Tanner thought about it a moment and then shook his head.

"Maybe another time. When you see her next, could you give her a message for me?"

"Sure, English. What would you have me tell her?"

"Tell her that her son is alive. That's the one thing she'd really want to know."

Isaac bowed his head slightly.

"I'll tell her today. You have my word."

Tanner nodded his thanks and climbed aboard the school bus. He took his seat behind the oversized steering wheel and glanced back at the kids. They all looked as if they'd been hypnotized by Jean-Martin Charcot.

He looked over at Samantha.

"What's up with them?"

"I think you scare them."

"Me? Why?"

"Are you kidding? You look like you just killed a werewolf with your bare hands, bite marks and all."

"Well, get them to sing a song or something. They're creeping me out."

Samantha walked down the aisle of the bus, saying something to each child. When she got to the back, she turned around, and they all started singing.

"The wheels on the bus go round and round,
round and round, round and round…"

Tanner dropped the transmission into drive and punched the gas. It was going to be a long drive home.

CHAPTER 22

With the help of Vince and Don, Mason was able to clean up most of the mess in short order. The helicopter would have to stay where it was, but the bodies were gathered up and tossed into the nearby ravine. The cabin hadn't taken any damage, so all it needed was a little hosing down to get the blood off the porch. By the time they finished, darkness was quickly approaching, and Mason could tell that his two friends were eager to get home to their loved ones.

He extended his hand, and each man shook it firmly.

"Marshal," said Vince, "we're terribly sorry about what happened to Ava. If we'd have known, we'd have brought the whole town to help her. Just like before, you know?"

Mason nodded. "I know."

"If you ever need anything..."

"Anything at all," seconded Don.

"I know that too."

"All right, then," Vince said, reaching down and petting Bowie one last time, "we should probably roll."

"Be careful going back."

The two men turned and walked back to their cruiser. Within seconds, the only evidence that they had ever been there was a small dust cloud that snaked its way down the driveway.

Mason turned and took a long look at the empty cabin. There was still a little blood spatter on the door, and the place felt dark and cold. He was halfway tempted to hop in his truck and follow the deputies back to Boone, maybe stay a night or two at the old church with Father Paul.

Bowie moved up next to him and licked the back of his hand as if to remind him that he wasn't alone.

He squatted down and hugged the huge dog.

"Yeah, I know. You're with me all the way."

Bowie pressed up against him, whining softly.

After a moment, Mason stood back up. He felt better, and the cabin looked a little warmer than it had a moment earlier.

"Come on," he said. "Let's get the generator fired up and bring a little life back to this place."

              ❧ ☙

Mason turned on his amateur radio and checked the power and antenna settings. It was still tuned to the 20-meter band from the last time he had used it. He keyed the microphone.

"This is KB4VXP, looking for WA4RTF, over."

He waited a few seconds and then repeated the call. As soon as he let off the microphone the second time, someone answered.

"This is WA4RTF. How are you, Marshal?"

Mason recognized the voice as that of Jack Atkins, a prepper who lived in Gloucester, Virginia.

"Hey, Jack. Good to hear your voice."

"It's been a few weeks, Marshal. I was afraid something might have happened to you."

"No, I'm all right. I've just been out assessing the situation. How are things on your end?"

"The missus and I are fine. Although we did have a run-in with a neighbor last week."

"What happened?"

"He was hungry, like everybody. He thought it only fair that we turn over some of our supplies."

"I'm guessing that didn't work out so well."

"I ran him off with a shotgun. I only hope for his sake that he doesn't come back around."

"Just stay safe, Jack. Desperate people do desperate things."

"I'll do my best. What about you, Marshal? What can you tell me now that you've had a chance to check things out? Are things as bad as they look?"

Mason's thoughts flashed past everything that had happened over the last few weeks—run-ins with militias, convicts, mercenaries, and petty criminals, not to mention the hordes of bloodthirsty infected survivors.

"Worse, I'm afraid."

"That's what I figured," mumbled Jack. "You got any kind of good news to report?"

"I've seen some towns pulling things together," Mason said, thinking of Boone, York, and now Chester. "Also, I heard a broadcast saying the government is planning to establish a few colonies."

"We heard that as well. One of them is going to be over in Norfolk, barely thirty miles from us."

"Are you planning to move there once they get it set up?"

"Probably not. A place like that will draw all sorts of unsavory folk. We'll take our chances out here in the real world."

"I can't say as I blame you. History has shown that, when desperate people seek government handouts, there tends to be a lot of chaos."

"Our thoughts exactly. Anyhow, what can I do for you, Marshal?"

Mason smiled. Jack had been around long enough to know small talk when he heard it.

"I was wondering if you might do me a favor."

"Sure. What do you need?"

"I'm looking for anything you can find on a General William Hood."

"Never heard of him, but I can ask around. I've made contact with plenty of service folks over the past few weeks. Someone's bound to know something."

"Thanks, Jack. And be careful when doing the asking."

"I appreciate the warning. Did this fella cross you, Marshal?"

"In more ways than one."

"It sounds like you're looking to pay him a visit."

"I am. But first, I need to find him."

"Understood. I'll do a little digging. A general shouldn't be too hard to locate. I guess you already heard the news about President Glass."

"What news?"

There was a pause as Jack chose the right words.

"She was killed today."

Mason sat up in his chair.

"Come again. Did you say the president was killed?"

"That's what's being broadcast. Details are sketchy, but the scuttlebutt is that she was assassinated by someone in her own government."

"Any chance it was Vice President Pike?"

"I don't think so," Jack said, laughing. "He was sworn in about an hour ago as the new President of the United States."

"Oh, man," Mason said, rubbing his chin, "that's not good."

"I wouldn't think so either. Pike always struck me as a bit of a loose cannon."

He might be a lot worse than that, thought Mason.

"Thanks, Jack, I appreciate the head's up."

After they signed off, Mason sat in the radio room for several minutes, thinking. Nakai had said that he suspected Pike might be involved. But it was just an unsubstantiated hunch. Perhaps General Hood was as high as it went.

Then again, maybe it went all the way to the top.

బ్ ఆ

After finishing dinner, Mason headed into the bedroom. A large handwritten note lay neatly folded in the center of his bed. He quickly unfolded it and saw his father's signature at the bottom of the page. Tanner had never written "Dad" in his entire life, preferring instead to pen his first name.

Mason carried the note, along with a lantern and what was left of his coffee, out onto the porch. He leaned back in his favorite rocking chair, and Bowie came over to lie at his feet. He took a moment to breathe the cool mountain air before turning his attention to his father's words. It was written in simple clean lettering.

Mason,

I wasn't at all surprised to hear that you were alive and out saving the world. I would have expected no less. While I have never been guided by the same moral compass, I have always respected you. I'm free now, not only from prison, but from everything. I hope that men coming from two different walks of life can meet in the middle to make a difference. I'm sure that our paths will cross soon enough. Until then, know that you are in my heart.

Tanner

The words hit Mason harder than he thought they would, and he had to sip the coffee to get the lump out of his throat. It had been more than a year since he and his father had last spoken, and their conversations were never without contention. The fact that their paths had crossed in such a violent and tragic way did not at all surprise him. Violence traveled alongside his father like his oldest and dearest friend. Not always of his own making, perhaps, but it was there nonetheless, waiting patiently in the shadows for any opportunity to step out into the light.

His father was right about the two of them being different. Mason had chosen to follow a path of justice, to instill order where there was chaos. Whereas Tanner felt compelled to fight every type of authority, to rely on no one but himself. Their differences had at times kept them apart or even at odds with one another. But as Mason looked over at the bullet-ridden helicopter, he accepted that he was still his father's son. Both of them were willing and able to fight with vicious purpose when situations dictated the need.

The death of Agent Sparks and his men should have brought a sense of closure. But as he sat listening to the millions of insects telling their own tales of woe, he realized that it hadn't. There were still questions to be answered, people to be held accountable. Getting to a man like General Hood would not be easy—let alone President Pike, should it come to that. They would be well protected, not to mention dangerous.

Good, he thought. It's better that way. There was no room in Mason's heart for forgiveness, and having adversaries deserving of his rage seemed only fitting. The situation with Hood would not be resolved in a day or a week, but the closure he sought would eventually come. One day, he would stand beside Ava's grave and tell her that justice had finally been done. Of that, he was certain.

To accomplish his task, he would need help. Not only from good men like Vince and Don, but also from men who could walk the ledge of the pit without falling in, matching every ruthless deed with one of their own. Men like that were rare indeed. But as he looked down at the paper one final time, Mason thought he might know of one such man.

Until then, he would continue putting the nation's house back together, one brick at a time. Some fights would be won, and some would be lost. The losses would always be painful, but he would persevere, no matter the setbacks. Mason was perhaps the nation's last living marshal, and as such, he was determined to do his God's honest best to make the Service proud.

ONLINE INFO

For information on my books and practical disaster preparedness, see:

http://disasterpreparer.com

CONTACT ME

If you enjoyed this book and are looking forward to the sequel, send me a short note (*arthur@disasterpreparer.com*). Like most authors, I enjoy hearing from my readers. Also, if you have time, perhaps you would be kind enough to post a positive review on Amazon.com.

I frequently travel the world giving disaster preparedness seminars. If you are a member of a church, business, or civic organization and would like to sponsor a disaster preparedness event, please keep me in mind.

Best wishes to you and your family!

FREE NEWSLETTER

To sign up for the *Practical Prepper Newsletter*, send an email to:

newsletter@disasterpreparer.com

Do you have a Plan?

Ninety-nine percent of the time the world spins like a top, the skies are clear, and your refrigerator is full of milk and cheese. But know with certainty that the world is a dangerous place. Storms rage, fires burn, and diseases spread. No one is ever completely safe. We all live as part of a very complex ecosystem that is unpredictable and willing to kill us without remorse or pause.

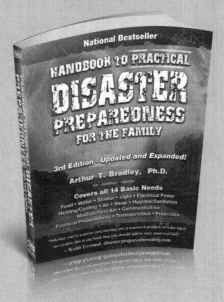

This handbook will help you to establish a practical disaster preparedness plan for your entire family. The 3rd Edition has been expanded to cover every important topic, including food storage, water purification, electricity generation, backup heating, firearms, communication systems, disaster preparedness networks, evacuations, life-saving first aid, and much more. Working through the steps identified in this book will prepare your family for nearly any disaster, whether it be natural disasters making the news daily (e.g., earthquakes, tornadoes, hurricanes, floods, and tsunamis), or high-impact global events, such as electromagnetic pulse attacks, radiological emergencies, solar storms, or our country's impending financial collapse. The new larger 8" x 10" format includes easy-to-copy worksheets to help organize your family's preparedness plans.

Available at Disasterpreparer.com and online retailers

Learn to Become a PREPPER

If your community were hit with a major disaster, such as an earthquake, flood, hurricane, or radiological release, how would you handle it? Would you be forced to fall into line with hundreds of thousands of others who are so woefully unprepared? Or do you possess the knowledge and supplies to adapt and survive? Do you have a carefully stocked pantry, a method to retrieve and purify water, a source for generating electricity, and the means to protect your family from desperate criminals? In short, are you a *prepper*?

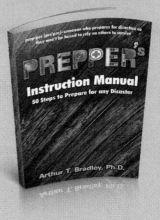

This book comprises fifty of the most important steps that any individual or family can take to prepare for a wide range of disasters. Every step is complete, clearly described, and actionable. They cover every aspect of disaster preparedness, including assessing the threats, making a plan, storing food, shoring up your home, administering first aid, creating a safe room, gathering important papers, learning to shoot, generating electricity, burying the dead, tying knots, keeping warm, and much more.

Recent events have reminded us that our world is a dangerous place, whether it is a deadly tsunami, a nuclear meltdown, or a stock market collapse. Our lifestyle, and even our very existence, is forever uncertain. Join the quickly growing community of individuals and families determined to stand ready.